FICTION HOUSE PRESS
PRESENTS

GALAXY SCIENCE FICTION

October 1950
Vol. 1, No. 1

This reprint edition is a facsimile of the original pulp magazine. Variations in printing and quality can be attributed to the original magazine which was printed on rough woodpulp paper. No attempt has been made to politically correct any language deemed inappropriate to the modern reader.

ISBN 978-1-64720-382-5

www.FictionHousePress.com
fictionhousepress@gmail.com

WHAT'S BETTER THAN MONEY?

Lots of things: Paid-up accident insurance for a hard-boiled pulp detective, for instance. . . . A stereoscopic full-color crystal ball for a swami. . . . A bathing suit with built-in curves for a flat-bottom non-dreamboat.

But for science fiction readers, such appealing plums lack *ingenuity*. Not so with the startling list we've prepared. For merely explaining a mystery (which no one has yet been able to explain satisfactorily) you can win the most exciting, the most extraordinary . . .

SCIENCE FICTION prizes ever offered in any contest!

We don't say this is the greatest science fiction contest there ever was; we want *you* to say it. And very far from incidental—some reader, somewhere, may have the actual answer to the key question:

What and Why Are Flying Saucers?

See Page 67 for Willy Ley's introduction to this baffling problem of our times . . . and Page 71 for the prizes. Remember, there is a $100 cash bonus for each of the winners of the first three prizes if their entries are accompanied by a susbcripton to GALAXY *Science Fiction*.

Galaxy
SCIENCE FICTION

Cover by David Stone
Illustrating The Hunting Asteroid Scene of Time Quarry

GALAXY *Science Fiction* is published monthly by World Editions, Inc. Main offices: 105 West 40th St., New York 18, N. Y. 25¢ per copy. Subscriptions (12 copies) $2.50 per year in the United States, Canada, Mexico, South and Central America and U. S. Possessions. Elsewhere $3.25. Application for entry as second-class matter is pending at the Post Office, Brooklyn, N.Y. President: George A. Gogniat. Vice-President: Marco Lombi. Secretary and Treasurer: Anne Swereda.

 173

October, 1950 Vol. 1, No. 1

CONTENTS

BOOK-LENGTH SERIAL—Installment 1

TIME QUARRY.. *by Clifford D. Simak* 4

NOVELETS

THE STARS ARE THE STYX........................ *by Theodore Sturgeon* 72

CONTAGION .... *by Katherine MacLean* 114

SHORT STORIES

THIRD FROM THE SUN........................... *by Richard Matheson* 61

LATER THAN YOU THINK........................ *by Fritz Leiber* 108

THE LAST MARTIAN.............................. *by Fredric Brown* 145

DARWINIAN POOL ROOM...................... *by Isaac Asimov* 152

FEATURES

EDITOR'S PAGE...................................... 2

FORECAST 107

GALAXY'S FIVE-STAR SHELF.................... *by Groff Conklin* 141

CONTEST ARTICLE

FLYING SAUCERS: Friend, Foe or Fantasy? *by Willy Ley* 67

Next Issue At Your Newsstand First Week in October

Printed in the U. S. A. Reg. U. S. Pat. Off.

For Adults Only

SCIENCE fiction, everybody agrees, or seems to, has finally come of age. Hollywood, radio, book publishers, and the slick magazines are all, with the usual degraded exceptions, buying and treating science fiction intelligently.

GALAXY *Science Fiction* proposes to carry the maturity of this type of literature into the science fiction magazine field, where it is now, unfortunately, somewhat hard to find. It establishes a compound break with both the lurid and the stodgy traditions of s-f magazine publishing. From cover design to advertising selections, GALAXY *Science Fiction* intends to be a mature magazine for mature readers . . . mature in reading; age alone is no assurance of maturity.

The cover design we are using is proof of our break with the amateur and/or shoddy tradition, and the way it was selected is typical of our respect for our potential readers. We presented a number of experimental cover designs to groups of fans, authors, artists, and persons with no interest at all in science fiction, and asked which they preferred. Three out of four consulted chose our present design . . . and explained that *they* liked it, but doubted if it had commercial appeal. Three votes out of every four, on a wide-scale survey, is commercial enough to satisfy us. We never were convinced, in any case, of the actual commercial appeal of naked maidens, prognathous youths in winter underwear of gold lamé, and monsters that can exist only on the nutrients found in India ink and Bristol board.

The cover, by David Stone, is the resolution of several personal conflicts. Long a science fiction fan, Stone is also an excellent artist who was weary of tearing covers off magazines to avoid embarrassment. His cover, he resolved, would not have to be hidden from either parents or friends. Having suffered thus ourselves, we agreed, and no reader will be ashamed to carry GALAXY.

If you will study our cover closely, preferably with a magnifying glass, you will find another reason for pride. Stone's fine painting has been reproduced by a *completely new and revolutionary engraving process!* It is a continuous tone method, developed by William Guth, one of the country's foremost experimenters in color reproduction. Like photography, this process uses a *granular* surface rather than mechanical dots, since no conventional screen is used at all. The Guth process allows imperceptible blending instead of the ordinary pattern or moire, which eliminates blurring through much more accurate registration, and makes possible more faithful color reproduction than any other engraving process known. We have to state that the above is the only information we can give; the patent is still pending.

Life is experimenting with the method . . . but GALAXY *Science Fiction* is the first magazine of any kind to use it.

A superb engraving process needs an equally superb cover stock. Therefore GALAXY *Science Fiction* is dressed in Champion Kromekote, an expensive and unusual coated paper. Kromekote was developed as a result of the long search for an ideal high finish paper, one that would duplicate the intense luster of the glossy photograph. The Champion Paper & Fibre Company solved the problem; Kromekote has a 20 per cent higher index of refraction than the costliest grade of enameled stock! It can also be soaked in water and still retain full color with practically no loss, an important quality to readers who dislike having to wash after reading a magazine.

Between William Guth's engraving process and Kromekote's incredible finish, artist and reader are assured fine color reproduction.

All this, of course, is merely a beautiful and dignified vehicle for science fiction itself. The novel, by Clifford D. Simak, is something that has been done far too seldom in s-f: a powerful story of suspense, mystery, ideas . . . and human emotion; Theodore Sturgeon's novelet is superb Sturgeon, recommendation enough, we think; and the short stories and illustrations were all selected for maturity, intelligence, and professional quality. Maintaining the standard of this first issue would not be easy even if we had the budget of a slick magazine, but our future issues promise to become even better.

As stated in the introduction to our contest, the fundamental purpose is to gain readers, but we also have a scientific intent. Flying Saucers, whether real or not, are a significant phenomenon of our times. If real, they have a vital function of some sort; if fantasy, they are noteworthy for psychological reasons. We do not have the answer, nor does Willy Ley. We hope, as he does, that our readers do, or that they can offer explanations which will suggest lines of research.

To conclude, we are not running a letter department in this issue—not because we have none, but because of their congratulatory and inspirational content. We would rather have a good fight than a bouquet any day, much as we like the odor of roses, because criticism is more important to the development of an idea . . . and GALAXY *Science Fiction* is an idea and a goal. Your ideas can help us achieve that goal.

—THE EDITOR

TIME QUARRY

By CLIFFORD D. SIMAK

Part I of a 3 part serial.

David Stone

One life should be enough to give for humanity... but humanity wanted Asher Sutton to keep making the sacrifice indefinitely!

THE man came out of the twilight when the greenish-yellow of the sun's last glow still lingered in the west. He paused at the edge of the patio and called.

"Mr. Adams, is that you?"

The chair creaked as Christopher Adams shifted his weight, startled by the voice. Then he remembered. A new neighbor had moved in across the meadow a day or two ago. Jonathon had told him . . . and Jonathon knew all the gossip within a hundred miles. Human gossip as well as android and robot gossip.

"Come on in," said Adams. "Glad you dropped around."

He hoped his voice sounded as

hearty and neighborly as he had tried to make it. For he wasn't glad. He was a little nettled, upset by this sudden shadow that came out of the twilight and walked across the patio.

This is my hour, he thought angrily. The one hour I give myself. The hour that I forget . . . forget the thousand problems that have to do with other star systems. Forget them and turn back to the green-blackness and the hush and the subtle sunset shadow-show that belong to my own planet. For here, on this patio, there are no mentophone reports, no robot files, no galactic co-ordination conferences . . . no psychological intrigue, no alien reaction charts. Nothing complicated or mysterious.

With half his mind, he knew the stranger had come across the patio and was reaching out a hand for a chair to sit in; and with the other half, once again, he wondered about the blackened bodies lying on the river bank on far-off Aldebaran XII, and the twisted machine that was wrapped around the tree.

Three humans had died there . . . three humans and two androids, and androids were almost human, different only in that they were manufactured instead of born. And humans must not die by violence unless it be by the violence of another human. Even then it must be on the field of honor, with all the formality and technicality of the *code duello,* or in the less polished affairs of revenge or execution.

For human life was sacrosanct. It had to be or there'd be no human life. Man was so pitifully outnumbered.

Violence or accident?

And accident was ridiculous.

There were few accidents, almost none at all. The near-perfection of mechanical performance, the almost human intelligence and reactions of machines to any known danger, long ago had cut accidents to an almost non-existent figure.

No modern machine would be crude enough to crash into a tree. A more subtle, less apparent danger, maybe. But never a tree.

So it must be violence.

And it could not be human violence, for human violence would have advertised the fact. Human violence had nothing to fear . . . there was no recourse to law, scarcely a moral code to which a human killer would be answerable.

THREE humans dead, fifty light years distant, and it became a thing of great importance to a man sitting on his patio on Earth. A thing of prime importance, for no human must die by other hands than human without a terrible vengeance. Human life must not be taken without a monstrous price anywhere in the galaxy, or the human race would end forever, and the great galactic brotherhood of intelligence would plummet down into the darkness and the distance that had scattered it before.

Adams slumped lower in his chair, forcing himself to relax, furious at himself for thinking . . . for it was his rule that in this time of twilight he thought of nothing . . . or as close to nothing as his restless mind could manage.

The stranger's voice seemed to come from far away and yet Adams knew he was sitting at his side.

"Nice evening," the stranger said.

Adams chuckled. "The evenings are always nice. The Weather boys don't let it rain until later on, when everyone's asleep."

In a thicket down the hill, a thrush struck up its evensong and the liquid notes ran like a quieting hand across a drowsing world. Along the creek a frog or two were trying out their throats. Far away, in some dim other-world, a whip-poor-will began his chugging question. Across the meadow and up the climbing hills, the lights came on in houses here and there.

"This is the best part of the day," said Adams.

HE DROPPED his hand into his pocket, brought out tobacco pouch and pipe. "Smoke?"

The stranger shook his head. "As a matter of fact, I am here on business."

Adams' voice turned crisp. "See me in the morning, then. I don't do business after hours."

The stranger said softly: "It's about Asher Sutton."

Adams' body tensed and his fingers shook as he filled his pipe. He was glad that it was dark so the stranger could not see.

"Sutton will be coming back," the stranger said.

Adams shook his head. "No chance. He went out twenty years ago."

"You haven't crossed him off?"

"No," said Adams slowly. "He still is on the payroll, if that is what you mean."

"Why?" asked the man. "Why do you keep him on?"

Adams tamped the tobacco in the bowl, considering. "Sentiment, I guess. Faith in Asher Sutton. Although the faith is running out."

"Just five days from now," the stranger said, "Sutton will come back." He paused a moment, then added: "Early in the morning."

"There's no way you could know a thing like that."

"But I do. It's recorded fact."

Adams snorted. "It hasn't happened yet."

"In my time it has."

Adams jerked upright in his chair. "In *your* time?"

"Yes," said the stranger quietly. "You see, Mr. Adams, I am your successor."

"Look here, young man. . . ."

"Not young man. I am half again your age. I am getting old."

"I have no successor," said Adams coldly. "There's been no talk of one. I'm good for another hundred years. Maybe more than that."

"Yes," the stranger said, "for

more than a hundred years. For much more than that."

Adams leaned back quietly in his chair. He put his pipe in his mouth and lit it with a hand that was suddenly steady.

"Let's take this easy," he said. "You say you are my successor . . . that you took over my job after I quit or died. That means you came out of the future. Not that I believe you for a moment, of course. But just for argument. . . ."

"There was a news item the other day," the stranger said. "About a man named Michaelson who claimed he went into the future."

"I read that. One second! How could a man know he went one second into time? How could he measure it and know? What difference would it make?"

"None," the stranger agreed. "Not the first time. But the next time he will go into the future five seconds. Five seconds, Mr. Adams. Five tickings of the clock. The space of one short breath. There must be a starting point for all things."

"Time travel?"

The stranger nodded.

"I don't believe it," Adams said. "In the last five thousand years we have conquered the galaxy. . . ."

"Conquer is not the right word, Mr. Adams."

"Well, taken over, then. Moved in. However you wish it. And we have found strange things. Stranger things than we ever dreamed. But never time travel." He waved his hand at the stars. "In all that space out there, no one had time travel. No one."

"You have it now," the stranger said. "Since two weeks ago. Michaelson went into time, one second into time. A start. That is all that's needed."

"All right," said Adams. "Let us say you are the man who in a hundred years or so will take my place. Let's pretend you traveled back in time. Then why come here?"

"To tell you that Asher Sutton will return."

"I would know it when he came," said Adams. "Why must I know now?"

"When he returns," the stranger said, "Sutton must be killed."

II

THE tiny, battered ship sank lower, slowly, like a floating feather, drifting down toward the field in the slant of morning sun. The bearded, ragged man in the pilot's chair sat tensed, not breathing.

Tricky, said his brain. Hard and tricky to handle so much weight, to judge the distance and the speed . . . hard to make the tons of metal float down against the savage pull of gravity. Harder even than the lifting of it, when there had been no consideration but that it should rise and move out into space.

For a moment the ship wavered and he fought it with every shred of will and mind . . . and then it floated once again, hovering just a few feet above the surface of the field.

He let it down, gently, so that it scarcely bumped when it touched the ground.

He sat rigid in the seat, slowly going limp, relaxing by inches, first one muscle, then another. Tired, he told himself. The toughest job I've ever done. Another few miles and I would have let the whole weight of the ship crash.

Far down the field was a clump of buildings. A ground car had swung away from them and was racing down the strip toward him. A breeze curled in through the shattered vision port and touched his face, reminding him. . . .

Breathe, he told himself. You must be breathing when they come. You must be breathing and you must walk out and you must smile at them. There must be nothing they will notice. Right away, at least. The beard and clothes will help some. They'll be so busy gaping at them that they will miss a little thing. But not breathing. They might notice if you weren't breathing.

Carefully, he pulled in a breath of air, felt the sting of it run along his nostrils and gush inside his throat, felt the fire of it when it reached his lungs.

Another breath and another one and the air had scent and life and a strange exhilaration. The blood throbbed in his throat and beat against his temples and he held his fingers to one wrist and felt it pulsing there.

Sickness came, a brief, stomach-retching sickness that he fought against, holding his body rigid, remembering all the things that he must do. The power of will, he told himself, the power of mind . . . the power that no man uses to its full capacity. The will to tell a body the things that it must do, the power to start an engine turning after years of doing nothing.

One breath and then another. And the heart is beating now, steadier, steadier.

Be quiet, stomach.

Get going, liver.

Keep pumping, heart.

It isn't as if you were old and rusted, for you never were. The other system took care that you were kept in shape, that you were ready at an instant's notice to be as you were.

But the switch-over was a shock. He had known that it would be. He had dreaded its coming, for he had known what it would mean: the agony of a new kind of life and metabolism.

IN HIS mind he held a blueprint of his body and all its working parts . . . a shifting, wobbly picture that shivered and blurred and ran color into color. But it steadied under the hardening of his mind, the driving of his will, and finally the blueprint was still and sharp and bright and he knew that the worst was over.

He clung to the ship's controls with hands clenched so fiercely, they almost dented metal, and perspiration poured down his body, and he was limp and weak. Nerves grew quiet and the blood pumped on, and he knew that he was breathing without even thinking of it.

For a moment longer he sat quietly in the seat, relaxing. The breeze came in the shattered port and brushed against his cheek. The ground car was coming very close.

"Johnny," he whispered, "we are home. We made it. This is my home, Johnny. The place I talked about."

But there was no answer, just a stir of comfort deep inside his brain, a strange, nestling comfort such as one may know when one is eight years old and snuggles into bed.

"Johnny!" he cried.

And he felt the stir again . . . a self-assuring stir like the feel of a dog's muzzle against a hand.

Someone was beating at the ship's door, beating with fists and crying out.

"All right," said Asher Sutton. "I'm coming. I'll be right along."

He reached down and lifted the attache case from beside the seat, tucked it underneath his arm. He went to the lock and twirled it open and stepped out on the ground.

There was only one man.

"Hello," said Asher Sutton.

"Welcome to Earth, sir," said the man, and the "sir" struck a chord of memory. Sutton's eyes went to the man's forehead and he saw the tattooing of the serial number, the only indication that this was a synthetic human being, an android.

Sutton had forgotten about androids. Perhaps a lot of other things as well. Little habit patterns that had sloughed away with the span of twenty years.

HE SAW the android staring at him, at the naked knee showing through the worn cloth, at the lack of shoes.

"Where I've been," said Sutton, sharply, "you couldn't buy a new suit every day."

"No, sir," said the android.

"And the beard," said Sutton, "is because I had nothing to shave with."

"I've seen beards before," the android told him.

Sutton stood quietly and stared at the world before him . . . at the upthrust of towers shining in the morning sun, at the green of park and meadow, at the darker green of trees and the blue and scarlet splashes of flower gardens on sloping terraces.

He took a deep breath and felt the air flooding in his lungs, seeking out all the distant cells that had been starved so long. And it was coming back to him, coming back again . . . the remembrance of life on Earth, of early morning sun and flaming sunsets, of deep blue sky and dew upon the grass, the swift blur of human talk and the lilt of human music.

"The car is waiting, sir," the android said. "I will take you to a human."

"I'd rather walk," said Sutton.

THE android shook his head. "The human is waiting and he is most impatient."

"Oh, all right," said Sutton.

The seat was soft and he sank into it gratefully, cradling the attache case carefully in his lap. He stared out of the window, fascinated by the green of Earth. *The green fields of Earth,* he said. Or was it *the green vales?* No matter now. It was a song written long ago, in the time when there had been fields on Earth, instead of parks, when Man had turned the soil for more important things than flower beds. In the day, thousands of years before, when Man had just begun to feel the stir of space within his soul. Long years before Earth had become the capital and the center of galactic empire.

A great starship was taking off at the far end of the field, sliding down the ice-smooth plastic skidway with the red-hot flare of booster jets frothing in its tubes. Its nose slammed into the upward curve of the take-off ramp and it was away, a rumbling streak of silver that shot into the blue. For a moment it flickered a golden red in the morning sunlight, and then was gone, vanished.

SUTTON brought his gaze back to Earth again, sat soaking in the sight of it as a man soaks in the first strong sun of spring after months of winter.

Far to the north towered the twin spires of the Justice Bureau, Alien Branch. And to the east the pile of gleaming plastics and glass that was the University of North America. And other buildings that he had forgotten . . . buildings for which he found he had no name, miles apart, with parks and homesites in between. The homes were masked by trees and shrubbery—none sat in barren loneliness—and, through the green of the curving hills, Sutton caught the glints of color that were roofs and walls.

The car slid to a stop before the Administration Building and the android opened the door. "This way, sir."

Only a few chairs in the lobby were occupied and most of those by humans. Humans or androids, thought Sutton, you can't tell the difference until you see their foreheads.

The sign upon the forehead, the brand of manufacture. The telltale mark that said: "This man is not a human, although he looks like one."

These are the ones who will listen to me. These are the ones who will pay attention. These are the ones who will save me against any future enmity that Man may raise against me.

For they are worse than the disinherited. They are not the has-beens; they are the never-weres. They are not born of woman, but of the laboratory. Their mother is a bin of chemicals and their father the ingenuity and technology of the creator race.

Android: An artificial human. A human made in the laboratory out of Man's own knowledge of chemicals and atomic and molecular structure and the strange reaction that is known as life.

Human in all but two respects—the mark upon the forehead and the ability to reproduce biologically.

Artificial humans to help the real humans, the biological humans, to carry the load of galactic empire, to make the thin line of humanity stronger, thicker. But kept in their place. Oh, yes, most definitely kept in their rightful place by psycho-conditioning and savagely enforced rules and laws.

THE corridor was empty. Sutton, his bare feet slapping on the floor, followed the android.

The door before which they stopped said:

THOMAS H. DAVIS
(Human)
Operations Chief

"In there," the android said.

Sutton walked in and the man behind the desk looked up.

"I'm a human," Sutton told him. "I may not look it, but I am."

The man jerked his thumb toward a chair. "Sit down."

Sutton sat.

"Why didn't you answer our signals?" Davis asked.

"My set was broken."

"Your ship has no identity."

"The rains washed it off," said Sutton, "and I had no paint."

"Rain doesn't wash off paint."

"Not Earth rain. Where I was, it does."

"Your motors?" asked Davis. "We could pick up nothing from them."

"They weren't working."

Davis' Adam's apple bobbed up and down. "Weren't working? How did you navigate?"

"With energy," said Sutton.

"Energy. . . ."

Sutton stared at him icily. "Anything else you want to know?"

Davis was confused. The answers were all wrong. He fiddled with a pencil. "Just the usual things, I guess." He drew a pad of forms before him.

"Name?"

"Asher Sutton."

"Origin of fli— Say, wait a minute! Asher Sutton?"

"That's right."

Davis flung the pencil on the desk, pushed away the pad. "Why didn't you tell me that first?"

"I didn't have a chance."

Davis was flustered. "If I had known. . . ."

"It's the beard," said Sutton.

"My father talked about you

often. Jim Davis. Maybe you remember him."

Sutton shook his head.

"Great friend of your father's. That is . . . they more or less knew one another."

"How is my father?" asked Sutton.

"Great," said Davis enthusiastically. "Getting along in years, but standing up. . . ."

"My father and mother," Sutton told him coldly, "died forty years ago. In the Argus pandemic." He heaved himself to his feet, faced Davis squarely. "If you're through, I'd like to go to my hotel. They'll find some room for me."

"Certainly, Mr. Sutton, certainly. Which hotel?"

"The Orion Arms."

Davis reached into a drawer, took out a directory, flipped the pages, ran a shaking finger down a column.

"Cherry 26-3489," he said. "The teleport is over there."

He pointed to a booth set flush into the wall, where a dematerializer could transport matter instantly to any other teleport booth anywhere on Earth.

"Thanks," said Sutton.

"About your father, Mr. Sutton. . . ."

"I know," said Sutton. "I'm glad you tipped me off."

He swung around and walked to the teleport. Before he closed the door, he looked back.

Davis was on the visaphone, talking rapidly.

III

TWENTY years had not changed the Orion Arms.

To Sutton, stepping out of the teleport, it looked the same as the day he had walked away. A little shabbier, but it was home, the quiet whisper of hushed activity, the dowdy furnishings, the finger-to-the lip, tiptoe atmosphere, the stiff respectability that he had remembered and dreamed about in the long years of alienness.

The life mural along the wall was the same as ever. A little faded now, but the same goatish Pan still chased, after twenty years, the same terror-stricken maiden across the self-same hills and dales. And the same rabbit hopped from behind a bush and watched the chase with all his customary boredom, chewing his everlasting cud of clover.

The self-adjusting furniture, bought before the management had considered throwing the hostelry open to the unhuman trade, had been out-of-date twenty years ago. But it still was there. It had been repainted, in soft, genteel pastels, its self-adjustment features still confined to human forms.

The spongy floor covering had lost some of its sponginess, and the Cetian cactus must have died at last, for a pot of frankly Terrestial geraniums now occupied its place.

The clerk snapped off the visaphone and turned back to the room.

"Good morning, Mr. Sutton," he

said, in his cultured android voice. Then he added, almost as an afterthought: "We've been wondering when you would show up."

"Twenty years," said Sutton drily, "is a long time to wonder."

"We've kept your old suite for you. We knew you would want it. Mary has kept it cleaned and ready for you ever since you left."

"That was nice of you, Ferdinand."

"You've hardly changed at all. Just the beard. I knew you the second that I turned and saw you."

"The beard and clothes," said Sutton. "The clothes are pretty bad."

"I don't suppose you have luggage, Mr. Sutton."

"No. Could I get something to eat?"

"Breakfast, perhaps? We still are serving breakfast. You always liked scrambled eggs for breakfast."

"That sounds all right," said Sutton. "Send them up with a change of clothes."

He turned slowly from the desk and walked to the elevator. He was about to close the door when a voice called: "Just a moment, please."

The girl was running across the lobby. Rangy and copper-haired, she slid into the lift, pressed her back against the wall.

"Thanks very much," she said. "Thanks so much for waiting."

Her skin, Sutton saw, was magnolia-white and her eyes were granite-colored with shadows deep within them. He closed the door softly. "I was glad to wait," he said. Her lips twitched just a little, and he added, "I don't like shoes. They cramp my feet."

He pressed the button savagely and the lift sprang upward. The lights ticked off the floors. Sutton stopped the cage. "This is my floor," he said.

HE HAD the door open and was halfway out, when she spoke to him. "Mister."

"Yes, what is it?"

"I didn't mean to laugh. I really-truly didn't."

"You had a right to laugh," said Sutton, and closed the door behind him. He stood for a moment, fighting down a sudden tenseness that seized him like a mighty fist.

Careful, he told himself, take it easy, boy. You are home at last. This is the place you dreamed of. Just a few doors down and you are finally home. You will reach out and turn the knob and push open the door and it will be there, just as you remembered it. The favorite chair, the life-paintings on the wall, the little fountain with the mermaids from Venus, and the windows where you can sit and fill your eyes with Earth.

But you can't get emotional. You can't go soft and scared.

For that chap back at the spaceport lied. And hotels don't keep rooms waiting for all of twenty years.

There is something wrong. I don't

know what, but something. Something terribly wrong.

He took a slow step . . . and then another, fighting down the tension, swallowing the dryness of excitement welling in his throat.

One of the paintings, he remembered, was a forest brook, with birds flitting in the trees. And at the most unexpected times one of the birds would sing, usually with the dawn or the going of the sun. And the water babbled with a happy song that held one listening.

He knew that he was running and he didn't try to stop. His fingers curled around the door knob and turned it.

The room was there . . . the favorite chair, the babble of the brook, the splashing of the mermaids. . . .

He caught the whiff of danger as he stepped across the threshold and he tried to turn and run, but he was too late. He felt his body crumpling forward to crash toward the floor.

"Johnny!" he cried and the cry bubbled in his throat. "Johnny!"

Inside his brain a voice whispered back: "It's all right, Ash. We're still joined."

Then darkness came.

IV

THERE was someone in the room and Sutton kept his eyelids down, kept his breathing slow.

Someone in the room was pacing quietly, stopping now before the window to look out, moving over to the mantlepiece to stare at the painting of the forest brook. And in the stillness of the room, Sutton heard the laughing babble of the painted stream against the splashing of the fountain, heard the faint bird notes that came from the painted trees, imagined that even from the distance that he lay he could smell the forest mold and the cool, wet perfume of the moss that grew along the stream.

The person in the room crossed back again and sat down in a chair. He whistled a tune, almost inaudibly. A funny, little lilting tune that Sutton had not heard before.

Someone gave me a going over, Sutton told himself. Knocked me out fast, with gas or powder, then gave me an overhauling. I seem to remember some of it . . . hazy and far away. Lights that glowed and a probing at my brain. And I might have fought against it, but I knew it was no use. And, besides, they're welcome to anything they found. Yes, they're welcome to anything they pried out of my mind. But they've found all they're going to find and they have gone away. They left someone to watch me and he still is in the room, waiting for me to wake up, probably.

Sutton stirred on the bed and opened his eyes, kept them glazed and only partly focused.

The man rose from the chair and Sutton saw that he was dressed in white. He crossed the room and leaned above the bed.

"All right now?" he asked.

Sutton raised a hand and passed it, bewildered, across his face. "Yes, I guess I am."

"You passed out," the man said.

"Something I forgot to eat."

THE man shook his head. "The trip, probably. It must have been a tough one."

"Yes," said Sutton. "Tough."

Go ahead, he thought. Go ahead and ask some more. Those are your instructions. Catch me while I'm groggy, pump me like a well. Go ahead and ask the questions and earn your lousy money.

But he was wrong. The man straightened up. "I think you'll be all right," he said. "If you aren't, call me. My card is on the mantle."

"Thanks, doctor," said Sutton.

He watched him walk across the room, waited until he heard the door click, then sat up in bed. His clothing lay in a pile in the center of the floor. His case? Yes, there it was, lying on a chair. Ransacked, no doubt, probably photostated. Spy rays, too, more than likely. All over the room. Ears listening and eyes watching.

But who? he asked himself. No one knew he was returning. No one could have known. Not even Adams. There was no way to know. There had been no way that he could let them know.

Funny. Funny the way Davis at the spaceport had recognized his name and told a lie to cover up. Funny the way Ferdinand pretended his suite had been kept for him for all these twenty years. Funny, too, how Ferdinand had turned around and spoken, as if twenty years were nothing.

Organized, said Sutton. Clicking like a relay system. Set and waiting. But why should anyone be waiting? No one knew when he'd be coming back. Or if he would come at all.

And even if someone did know, why go to all the trouble?

For they could not know, he thought . . . they could not know the thing I have, they could not even guess. Even if they did know I was coming back, incredible as it might be that they should know, even that would be more credible by a million times than that they should know the real reason for my coming.

And knowing, he said, they would not believe.

His eyes found the attache case lying on the chair, and stared at it.

And knowing, he said again, they would not believe.

When they look the ship over, of course, they will do some wondering. Then there might be some excuse for the thing that happened. But they didn't have time to look at the ship. They didn't wait a minute. They were laying for me and they gave me the works from the second that I landed.

Davis shoved me into a teleport and grabbed his phone like mad.

And Ferdinand knew that I was on the way, he knew he'd see me when he turned around. And the girl— the girl with the granite eyes?

Sutton got up and stretched. A bath and shave, first of all, he told himself. And then some clothes and breakfast. A visor call or two.

Don't act as if you've got the wind up, he warned himself. Act naturally. Talk to yourself. Pinch out a blackhead. Scratch your back against a door casing. Act as if you think you are alone.

But be careful.

There is someone watching.

V

SUTTON was finishing breakfast when the android came.

"My name is Herkimer," the android told him, "and I belong to Mr. Geoffrey Benton."

"Mr. Benton sent you here?"

"Yes. He sends a challenge."

"A challenge?"

"Yes. You know, a duel."

"But I am unarmed."

"You cannot be unarmed," said Herkimer.

"I never fought a duel in all my life," said Sutton. "I don't intend to now."

"You are vulnerable."

"What do you mean, vulnerable? If I go unarmed. . . ."

"But you cannot go unarmed. The code was changed just a year or two ago. No man younger than a hundred years can go unarmed."

"But if one does?"

"Why, then," said Herkimer, "anyone who wants to can pot him like a rabbit."

"You are sure of this?"

Herkimer dug into his pocket, brought out a tiny book. He wet his finger and fumbled at the pages. "It's right here."

"Never mind," said Sutton. "I will take your word."

"You accept the challenge, then?"

Sutton grimaced. "I suppose I have to. Mr. Benton will wait, I presume, until I buy a gun."

"No need of that," Herkimer told him brightly. "I brought one along. Mr. Benton always does that. Just a courtesy, you know. In case someone hasn't got one."

He reached into his pocket and held out the weapon. Sutton took it and laid it on the table. "Awkward looking thing," he said.

Herkimer stiffened. "It's traditional. The finest weapon made. Shoots a .45 caliber slug. Hand-loaded ammunition. Sights are tested in for fifty feet."

"You pull this?" asked Sutton, pointing.

Herkimer nodded. "It is called a trigger. And you don't pull it. You squeeze it."

"Just why does Mr. Benton challenge me?" asked Sutton. "I don't even know the man."

"You are famous," said Herkimer.

"Not that I have heard of."

"You are an investigator," Herkimer pointed out. "You have just come back from a long and perilous mission. You're carrying a mysterious attache case. And there are reporters waiting in the lobby to interview you."

Sutton nodded. "I see. When Benton kills someone, he likes him to be famous."

"Of course. More publicity."

"But I don't know your Mr. Benton. How will I know who I'm supposed to shoot at?"

"I'll show you," said Herkimer, "on the televisor." He stepped to the desk, dialed a number and stepped back. "That's him."

In the screen a man was sitting before a chess table. The pieces were in mid-game. Across the board stood a beautifully machined robotic. The man reached out a hand, thoughtfully played his knight. The robotic clicked and chuckled. It moved a pawn. Benton's shoulders hunched forward and he bent above the board. One hand came around and scratched the back of his neck.

"Oscar's got him worried," said Herkimer. "He always has him worried. Mr. Benton hasn't won a single game in the last ten years."

"Why does he keep on playing?"

"Stubborn," said Herkimer. "But Oscar's stubborn, too." He made a motion with his hand., "Machines can be so much more stubborn than humans. It's the way they're built."

"But Benton must have known, when he had Oscar fabricated, that Oscar would beat him," Sutton pointed out. "A human simply can't beat a robotic expert."

"Mr. Benton knew that," said Herkimer, "but he didn't believe it. He wanted to prove otherwise."

"Egomaniac," said Sutton.

Herkimer stared at him calmly. "I believe that you are right, sir. I've sometimes thought the same myself."

SUTTON brought his gaze back to Benton, who was still hunched above the board, the knuckles of one hand thrust hard against his mouth. The veined face was scrubbed and pink and chubby and the brooding eyes, thoughtful as they were, still held a fat twinkle of culture and good fellowship.

"You'll know him now?" asked Herkimer.

Sutton nodded. "Yes, I think I can pick him out. He doesn't look too dangerous."

"He's killed sixteen men," Herkimer said stiffly. "He plans to lay away his guns when he makes it twenty-five." He looked straight at Sutton and said: "You're the seventeenth."

"I'll try to make it easy for him."

"How would you wish it, sir?" asked Herkimer. "Formal or informal?"

"Let's make it catch-as-catch-can."

Herkimer was disapproving. "There are certain conventions. . . ."

"You can tell Mr. Benton," said Sutton, "that I don't plan to ambush him."

Herkimer picked up his cap, put it on his head. "The best of luck, sir."

"Why, thank you, Herkimer," said Sutton.

THE door closed and Sutton was alone. He turned back to the screen. Benton played to double up his rooks. Oscar chuckled at him, slid a bishop three squares along the board and put Benton's king in check.

Sutton snapped the visor off.

He scraped a hand across his now-shaved chin.

Coincidence or plan?

One of the mermaids had climbed to the edge of the fountain and balanced her three-inch self precariously. She whistled at Sutton. He turned at the sound and she dived into the pool, swam in circles, mocking him with obscene gestures.

Sutton leaned forward, reached into the visor rack, brought out the INF-JAT directory, flipped the pages swiftly.

INFORMATION—Terrestrial
Culinary
Culture
Customs

That would be it. Customs.

He found DUELING, noted the number and put back the book. He reset the dial and snapped the tumbler for direct communication.

A robot's streamlined, metallic face filled the plate. "At your service, sir," it said.

"I have been challenged to a duel," said Sutton.

The robot waited for the question.

"I don't want to fight a duel," said Sutton. "Is there any way, legally, for me to back out? I'd like to do it gracefully, too, but I won't insist on that."

"There is no way," the robot said.

"No way at all?"

"You are under one hundred?" the robot asked.

"Yes."

"You are sound of mind and body?"

"I think so."

"You are or you aren't. Make up your mind."

"I am," said Sutton.

"You do not belong to any *bona fide* religion that prohibits killing?"

"I presume I could classify myself as a Christian," said Sutton. "Isn't there a Commandment against killing?"

The robot shook his head. "It doesn't count."

"It's clear and specific," Sutton argued. "It says one should not kill."

"It does," the robot told him. "But it has been discredited. You humans never obeyed it. You either obey a law or you forfeit it."

"I guess I'm sunk then," said Sutton.

"According to the revision of the year 7990," said the robot, "arrived at by convention, any human under the age of one hundred, of male sex, sound in mind and body, unhampered by religious bonds or belief, which are subject to a court of inquiry, must fight a duel whenever challenged."

"I see."

"The history of dueling," said the robot, "is very interesting."

"It's barbaric," said Sutton.

"Perhaps so. But you humans are still barbaric in many other ways as well."

"You're impertinent."

"I'm sick and tired," the robot said. "Sick and tired of the smugness of you humans. You say you've outlawed war and you haven't, really. You've just fixed it so no one dares to fight you. You say you have abolished crime and you have, except for human crime. And a lot of the crime you have abolished isn't crime at all, except by human standards."

"You're taking a long chance, friend," warned Sutton, "talking the way you are."

"You can pull the plug on me," the robot told him, "any time you want to. Life isn't worth it, the kind of job I have."

HE SAW the look on Sutton's face and hurried on.

"Try to see it this way, sir. Through all his history, Man has been a killer. He was smart and brutal, even from the first. He was a puny thing, but he found how to use a club and rocks, and when the rocks weren't sharp enough, he chipped them so they were. There were things, at first, he should not by rights have killed. They should have killed him. But he was smart and he had the club and flints and he killed the mammoth and the sabertooth and other things he could not have faced bare-handed. So he won the Earth from the animals. He wiped them out, except the ones he allowed to live for the service that they gave him. And even as he fought with the animals, he fought with others of his kind. After the animals were gone, he kept on fighting . . . man against man, nation against nation."

"But that is past," said Sutton. "There hasn't been a war for more than a thousand years. Humans have no need of fighting now."

"That is just the point," the robot insisted. "There is no more need of fighting, no more need of killing. Oh, once in a while, perhaps, on some far-off planet, where a human must kill to protect his life or to uphold human dignity and power. But, by and large, there is no need of killing.

"And yet you kill. You must kill. The old brutality is in you. You are drunk with power and killing is a sign of power. It has become a habit with you . . . a thing you've carried from the caves. There's nothing left to kill but one another, so you kill one another and you call it dueling. You know it's wrong, and you're hypocritical about it. You've set up a fine system of semantics to make it sound respectable and brave and noble. You call it traditional and chivalric . . . and even if you don't call it that in so many words, that is what you think. You cloak it with the trappings of your vicious past, you dress it up with words, and the words are only tinsel."

"Look," said Sutton, "I don't want to fight this duel. I don't think it's. . . ."

There was vindictive glee in the robot's voice. "But you've got to fight it. There's no way to back out. Maybe you would like some pointers. I have all sorts of tricks. . . ."

"I thought you didn't approve of dueling."

"I don't," the robot said. "But it's my job. I'm stuck with it. I try to do it well. I can tell you the personal history of every man who ever fought a duel. I can talk for hours on the advantages of rapiers over pistols. Or if you'd rather I argued for pistols, I can do that, too. I can tell you about the old American West gun slicks and the Chicago gangsters and the handkerchief and dagger duels and. . . ."

"No, thanks," said Sutton.

"You aren't interested?"

"I haven't got the time."

"But, sir," the robot pleaded, "I don't get a chance too often. I don't get many calls. Just an hour or so. . . ."

"No," said Sutton firmly.

"All right, then. Maybe you'd tell me who has challenged you."

"Benton. Geoffrey Benton."

The robot whistled.

"Is he that good?" asked Sutton.

"All of it," the robot said.

Sutton shut the visor off.

He sat quietly in his chair, staring at the gun. Slowly he reached out a hand and picked it up. The butt fitted snugly in his hand. His finger curled around the trigger. He lifted it and sighted at the door knob.

It was easy to handle. Almost like it was a part of him. There was a feel of power within it . . . of power and mastery. As if he suddenly were stronger and greater . . . and more dangerous.

He sighed and laid it down. The robot had been right.

He reached out to the visor, pushed the signal for the lobby desk. Ferdinand's face came in.

"Anyone waiting down there for me, Ferdinand?"

"Not a soul," said Ferdinand.

"Anyone asked for me?"

"No one, Mr. Sutton."

"No reporters? No photographers?"

"No, Mr. Sutton. Were you expecting them?"

Sutton didn't answer. He cut off, feeling very silly.

VI

MAN was spread thin throughout the galaxy. A lone man here, a handful there. Slim creatures of bone and brain and muscle to hold a galaxy in check. Slight shoulders to hold up the cloak of human greatness spread across the light years.

For Man had flown too fast, had driven far beyond his physical capacity. Not by strength did he hold his starry outposts, but by something else . . . by depth of human character, by his colossal conceit, by his ferocious conviction that Man was the greatest living thing the galaxy had spawned. All this in spite of many evidences that he was not . . . evidence that he cast aside, scornful of any greatness that was not ruthless and aggressive.

Too thin, Christopher Adams told himself. Too thin and stretched too far. One man backed by a dozen androids and a hundred robots could hold a solar system. Could hold it until there were more men or until something cracked.

In time there'd be more men, if the birth rate increased. But it would be many centuries before the line could grow much thicker, for Man only held the keypoints . . . one planet in an entire system, and not in every system. Man had leapfrogged since there weren't men enough, had set up strategic spheres of influence, had bypassed all but the richest, most influential systems.

THERE was room to spread, room for a million years. If there were any humans left by then.

If the life on those other planets let the humans live, if there never came a day when they would be willing to pay the terrible price of wiping out mankind.

The price would be high, said Adams, talking to himself, but it could be done. Just a few hours' job. Humans in the morning, no humans left by night. What if a thousand others died for every human death . . . or ten thousand, or a hundred thousand? Under certain circumstances, such a price might be cheap.

There were islands of resistance even now where one walked carefully . . . or even walked around. Like 61 Cygni, for example.

It took judgment . . . and some tolerance . . . and a great measure of latent brutality, but, most of all, conceit, the absolute, unshakable conviction that Man was sacrosanct, that he could not be touched, that he could die only individually.

But five had died, three humans and two androids, beside a river that flowed on Aldebaran XII, just a few short miles from Andrelon, the planetary capital.

They had died of violence, of that there was no question.

Adams' eyes sought out the paragraph of Thorne's latest report:

Force had been applied from the outside. We found a hole burned through the atomic shielding of the engine. The force must have been controlled or it would have resulted in absolute destruction. The automatics got in their work and headed off the blast, but the machine went out of control and smashed into the tree. The area was saturated with intensive radiation.

Good man, Thorne, thought Adams. He won't let a single thing be missed. He had those robots in there before the place was safe for humans.

But there wasn't much to find . . . not much that gave an answer. Just a batch of question marks.

Five had died, and when that was said, that was the end of fact. For they were burned and battered and there were no features left, no fingerprints or eyeprints to match against the records.

A few feet away from the strewn blackness of the bodies, the machine had smashed into a tree. A machine that, like the men, was without a record. A machine without a counterpart in the known galaxy and, so far at least, a machine without a purpose.

Thorne would give it the works. He would set it up in solidographs, down to the last shattered piece of glass and plastic. He would have it analyzed and diagramed and the robots would put it in scanners that would peel it and record it molecule by molecule.

And they might find something. Just possibly they might.

Adams shoved the report to one side and leaned back in his chair. Idly, he spelled out his name lettered across the office door, reading backward slowly and with exaggerated care. As if he'd never seen the name before. As if he did not know it. Puzzling it out.

And then the line beneath it:

SUPERVISOR, ALIEN
RELATIONS BUREAU
Space Sector 16

And the line beneath that:

Department of Galactic
Investigation (Justice)

EARLY afternoon sunlight slanted through a window and fell across his head, highlighting the clipped silver mustache, the whitening temple hair.

Five men had died. . . .

He wished that he could get it out of his mind. There was other work. This Sutton thing, for instance. The reports on that would be coming in within an hour or so.

But there was a photograph . . . a photograph from Thorne, that he could not forget.

A smashed machine and broken bodies and a great smoking gash sliced across the turf. The silver river flowed in a silence that one knew was there even in the photograph, and far in the distance the spidery web of Andrelon rose against a pinkish sky.

Adams smiled softly to himself. Aldebaran XII, he thought, must be a lovely world. He never had been there and he never would be there . . . for there were too many planets for one man to even dream of seeing all.

Someday, perhaps, when the teleports would transmit matter instantly across light years instead of puny miles . . . perhaps then a man might just whisk across to any planet that he wished, for a day or hour, or just to say he'd been there.

But Adams didn't need to be there. He had eyes and ears there, as he had on every occupied planet within the entire galactic sector.

Thorne was there, and Thorne was an able man. He wouldn't rest until he'd wrung the last ounce of information from the broken wreck and bodies.

I wish I could forget it, Adams told himself. It's important, yes, but not all-important.

A buzzer hummed at Adams and he flipped up a tumbler on his desk. "What is it?"

A female android voice answered: "It's Mr. Thorne, sir, on the mentophone from Andrelon."

"Thank you, Alice," Adams said.

He clicked open a drawer and took out the mentophone cap, placed it on his head, adjusted it with steady fingers. Thoughts flickered through his brain, disjointed, random thought, enormously amplified by the Electro-Neuron Boosting Stations. Ghost thoughts drifting through the universe—residual flotsam from the minds of men and creatures back to the unguessable past.

Adams flinched. I'll never get used to it, he told himself. I will always duck, like the kid who anticipates a cuffing.

The ghost thoughts peeped and chittered at him.

Adams closed his eyes and settled back. "Hello, Thorne," he thought.

Thorne's thought came in, thinned and tenuous over the distance of more than fifty light years.

"That you, Adams?"

"Yes, it's me. What's up?"

A high, sing-song thought came in and skipped along his brain: *Spill the rattle . . . pinch the fish . . . oxygen is high-priced.*

Adams forced the unwanted thought out of his brain, built up his concentration. "Start over again, Thorne. A ghost thought came along and blotted you out."

Thorne's thought was louder now, more distinct. "I wanted to ask you about a name. Seems to me I heard it once before, but I can't be sure."

"What name?"

Thorne was spacing his thoughts now, placing them slowly and with emphasis to cut through the static. "The name is Asher Sutton."

ADAMS sat bolt upright in his chair. His mouth flapped open. "What?" he roared.

"Walk west," said a voice in his brain. *"Walk west and then straight up."*

Thorne's thought came in . . . "it was the name that was on the fly leaf. . . ."

"Start over," Adams concentrated. "Start over and take it slow. I couldn't hear a thing you thought."

Thorne's thoughts came slowly, intense mental power behind each word: "It was like this. You remember that wreck we had out here? Five men killed. . . ."

"Yes, yes. Of course I remember it."

"Well, we found a book, or what once had been a book, on one of the corpses. The book was burned, scorched through and through by radiation. The robots did what they could with it, but that wasn't much. A word here and there. Nothing you could make any sense out of. . . ."

The thought static purred and rumbled. Half thoughts cut through. Rambling thought-snatches that had no human sense or meaning—that could have had no human sense or meaning even if they had been heard in their entirety.

"Start over," Adams thought desperately. "Start over."

"You know about this wreck. Five men. . . ."

"Yes, yes. I got that much. Up to the part about the book. Where does Sutton come in?"

"That was about all the robotics could figure out," Thorne told him. "Just three words. 'By Asher Sutton.' Like he might have been the author. Like the book might have been written by him. It was on one of the first pages. The title page, maybe. Such and such a book by Asher Sutton."

There was silence. Even the ghost voices were still for a moment. Then a piping, lisping thought came in . . . a baby thought, immature and puling. And the thought was without context, untranslatable, almost meaningless . . . but hideous and nerve-wrenching in its alien imbecility.

Adams felt the sudden chill of fear slice into his marrow. He grasped the chair arms with both his hands and hung on tight while the degraded mindlessness babbled in his brain.

SUDDENLY the thought was gone. Fifty light years of space whistled in the cold.

Adams relaxed, felt the perspiration running from his armpits, trickling down his ribs. "You there, Thorne?" he asked.

"Yes. I caught some of that one, too."

"Pretty bad, wasn't it?"

"I've never heard much worse," Thorne told him. There was a moment's silence. Then Thorne's thoughts took up again. "Maybe I'm just wasting time. But it seemed to me I remembered that name."

"You have," Adams thought back. "Sutton went to 61 Cygni."

"Oh, he's the one!"

"He got back this morning."

"Couldn't have been him, then. Someone else by the same name."

"Must have been," thought Adams.

"Nothing else to report," Thorne told him. "The name just bothered me."

"Keep at it," Adams thought. "Let me know anything that turns up."

"I will," Thorne promised. "Good-bye."

"Thanks for calling."

ADAMS lifted off the mentophone cap. He opened his eyes and the sight of the room, commonplace and Earthly, with the sun streaming through the window, was almost a physical shock.

He sat limp in his chair, thinking, remembering.

The man had come at twilight, stepping out of the shadows onto the patio, and he had sat down in the darkness and talked like any other man. Except the things he said.

When he returns, Sutton must be killed. I am your successor.

Crazy talk. Unbelievable. Impossible.

And, still, maybe I should have listened. Maybe I should have heard him out instead of flying off the handle.

Except that you don't kill a man who comes back after twenty years.

Especially a man like Sutton.

Sutton is a good man. One of the best the Bureau has. Slick as a whistle, well grounded in alien psychology, an authority on galactic politics. No other man could have done the Cygnian job as well.

If he did it.

I don't know that, of course. But he'll be in tomorrow and he'll tell me all about it.

A man is entitled to a day's rest after twenty years.

Slowly, Adams reached out an almost reluctant hand and snapped up a tumbler.

Alice answered.

"Send me in the Asher Sutton file."

"Yes, Mr. Adams."

Adams settled back in his chair.

The warmth of the sun felt good across his shoulders. The ticking of the clock was comforting after the ghost voices whispering out in space. Thoughts that one could not pin down, that one could not trace back and say: "This one started here and then."

Although we're trying, Adams thought. He chuckled to himself at the weirdness of the project.

Thousands of listeners listening in on the random thoughts of random time and space, listening in for clues, for hints, for leads. Seeking a driblet of sense from the stream of gibberish . . . hunting the word or sentence or disassociated thought that might be translated into a new philosophy or a new technique or a new science . . . or a new something that the human race had never even dreamed of.

A new concept, said Adams, talking to himself. An entirely new concept.

Adams scowled to himself.

A new concept might be dangerous. This was not the time for anything that did not fit into human society, that did not match the pattern of human thought and action.

There must be no confusion.

There must be nothing but the sheer, bulldog determination to hang on, to sink in one's teeth and stay. To maintain the *status quo*.

Later, someday, many centuries from now, there would be a time and place and room for a new concept. When Man's grip was firmer, when the line was not too thin, when a mistake or two would not spell disaster.

Man, at the moment, controlled every factor. He held the edge at every point . . . a slight edge, admitted, but certainly an edge. And it must stay that way. There must be nothing that would tip the scale in the wrong direction. Not a word or thought, not an action or a whisper.

The desk buzzer lighted up and snarled at him.

"Yes?" said Adams.

Alice's words tumbled over one another. "The file, sir. The Sutton file."

"What about the Sutton file? Bring it in here."

"It's gone, sir."

"Someone is using it."

"No, sir, not that. It has been stolen."

Adams jerked straight upright. "Stolen!"

"That is right, sir. Twenty years ago."

"But twenty years. . . ."

"We checked the security points," said Alice. "It was stolen three days after Mr. Sutton set out for 61 Cygni."

VII

THE lawyer told Sutton his name was Wellington. He had painted a thin coat of plastic lacquer over his forehead to hide the tattoo, but the mark of the manufacture showed through, provided one looked closely.

He laid his hat very carefully on a table, sat down meticulously in a chair and placed his briefcase across his knee. He handed Sutton a rolled-up paper.

"Your newspaper, sir," he said. "It was outside the door. I thought that you might want it."

"Thanks," said Sutton.

Wellington cleared his throat. "You are Asher Sutton?" he asked.

Sutton nodded.

"I represent a certain robot who commonly went by the name of Buster. You may remember him."

Sutton leaned quickly forward. "Remember him? Why, he was a second father to me. Raised me after both my parents died. He has been with the Sutton family for almost four thousand years."

Wellington cleared his throat again. "Quite so."

Sutton leaned back in his chair, crushing the newspaper in his grip. "Don't tell me . . ."

Wellington waved a sober hand. "No, he's in no trouble. Not yet, that is. Not unless you choose to make it for him."

"What has he done?" asked Sutton.

"He has run away."

"Good Lord! Run away? Where to?"

Wellington squirmed uneasily in the chair. "To one of the Tower stars, I believe."

"But," protested Sutton, "that's way out. Out almost to the edge of the galaxy."

Wellington nodded. "He bought himself a new body and a ship and stocked it up . . ."

"With what? asked Sutton. "Buster had no money."

"Oh, yes, he had. Money he had saved over—what was it you said?—four thousand years or so. Tips from guests, Christmas presents, one thing and another. It would all count up . . . in four thouand years. Placed at interest, you know."

"But why?" asked Sutton. "What does he intend to do?"

"He took out a homestead on a planet. He didn't sneak away. He filed his claim, so you can trace him if you wish. He used the family name, sir. That worried him a little. He hoped you wouldn't mind."

Sutton shook his head. "Not at all. He has a right to that name, as good a right as I have myself."

"You don't mind, then?" asked Wellington. "About the whole thing, I mean? After all, he was your property."

"No," said Sutton, "I don't mind. But I was looking forward to seeing him again. I called the old home place, but there was no answer. I thought he might be out."

Wellington reached into the inside pocket of his coat. "He left you a letter," he said, holding it out.

Sutton took it. It had his name written across its face. He turned it over, but there was nothing more.

"He also," said Wellington, "left an old trunk in my custody. Said it contained some old family papers that you might find of interest."

Sutton sat quietly staring across the room, seeing nothing.

There had been an apple tree at the gate, and each year young Ash Sutton had eaten the apples when they were green, and Buster had nursed him each time gently through the crisis and then had whaled him good and proper to teach him respect for his human metabolism. And when the kid down the road had licked him on the way home from school, it had been Buster who had taken him out in the backyard and taught him how to fight with head as well as hands.

Sutton clenched his fists unconsciously, remembering the surge of satisfaction, the red rawness of his knuckles. The kid down the road, he recalled, had nursed a black eye for a week and become his fastest friend.

"About the trunk, sir?" asked Wellington. "You will want it delivered?"

"Yes," said Sutton, "if you please."

"It will be here tomorrow morning." The android picked up his hat and rose. "I want to thank you, sir, for my client. He assured me you would be reasonable."

"Not reasonable," said Sutton. "Just fair. He took care of us for many years. He has earned his freedom."

"Good day, sir," said Wellington.

"Good day," said Sutton. "And thank you very much."

One of the mermaids whistled at Sutton. Sutton told her. "One of these days, my beauty, you'll do that once too often."

She thumbed her nose at him and dived into the fountain.

The door clicked shut as Wellington left.

Slowly, Sutton tore the letter open, spread out the single page:

Dear Ash—I went to see Mr. Adams today and he told me

that he was afraid that you would not come back, but I told him that I knew you would. So I'm not doing this because I think you won't come back and that you will never know . . . because I know you will. Since you left me and struck out on your own, I have felt old and useless. In a galaxy where there were many things to do, I was doing nothing. You told me you just wanted me to live on at the old place and take it easy, and I knew you did that because you were kind and would not sell me even if you had no use for me. So I'm doing something I have always wanted to do. I am filing on a planet. It sounds like a pretty good planet and I should be able to do something with it. I shall fix it up and build a home and maybe someday you will come and visit me.

P. S. If you ever want me, you can find out where I am at the homestead office.

GENTLY, Sutton folded the sheet, put it in his pocket.

He sat idly in the chair, listening to the purling of the stream that gushed through the painting hung above the fireplace. A bird sang and a fish jumped in a quiet pool around the bend, just outside the frame.

Tomorrow, he thought, I will see Adams. Maybe I can find out if he's behind what happened. Although why should he be? I'm working for him. I'm carrying out his orders.

He shook his head. No, it couldn't be Adams.

But it must be someone. Someone who had been laying for him, who even now was watching.

He shrugged mental shoulders, picked up the newspaper and opened it.

It was the *Galactic Press* and in twenty years its format had not changed. Conservative columns of gray type ran down the page, broken only by laconic headings. Earth news started in the upper left-hand corner of the front page, followed by Martian news, by Venusian news, by the column from the asteroids, the column and a half from the Jovian moons . . . then the outer planets. News from the rest of the galaxy, he knew, could be found on the inside pages. A paragraph or two to each story. Like the old community personal columns in the country papers of many centuries before.

Still, thought Sutton, smoothing out the paper, it was the only way it could be handled. There was so much news . . . news from many worlds, from many sectors . . . human news, android and robot news, alien news. The items had to be boiled down, condensed, compressed, making one word do the job of a hundred.

There were other papers, of course, serving isolated sections, and these would give the local news in more detail. But on Earth there was need of galactic-wide news coverage

. . . for Earth was the capital of the galaxy, a planet that was nothing but a capital, a planet that grew no food, allowed no industries, that made its business nothing but government. A planet whose every inch was landscaped and tended like a lawn or park or garden.

Sutton ran his eye down the Earth column. An earthquake in eastern Asia. A new underwater development for the housing of alien employes and representatives from watery worlds. Delivery of three new star ships to the Sector 19 run. And then:

> *Asher Sutton, special agent of the department of galactic investigation, returned today from 61 Cygni, to which he was assigned twenty years ago. Hope of his return had been abandoned. Immediately upon his landing, a guard was thrown around his ship and he was in seclusion at the Orion Arms. All attempts to reach him for a statement failed. Shortly after his arrival, he was called out by Geoffrey Benton. Mr. Sutton chose a pistol and informality.*

Sutton read the item again. *All attempts to reach him . . .*

Herkimer had said there were reporters and photographers in the lobby, and ten minutes later Ferdinand had sworn there weren't. He had had no calls. There had been no attempt to reach him. Or had there? Attempts that had been neatly stopped. Stopped by the same person who had lain in wait for him, the same power that had been inside the room when he stepped across the threshold.

He dropped the paper to the floor, sat thinking.

He had been drugged and searched, an attempt made to probe his mind. His attache case had been ransacked. He had been challenged by one of Earth's foremost duelists. The old family robot had run away . . . or been persuaded to run away. Attempts by the press to reach him had been stopped cold.

The visor purred at him.

A call. The first since he had arrived.

HE SWUNG around in his chair and flipped up the switch.

A woman's face came in. Granite eyes and skin magnolia white, hair a copper glory.

"My name is Eva Armour," she said. "I am the one who asked you to hold the elevator."

"I recognized you," said Sutton.

"I called to make amends."

"There is no need . . ."

"But there is, Mr. Sutton. You thought I was laughing at you and I really wasn't."

"I looked funny," Sutton told her. "It was your privilege to laugh."

"Will you take me out to dinner?" she asked.

"Certainly," gasped Sutton. "I would be delighted to."

"And someplace afterward," she suggested. "We'll make an evening of it."

"Gladly."

"I'll meet you in the lobby at seven," she said. "And I won't be late."

The visor faded and Sutton sat stiffly in the chair.

We'll make an evening of it, he said, talking to himself, and you'll be lucky if you're alive tomorrow.

VIII

ADAMS silently faced the four men who had come into his office, trying to make out what they might be thinking. But their faces gave no indication.

Clark, the space construction engineer, clutched a field book in his hand and his face was set and stern. There was no foolishness about Clark . . . ever.

Anderson, anatomist, big and rough, was lighting his pipe and, for the moment, that seemed to him the most important thing in all the worlds.

Blackburn, the psychologist, frowned at the glowing tip of his cigarette, and Shulcross, the language expert, sprawled sloppily in his chair like a bored youngster.

They found something, Adams told himself. They found plenty and some of it has them tangled up.

"Clark," said Adams, "suppose you start us out."

"We looked the ship over," Clark told him, "and we found it couldn't fly."

"But it did," said Adams. "Sutton brought it home."

Clark shrugged, "He might as well have used a log. Or a hunk of rock. Either one would have served the purpose. Either one would fly just as well, or better, than that heap of junk."

"Junk?"

"The engines were washed out," said Clark. "The safety automatics were the only things that kept them from atomizing. The ports were cracked, some of them were broken. One of the tubes was busted off and lost. The whole ship was twisted out of line."

"That sounds like a wreck," Adams objected.

"It had struck something." Clark declared. "Struck it hard and fast. Seams were opened, the structural plates were bent, the whole thing was twisted out of kilter. Even if you could start the engines, the ship would never handle. Even with the tubes okay you couldn't set a course. Give it any drive and it would simply corkscrew."

Anderson cleared his throat. "What would have happened to Sutton if he'd been in it when it it was struck?"

"He would have died," said Clark.

"You are positive of that?"

"No question. Even a miracle wouldn't have saved him. We thought of that, so we worked it out. We rigged up a diagram and we used the most conservative force factors to show theoretic effects . . ."

Adams interrupted. "But he must have been in the ship."

Clark shook his head stubbornly. "If he was, he died. Our diagram shows he didn't have a chance. If one force didn't kill him, a dozen others would."

"Sutton came back," Adams said.

THE two stared at one another, half angrily.

Anderson broke the silence. "Had he tried to fix it up?"

Clark shook his head. "Not a mark to show he did. There would have been no use trying. Sutton didn't know a thing about mechanics. Not a single thing. I checked on that. He had no training, no natural inclination. And it takes a man with savvy to repair an atomic engine. Just to fix it, not rebuild it. And this crash would have called for complete rebuilding."

Shulcross spoke for the first time, softly, quietly, not moving from his awkward slouch. "Maybe we're starting in the middle. If we started at the beginning, laid the groundwork first, we might get a better idea of what really happened."

They looked at him, all of them, wondering what he meant. Shulcross saw it was up to him to go ahead. He spoke to Adams: "Do you have any idea of what sort of place this Cygnian world might be where Sutton went?"

Adams smiled wearily. "We've never been able to get close enough to know. It's the seventh planet of 61 Cygni. It might have been any one of the system's sixteen planets, but mathematically it was figured out that the seventh planet had the best chance of sustaining life."

He paused and looked around the circle of faces and saw that they were waiting for him to go on.

"Sixty-one," he said, "is a near neighbor of ours. It was one of the first suns that Man headed for when he left the solar system. Ever since it has been a thorn in our sides."

Anderson grinned. "Because we couldn't crack it."

Adams nodded. "That's right. A secret system in a galaxy that held few secrets from Man anytime he wanted to go out and take the trouble to solve them. We've run into all sorts of weird things, of course. Planetary conditions that, to this day, we haven't licked. Weird, dangerous life. Economic systems and psychological concepts that had us floored and still give us a headache every time we think of them. But we were always able, at the very least, to see the thing that gave us trouble, to know the thing that licked us. With Cygni it was different. We couldn't even get there.

"The planets are either cloud-covered or screened, for we've never seen the surface of a single one of them. And when you get within a few billion miles of the system you start sliding." He turned to Clark. "That's the right word, isn't it?"

"There's no word for it," Clark told him, "but sliding comes as close as any. You aren't stopped and you aren't slowed, but you are deflected. As if the ship had hit ice, although it feels slicker than ice. Whatever it is, it doesn't register. There's no sign of it, nothing that you can see, nothing that makes even the faintest flicker on the instruments, but you hit it and you slide off course. You correct and you slide off course again. In the early days, it drove men batty trying to reach the system and never getting a mile nearer than a certain imaginary line."

"As if," said Adams, "someone had taken his finger and drawn a deadline around the system."

"Something like that," said Clark.

"But Sutton got through," said Anderson.

"I don't like it," Clark declared. "I don't like a thing about it. Someone got a brainstorm. Our ships are too big, they said. If we use smaller ships, we might squeeze through. As if the thing that kept us off was a mesh holding back the big jobs."

"Sutton got through," said Adams stubbornly. "They launched him in a lifeboat and he got through where the big ships couldn't."

CLARK shook his head, just as stubbornly. "It doesn't make sense. Smallness and bigness wouldn't have a thing to do with it. There's another factor somewhere, a factor we've never even thought of. Sutton got through, all right, and he crashed and if he was in the ship when it crashed, he died. But he didn't get through only because his ship was small. It was for some other reason."

The men sat tense, thinking, waiting.

"Why Sutton?" Anderson asked, finally.

Adams answered quietly. "The ship was small. We could only send one man. We picked the man we thought could do the best job if he did get through."

"And Sutton was the best man?"

"He was," said Adams.

Anderson said amiably: "Well, apparently he was. He got through."

"Or was let through," said Blackburn.

"Not necessarily," said Anderson.

"It follows," Blackburn contended. "Why did we want to get into the Cygnian system? To find out if it was dangerous. That was the idea, wasn't it?"

"That was the idea," Adams agreed. "Anything unknown is potentially dangerous. You can't write it off until you are sure. Those were Sutton's instructions: Find out if 61 is dangerous."

"And, by the same token, they'd want to find out about us," Blackburn said. "We'd been prying and poking at them for several thousand years. They might have wanted to find out about us as badly as we did about them."

Anderson nodded. "I see what you mean. They'd chance one man, if they could haul him in, but they wouldn't let a full-armed ship and a fighting crew get in shooting distance."

"Exactly," said Blackburn.

Adams dismissed the line of talk abruptly, said to Clark: "You spoke of dents. Were they made recently?"

"Twenty years ago looks right to me. There was a lot of rust. Some of the wiring was getting pretty soft."

"Let us suppose, then," said Anderson, "that Sutton, by some miracle, had the knowledge to fix the ship. Even so, he would have needed materials."

"Plenty of them," said Clark.

"The Cygnians could have supplied them," Shulcross suggested.

"If there are any Cygnians," said Anderson.

"I don't believe they could," Blackburn declared. "A race that hides behind a screen would not be mechanical. If they knew mechanics, they would go out into space instead of shielding themselves from space. I'll make a guess the Cygnians are non-mechanical."

"But the screen," Anderson prompted.

"It wouldn't have to be mechanical," Blackburn said flatly. "Some energy force or other we don't know about."

Clark smacked his open palm on his knee. "What's the use of all this speculation? Sutton didn't repair that ship. He brought it back, somehow, without repair. He didn't even try to fix it. There are layers of rust on everything and there's not a wrench mark on it."

Shulcross leaned forward. "One thing I don't get: Clark says some of the ports were broken. That means Sutton navigated eleven light years without air to breathe."

"He used a suit," said Blackburn.

Clark said quietly: "There weren't any suits." He looked around the room, almost as if he feared some one outside the little circle might be listening. "And that isn't all. There wasn't any food and there wasn't any water."

Anderson tapped out his pipe against the palm of his hand and the hollow sound of tapping echoed in the room. Carefully, deliberately, almost as if he forced himself to concentrate upon it, he dropped the ash from his hand into a tray.

"I might have the answer to that one," he said. "At least a clue. There is still a lot of work to do before we have the answer. And, then, we can't be sure." He was aware of the eyes upon him. "I hesitate to say the thing I have in mind."

NO ONE spoke a word.

The clock on the wall ticked the seconds off.

From far outside the open window, a locust hummed in the quiet of afternoon.

"I don't think," said Anderson, "that the man is human."

The clock ticked on. The locust shrilled to tense silence.

Adams finally spoke. "But the

fingerprints checked. The eyeprints, too."

"Oh, it's Sutton, all right," Anderson admitted. "There is no doubt of that. Sutton on the outside. Sutton in the flesh. The same body, or at least part of the same body, that left Earth twenty years ago."

"What are you getting at?" asked Clark. "If he's the same, he's human."

"You take an old spaceship," said Anderson, "and you juice it up. Add a gadget here and another there, eliminate one thing, modify another. What have you got?"

"A rebuilt job," said Clark.

"That's just the phrase I wanted," Anderson told them. "Someone or something has done the same to Sutton. He's a rebuilt job. And the best human job I have ever seen. He's got two hearts and his nervous system's haywire . . . well, not haywire exactly, but different. Certainly not human. And he's got an extra circulatory system. Not a circulatory system, either, but that is what it looks like. Only it's not connected with the heart. Right now, I'd say, it's not being used. Like a spare system. One system starts running down and you can switch to the spare one while you tinker with the first."

ANDERSON pocketed his pipe, rubbed his hands together almost as if he were washing them.

"Well, there," he said, "you have it."

Blackburn blurted out: "It sounds impossible."

Anderson appeared not to have heard him, and yet answered him. "We had Sutton under for the best part of an hour and we put every inch of him on tape and film. It takes some time to analyze a job like that. We aren't finished yet. But we failed in one thing. We used a psychonometer on his mind and we didn't get a nibble. Not a quaver, not a thought. Not even mental seepage. His mind was closed, tight shut."

"Some defect in the meter," Adams suggested.

"No," said Anderson. "We checked that." He looked around the room, from one face to another. "Maybe you don't realize the implication. When a man is drugged or asleep . . . or in any case where he is unaware, a psychonometer will turn him inside out. It will dig out things that his waking self would swear he didn't know. Even when a man fights against it, there is a certain seepage and that seepage widens as his mental resistance wears down."

"But it didn't work with Sutton," Shulcross said.

"That's right. It didn't work with Sutton. I tell you, the man's not human."

"And you think he's different enough, physically, so that he could live in space without air, food and water?"

"I don't know," said Anderson.

He licked his lips and stared around the room. "I don't know. I simply don't."

Adams spoke softly. "We must not get upset. Alienness is no strange thing to us, Once it might have been, when the first humans went out into space. But today. . . ."

Clark interrupted impatiently. "Alien things themselves don't bother me. But when a man turns alien. . . ." He gulped, appealed to Anderson. "Do you think he's dangerous?"

"Possibly," said Anderson.

"Even if he is, he can't do much to harm us," Adams told them calmly. "That place of his is simply clogged with spy rigs."

"Any reports in yet?" asked Blackburn.

"Just general. Nothing specific. Sutton has been taking it easy. Had a few calls. Made a few himself. Had a visitor or two."

"He knows he's being watched," said Clark. "He's putting on an act."

"There's a rumor around," said Blackburn, "that Benton challenged him."

Adams nodded. "Yes, he did. Ash tried to back out of it. That doesn't sound as if he's dangerous."

"Maybe," speculated Clark, almost hopefully, "Benton will close our case for us."

Adams smiled thinly. "Somehow I think Ash may have spent the afternoon thinking up a dirty deal for our Mr. Benton."

Anderson had fished the pipe out of his pocket, was loading it from his pouch. Clark was fumbling for a cigarette.

ADAMS looked at Shulcross. "You have something?"

The language expert nodded. "But it's not too exciting. We opened Sutton's case and we found a manuscript. We photostated it and replaced it exactly as it was. But so far it hasn't done us any good. We can't read a word of it."

"Code," said Blackburn.

Shulcross shook his head. "If it was code, our robots would have cracked it in an hour or two. But it's not a code. It's language. And until you get a key, a language can't be cracked."

"You've checked, of course."

Shulcross smiled glumly. "Back to the old Earth languages . . . back to Babylon and Crete. We cross-checked every lingo in the galaxy. None of them came close."

"Language," said Blackburn. "A new language. That means Sutton found something."

"Sutton would," said Adams. "He's the best agent I ever had."

Anderson stirred restlessly in his chair. "You like Sutton?" he asked.

"I do," said Adams.

"Adams," said Anderson, "I've been wondering. It's a thing that struck me funny from the first."

"Yes, what is it?"

"You knew Sutton was coming back. Knew almost to the minute

when he would arrive. And you set a mousetrap for him. How come?"

"Just a hunch," said Adams.

For a long moment all four of them sat looking at him. Then they saw he meant to say no more. They rose and left the room.

IX

ACROSS the room a woman's laughter floated, sharp-edged with excitement.

The lights changed from the dusk-blue of April to the purple-gray of madness, and the room was another world that floated in a hush that was not exactly silence. Perfume came down a breeze that touched the cheek with ice . . . perfume that called to mind black orchids in an outland of breathless terror.

The floor swayed beneath Sutton's feet and he felt Eva's small fist digging hard into his arm.

The Zag spoke to them—an android with specialized psychic development—and his words were dead and hollow sounds dripping from a mummied husk. "What is it that you wish? Here you live the lives you yearn for . . . find any escape that you may seek . . . possess the things you dream of."

"There was a stream," said Sutton. "A little creek that ran. . . ."

The light changed to green, a faery green that glowed with soft, quiet life, exuberant, springtime life and the hint of things to come, and there were trees, trees that were fringed and haloed with the glistening, sun-kissed green of first-bursting buds.

Sutton wiggled his toes and knew the grass beneath them, the first tender grass of spring, and smelled the hepaticas and bloodroot that had almost no smell at all . . . and the stronger scent of sweet Williams blooming on the hill across the creek.

He told himself: "It's too early for sweet Williams to be in bloom."

The creek gurgled at him as it ran across the shingle down into the Big Hole, and he hurried forward across the meadow grass, cane pole tight-clutched in one hand, the can of worms in the other.

A bluebird flashed through the trees that climbed the bluff across the meadow and a robin sang high in the top of the mighty elm that grew above the Big Hole.

Sutton found the worn place in the bank, like a chair with the elm's trunk serving as a back, and he sat down in it and leaned forward to peer into the water. The current ran strong and dark and deep.

Sutton drew in his breath and held it with pent-up anticipation. With shaking hands he found the biggest worm and pulled it from the can, baited up the hook.

Breathlessly, he dropped the hook into the water, canted the pole in front of him for easy handling. The bobber drifted down the swirling slide of water, floated in an eddy where the current turned back upon itself. It jerked, almost disappeared, then bobbed to the surface and floated once again.

Sutton leaned forward, arms aching with tension. But even through the tension, he knew the goodness of the day. The water talked to him and he felt himself grow and become a being that comprehended and became a part of the clean, white ecstasy that was the hills and stream and meadow . . . earth, cloud, water, sky and sun.

And the bobber went clear under!

He felt the weight and strength of the fish that he had caught. It sailed in an arc above his head and landed in the grass behind him. He laid down his pole, scrambled to his feet and ran.

The chub flopped in the grass and he grabbed the line and held it up. It was a whopper! Sobbing in excitement, he dropped to his knees and grasped the fish, removed the hook with fingers that fumbled in their trembling.

"Hello," said a childish voice.

Sutton twisted around, still on his knees.

A LITTLE girl stood by the elm tree, and it seemed for a moment that he had seen her somewhere before. But then he realized that she was a stranger and he frowned a little, for girls were no good when it came to fishing. He hoped she wouldn't stay. It would be just like a girl to hang around and spoil the day for him.

"I am . . . ," she said, speaking a name he did not catch, for she lisped a little.

He did not answer.

"I am eight years old," she said.

"I am Asher Sutton," he told her, "and I am ten . . . going on eleven."

She stood and stared at him, one hand plucking nervously at the figured apron that she wore. The apron, he noticed, was clean and starched, very stiff and prim, and she was messing it all up with her nervous plucking.

"I am fishing," he said and tried very hard to keep from sounding too important. "And I just caught a whopper."

He saw her eyes go large in sudden terror at the sight of something that came up from behind him and he wheeled around, no longer on his knees, but on his feet, and his hand was snaking into the pocket of his coat.

The place was purple-gray and there was shrill woman-laughter and there was a face in front of him . . . a face he had seen that afternoon and never would forget.

A fat and cultured face that twinkled even now with good fellowship, twinkled despite the deadly squint, and the gun already swinging upward in his hairy, pudgy fist.

Sutton felt his own fingers touch the grip on the gun he carried, felt them tighten around it and jerk it from the pocket. But he was too late, he knew, to beat the *spat* of flame from a gun that had long seconds start.

Anger flamed within him, cold, desolate, deadly anger. Anger at the pudgy fist, at the smiling face . . . the face that would smile across a chess board or from behind a gun. The smile of an egotist who would try to beat a robotic that was designed to play a perfect game of chess . . . an egotist who believed that he could shoot down Asher Sutton.

THE anger, he realized, was something more than anger . . . something greater and more devastating than the mere working of human adrenal. It was a part of him and something that was more than

him, more than the mortal thing of flesh and blood that was Asher Sutton. A terrible thing plucked from non-humanity.

The face before him melted . . . or it seemed to melt. It changed and the smile was gone, and Sutton felt the anger whip from his brain and slam bullet-hard against the wilting personality that was Geoffrey Benton.

Benton's gun coughed loudly and the muzzle-flash was blood red in the purple light. Then Sutton felt the thud of his own gun slamming back against the heel of his hand as he pulled the trigger.

Benton was falling, twisting forward, bending at the middle as if he had hinges in his stomach, and Sutton caught one glimpse of the purple-tinted face before it dropped to the floor. There were surprise and anguish and a terrible over-riding fear printed on the features that had been twisted out of shape.

The crashing of the guns had smashed the place to silence, and through the garish light that swirled with powder smoke, Sutton saw the white blobs of many faces staring at him. Faces that mostly were without expression, although some of them had mouths and the mouths were round and open.

He felt a tugging at his elbow and he moved, guided by the hand upon his arm. Suddenly he was limp and shaken and the anger was no more and he told himself: "I have just killed a man."

"Quick," said Eva Armour's voice.

"We must get out of here. They'll be swarming at you now. The whole hell's pack of them."

"It was you," he told her. "I remember now. I didn't catch the name at first. You mumbled it . . . or I guess you lisped, and I didn't hear it."

The girl tugged at his arm. "They had Benton-conditioned to kill you. They figured that was all they needed. They never dreamed you could match him in a duel."

"You were the little girl," Sutton told her blankly. "You wore a checkered apron and you kept twisting it nervously."

"What in heaven's name are you talking about?"

"I was fishing," Benton said, "and I had just caught a big one when you came along . . ."

"You're crazy," said the girl. "Fishing? Here?"

She pushed open a door and pulled him out and the cool air of night slapped him briskly and shockingly across the face.

"Wait a second," he cried. He wheeled around and caught the girl's arms roughly in his hands. "They?" he yelled at her. "What are you talking about? Who are they . . ."

She stared at him wide-eyed. "You mean you don't know?"

He shook his head, bewildered.

"Poor Ash," she said.

Her copper hair was a reddish flame, burnished and alive in the flicker of the sign that flashed on and off above the Zag House facade:

DREAMS TO ORDER
Live the Life You Missed!
Dream Up a Tough One for Us!

AN android doorman spoke to them softly. "You wished a cab, sir?" Even as he spoke, the car was there, sliding smoothly and silently up the driveway, like a black beetle winging from the night. The doorman reached out a hand and swung wide the door. "Quick is the word," he said.

There was something in the soft, slurred tone that made Sutton move. He stepped inside the car and pulled Eva after him. The android slammed the door.

Sutton tramped on the accelerator and the car screamed down the curving driveway, slid into the highway, roared with leashed impatience as it took the long road curving toward the hills.

"Where?" asked Sutton.

"Back to the Arms," she said. "They wouldn't dare to try for you there. Your room is rigged with rays."

Sutton chuckled. "I have to be careful or I would trip on them. But how come you know?"

"It is my job to know."

"Friend or foe?" he asked.

"Friend," she said.

He turned his head and studied her. She had slumped down in the seat and was a little girl again . . . but she didn't have a checkered apron and she wasn't nervous.

"I don't suppose," said Sutton,

"that it would be any use for me to ask you questions?"

She shook her head.

"If I did, you'd probably lie to me."

"If I wanted to," she said.

"I could shake it out of you."

"You could, but you won't. You see, Ash, I know you very well."

"You just met me yesterday."

"Yes, I know," she said, "but I've studied you for all of twenty years."

X

THE trunk came in the morning when Sutton was finishing his breakfast.

It was old and battered, the ancient rawhide covering hanging in tatters to reveal the marred steel skeleton, flecked here and there with rust. A key was in the lock and the straps were broken. Mice had gnawed the leather completely off one end.

Sutton remembered it. It was the one that had stood in the far corner of the attic when he had been a boy and gone there to play on rainy afternoons..

He picked up the neatly folded copy of the morning edition of the *Galactic Press* that had come with his breakfast tray and shook it out.

The article he was looking for was on the front page, the third item in the Earth news column:

Mr. Geoffrey Benton was killed last night in an informal meeting at one of the amusement centers in the university district. The victor was Mr. Asher Sutton, who returned only yesterday from a mission to 61 Cygni.

There was a final sentence, the most damning that could be written of a duelist:

Mr. Benton fired first and missed.

Sutton folded the paper again and laid it carefully on the table. He lit a cigarette.

I thought it would be me, he told himself. I never fired a gun like that before . . . scarcely knew such a gun existed. Of course, I didn't really kill Benton. He killed himself. If he hadn't missed . . . and there was no excuse for missing . . . the item would have read the other way around.

We'll make an evening of it, the girl had said, and she probably knew. We'll have dinner and make an evening of it and Geoffrey Benton will kill you by appointment at the Zag House.

YES, said Sutton to himself, she might have known. She knows too many things. About the spy traps in this room, for instance. And about someone who had Benton psychologically conditioned to challenge me and kill me.

She said friend when I asked her friend or foe, but a word is an easy thing. There is no way to know if it is true or false.

She said she had studied me for twenty years and that is false, of course, for twenty years ago I was setting out for Cygni and I was unimportant. Just a cog in a great machine. I am unimportant still, unimportant to everyone but myself, and to a great idea that no human but myself could possible know about. For no matter if the manuscript was photostated; there is not a soul can read it.

He snubbed out the cigarette and rose and walked over to the trunk. The lock was rusty and the key turned hard, but he finally got it open and lifted up the lid.

The trunk was half full of papers neatly piled. Sutton, looking at them, chuckled. Buster always was a methodical soul. But, then, all robots were methodical. It was the nature of them. Methodical and—what was it Herkimer had said?—stubborn.

He squatted on the floor beside the trunk and rummaged through the contents. Old letters tied neatly in bundles. An old notebook from his college days. A sheaf of clipped-together documents that undoubtedly were outdated. A scrapbook littered with clippings that had not been pasted up. An album half filled with a cheap stamp collection.

He squatted back on his heels and turned the pages of the album lovingly, childhood memories coming back again. Cheap stamps because he had had no money to buy the better ones. Gaudy ones because they had appealed to him. The stamp craze, he remembered, had lasted two years . . . three years at the most. He had pored over catalogs, had traded, picked up the strange lingo of the hobby . . . perforate, imperforate, shades, watermarks, intaglio.

He smiled at the happiness of memory. There had been stamps he'd wanted, but could never have, and he had studied the illustrations of them until he knew each one by heart. He lifted his head and stared hard at the wall and tried to remember what some of them were like, but there was no recollection. The once all-important thing had been buried by more than fifty years of other all-important matters.

HE LAID the album to one side, went at the trunk again.

More notebooks and letters. Loose clippings. A curious-looking wrench. A well chewed bone that at one time probably had been the property and the solace of some loved but now forgotten family dog.

Junk, said Sutton. Buster could have saved a lot of time by simply burning it.

A couple of old newspapers. A moth-eaten pennant. A bulky letter that never had been opened. Sutton tossed it on top of the rest of the litter he had taken from the trunk, then hesitated, put out his hand and picked it up again.

That stamp looked queer. The color, for one thing.

Memory ticked within his brain and he saw the stamp as he had seen it when a lad . . . not the stamp itself, of course, but the illustration of it in a catalog.

He bent above the letter and caught a sudden, gasping breath.

The stamp was old, incredibly old . . . incredibly old and worth . . . good Lord, how much was it worth?

He tried to make out the postmark, but it was faint with time.

He got up slowly and carried the letter to the table, bent above it, puzzling out the town name.

BRIDGEP WIS

Bridgeport, probably. And WIS? Some political division lost in the mist of time.

July 198

July, 1980—something!

Sutton's hand shook.

AN unopened letter, mailed 6,000 years ago. Tossed in with this heap of junk. Lying cheek by jowl with a tooth-scarred bone and a funny wrench.

An unopened letter . . . and with a stamp that was worth a fortune.

Sutton read the postmark again. Bridgeport, Wis. July, it looked like 11 . . . July 11, 198—. The missing numeral in the year was too faint to make out. Maybe with a good glass it could be done.

The address, faded but still legible, said:

Mr. John H. Sutton
Bridgeport
Wisconsin

So that was what WIS was. Wisconsin.

And the name was Sutton.

Of course, it would be Sutton.

What had Buster's android lawyer said? A trunk full of family papers.

I'll have to look into historic geography, Sutton thought. I'll have to find out just where Wisconsin was.

But John H. Sutton. That was another matter. Just another Sutton. One who had been dust these many years. A man who sometimes forgot to open up his mail.

Sutton turned the letter and examined the flap. There was no sign of tampering. The adhesive was flaking with age and when he ran a fingernail along one corner, the mucilage came loose in a tiny shower of powder. The paper, he saw, was brittle and would require careful handling.

A trunk full of family papers, the android Wellington had said when he came into the room and balanced himself very primly on the edge of a chair and laid his hat precisely on the table top.

And it was a trunk full of junk instead. Bones and wrenches and paper clips and clippings. Old notebooks and letters and a letter that had been mailed 6,000 years ago and never had been opened.

Did Buster know about the letter?

But even as he asked himself the question, Sutton knew that Buster did.

And he had tried to hide it . . . and he had succeeded. He had tossed it in with other odds and ends, knowing that it would be found, but by the man for whom it was intended. For the trunk was deliberately made to appear of no importance. It was old and battered and the key was in the lock and it said there's nothing important inside, but if you want to waste your time, why, go ahead and look. And if anyone had looked, the clutter would have seemed worthless.

SUTTON reached out and tapped the letter lying on the table.

John H. Sutton, an ancestor sixty centuries removed. His blood runs in my veins, though many times diluted. But he was a man who lived and breathed and ate and died, who saw the sunrise against the green Wisconsin hills . . . if Wisconsin had any hills, wherever it was. He felt the heat of summer and shivered in the cold of winter. He worried about many things, both big and small and most of them would be small, the way worries usually are.

A man like me, although there would be minor differences. He had a vermiform appendix and it may have caused him trouble. He had wisdom teeth and they may have caused him trouble, too. And he probably died at eighty or earlier. And when I am eighty, Sutton thought, I will be just entering my prime.

But there would be compensations. John H. Sutton would have lived closer to the Earth, for the Earth was all he had. He would have been unplagued by alien psychology and Earth would have been a living place instead of a governing place where not a thing is grown for its economic worth, not a wheel is turned for economic purpose. He could have chosen his life work from the whole broad field of human endeavor instead of being forced into governmental work, into the job of governing a thin cobweb of galactic empire.

And somewhere, lost now, there were Suttons before him, and after him—lost, too—many other Suttons. The chain of life runs smoothly from one generation to the next, and none of the links stands out, except, here and there, a link one sees by accident. By the accident of history, or the accident of myth, or the accident of not opening a letter.

The door bell chimed and Sutton, startled, scooped up the letter and slid it into the inside pocket of his coat.

"Come in," he called.

It was Herkimer. "Good morning, sir," he said.

Sutton glared at him. "What do you want?"

"I belong to you," Herkimer told him blandly. "I'm part of your third of Benton's property."

"My third. . . ." And then he remembered.

It was the law. Whoever kills another in a duel inherits one third of the dead man's property. That was a law he had forgotten.

"I hope you don't object," said Herkimer. "I am easy to get along with and very quick to learn and I like to work. I can cook and sew and run errands and I can read and write."

"And put the finger on me."

"Oh, no, I never would do that."

"Why not?"

"Because you are my master."

"We'll see," Sutton remarked sourly.

"But I'm not all," said Herkimer. "There are other things. There's a hunting asteroid stocked with the finest game, and a spaceship. A small one, it's true, but very serviceable. There are several thousand dollars and an estate out on the West Coast and some wildcat planetary development stock and a number of other small things, too numerous to mention." Herkimer brought out a notebook. "I have them written out if you would care to listen."

"Not now," said Sutton. "I have work to do."

Herkimer brightened. "Something I could do, no doubt? Something I could help with?"

"Nothing," said Sutton. "I am going to see Adams."

"I could carry your case. That one over there."

"I'm not taking the case."

"But, sir. . . ."

"You sit down and fold your hands and wait until I get back."

"I'll get into mischief," the android warned. "I just know I will."

"All right, then, there is something you can do. That case you mentioned. You can watch it."

"Yes, sir," said Herkimer, plainly disappointed.

"And don't waste your time trying to read what's in it," said Sutton. "You won't be able to."

"Oh," said Herkimer, still more disappointed.

"There's another thing. A girl by the name of Eva Armour lives in this hotel. Know anything about her?"

HERKIMER shook his head. "But I have a cousin. . . ."

"A cousin? An android with a cousin?"

"Yes, sir. She was made in the same laboratory as me and that makes her my cousin."

"You have a lot of cousins, then."

"Yes," said Herkimer, "I have many thousands and we stick together. Which," he said, very sanctimoniously, "is the way it should be with families."

"You think this cousin might know something?"

Herkimer shrugged. "She works in the hotel. She might know something."

Sutton turned to the door.

"You are to be congratulated, sir," said Herkimer. "You gave a very good account of yourself last night."

Sutton turned back to the room. "Benton missed," he said. "I couldn't help but kill him."

Herkimer nodded. "But it isn't only that, sir. This happens to be the first time I ever heard of a man being killed by a bullet in the arm."

"In the *arm?"*

"Precisely, sir. The bullet smashed his arm, but it didn't touch him otherwise. And he died."

XI

ADAMS thumbed the lighter and waited for the flame to steady. His eyes were fixed on Sutton and there was no softness in them, but there were softness and irritability and a faint unsureness in the man himself, hidden well, but undeniably there.

That staring, Sutton told himself, is an old trick of his. He glares at you and keeps his face frozen like a sphinx and if you aren't used to him and on to all his tricks, he'll have you thinking that he knows everything.

But he doesn't do the glaring quite as well as he use to do it. There's strain in him now and there was no strain in him twenty years ago. Just granite, and the granite is beginning to weather. There's something on his mind. There's something that isn't going well.

Adams passed the lighter flame over the loaded bowl of his pipe, back and forth, deliberately taking his time, making Sutton wait.

"You know, of course," said Sutton, speaking quietly, "that I can't be frank with you."

The lighter flame snapped off and Adams straightened in his chair. "Eh?" he asked.

Sutton grinned mentally. A passed pawn, he told himself. That's what Adams is . . . a passed pawn.

He said aloud: "You know by now, of course, that I came back in a ship that could not fly. You know I had no spacesuit and that the ports were broken and the hull was riddled. I had no food and air and water, and 61 is eleven light years away."

Adams nodded bleakly. "Yes, we know all that."

"How I got back or what happened to me has nothing to do with my report and I don't intend to tell you."

Adams rumbled at him, "Then why mention it at all?"

"Just so you won't ask a lot of questions that will get no answer. It will save a lot of time."

Adams leaned back and puffed his pipe contentedly. "You were sent out to get information, Ash. Any kind of information. Anything that would make Cygni more understandable. You represented Earth and you were paid by Earth and you surely owe Earth something."

"I owe Cygni something, too," replied Sutton. "I owe Cygni my life. My ship crashed and I was killed."

Adams nodded. "Yes, that is what Clark said. He told me you were killed. Clark is a space construction engineer. Sleeps with ships and blueprints. He studied your ship and he calculated a graph of force co-ordinates. He reported that if you were inside the ship when it hit, you had to be dead."

"It's wonderful," said Sutton, drily, "what a man can do with figures."

Adams prodded him again. "Anderson said you weren't human."

"I suppose Anderson could tell that by looking at the ship."

Adams nodded. "No food, nor air. It was the logical conclusion for anyone to draw."

Sutton shook his head. "Anderson is wrong. If I weren't human, you never would have seen me. I would not have come back at all. But I was homesick for Earth and you were expecting a report."

"You took your time," Adams accused.

"I had to be sure. I had to know. I had to be able to come back and tell you if the Cygnians were dangerous or if they weren't."

"And which is it?"

"They aren't dangerous."

ADAMS waited and Sutton was silent.

Finally Adams said: "And that is all?"

"That is all," said Sutton.

Adams tapped his teeth with the bit of his pipe. "I'd hate to have to send another man out to check up. Especially after I had told everyone you'd bring back all the data."

"It wouldn't do any good," said Sutton. "No one could get through."

"You did."

"Yes, and I was the first. And because I was the first, I also will be the last."

Across the desk, Adams smiled winterly. "You were fond of those people, Ash."

"They aren't people."

"Well . . . beings, then."

"They aren't even beings. It's hard to tell you exactly what they are. You'd laugh if I said what I really think they are."

Adams grunted. "Try me."

"Symbiotic abstractions. That's as close as I can come."

Adams didn't laugh. "You mean they really don't exist?"

"Oh, they exist, all right. They form symbiotic relationships that help them and their alien hosts. Not like parasites, unless maybe like the bacteria that release nitrogen in the soil for plants to live on. Only the bacteria and the plants are separate. They and their hosts aren't, and each helps the other."

"But they're abstractions," Adams repeated. "They can't exist."

"Not as we know the word," Sutton said. "They do, though."

"And no one can get through again?"

Sutton leaned forward. "Why don't you cross Cygni off your list? Pretend it isn't there. There's no danger from Cygni. The Cygnians, will never bother Man, and Man will never get there again. There's no use trying."

"They aren't mechanical?"

"No," said Sutton. "An abstraction can't be mechanical."

Adams changed the subject. "How old are you, Ash?"

"Fifty-nine."

"Just a kid," said Adams. "Just getting started." His pipe had gone out and he worried the tobacco with his finger, scowling at it. "What do you plan to do?" he asked.

"I have no plans."

"You want to stay on with the Service, don't you?"

"That depends on how you feel about it. I had presumed, of course, that you wouldn't want me."

"We owe you twenty years back pay," said Adams, almost kindly. "It's waiting for you. You can pick it up when you go out. You also have three or four years leave coming to you. Why don't you take it now?"

Sutton said nothing.

"Come back later on," said Adams. "We'll have another talk."

"I won't change my mind."

"No one will ask you to."

Sutton stood up slowly.

"I'm sorry," Adams said, "that I haven't your confidence."

"I went out to do a job," Sutton told him crisply. "I've done that job. I've made my report."

"So you have."

"I suppose," said Sutton, "you will keep in touch with me."

Adams' eyes twinkled grimly. "Certainly, Ash. I shall keep in touch with you."

XII

SUTTON sat quietly in the room and forty years were canceled from his life. It was like going back all of forty years . . . even to the teacups.

Through the open windows of Dr. Raven's study came young voices and the sound of students' feet tramping past along the walk. The wind talked in the elms and it was a sound with which he was familiar. Far off a chapel bell tolled and there was girlish laughter just across the way.

Dr. Raven handed him his teacup. "I think that I am right. Three lumps and no cream."

"Yes, that's right," said Sutton, astonished that he should remember.

But remembering, he told himself, was easy. I seem to be able to remember almost everything. As if the old habit patterns had been kept bright and polished in my mind through all the alien years. Waiting, like a set of cherished silver standing on a shelf, until it was time for them to be used again.

"I remember little things," said Dr. Raven. "Little, inconsequential things, like how many lumps of sugar and what a man said sixty years ago, but I don't do so well, sometimes, at the big things . . . the things a man really should remember."

The white marble fireplace flared

to the valuted ceiling and the university's coat of arms upon its polished face was as bright as the last day Sutton had seen it.

"I SUPPOSE," he said, "you wonder why I came."

"Not at all," said Dr. Raven. "All my boys come back to see me. And I am glad to see them. It makes me feel so proud."

"I've been wondering myself," said Sutton. "And I guess I know what it is, but it is hard to say."

"Let's take it easy, then," said Dr. Raven. "Remember, the way we used to. We sat and talked around a thing and finally, before we knew it, we had found the core."

Sutton laughed shortly. "Yes, I remember, doctor. Fine points of theology. The vital differences in comparative religions. Tell me this. You have spent a lifetime at it; you know more about religions, Earthly and otherwise, than any man on Earth. Have you been able to keep one faith? Have you been tempted from the teachings of your race?"

Dr. Raven set down his teacup. "I might have known you would embarrass me. You used to do it all the time. You had the uncanny ability to hit exactly on the question that a man found hardest to answer."

"I won't embarrass you any longer," Sutton told him. "I take it that you have found some good—one might say superior—points in alien religions."

"You found a new religion?"

"No," said Sutton. "Not a religion."

The chapel bell kept on tolling and the girl who had laughed was gone. The footsteps along the walk were far off in the distance.

"Have you ever felt," asked Sutton, "as if you sat on God's right hand and heard a thing you knew you were never meant to hear?"

Dr. Raven shook his head. "No, I don't think I ever have."

"If you did, what would you do?"

"I think," said Dr. Raven, "that I might be as troubled by it as you are."

"We've lived by faith alone," said Sutton, "for ten thousand years at least. More—much more. For it must have been a glimmer of some sort of faith that made the Neanderthaler paint corpses' shin bones red and nest the skulls so they faced toward the east."

"Faith," said Dr. Raven gently, "is a powerful thing."

"Yes, powerful," Sutton agreed, "but even in its strength it is our own confession of weakness. Our own admission that we are not strong enough to stand alone, that we must have a hope and conviction that there is some greater power which will lend us aid and guidance."

"You haven't grown bitter, Ash?"

"Not bitter."

Somewhere a clock was ticking, loud in the sudden hush.

"Doctor," said Sutton, "what do you know of destiny?"

"It's strange to hear you talk of

destiny," said Dr. Raven. "You always were a man who never was inclined to bow to destiny."

"I mean documentary destiny," Sutton explained. "Not the abstraction, but the actual belief in destiny. What do the records say?"

"There always have been men who believed in destiny," said Dr. Raven. "Some of them, it would appear, with some justification. But mostly they didn't call it destiny. They called it luck or a hunch or inspiration or something else. There have been historians who wrote of manifest destiny, but those were no more than words. Of course, there were some fanatics who preached destiny, but practiced fatalism."

"But there is no evidence of a thing called destiny? An actual force? A living vital thing?"

Dr. Raven shook his head. "None that I know of, Ash. Destiny, after all, is just a word. It isn't something that you can pin down. Faith, too, at one time may have been no more than a word, just as destiny is today. But millions of people and thousands of years made it a real force, a thing that can be defined and invoked and lived by."

"But hunches and luck," protested Sutton. "Those are just happenstance."

"They might be glimmerings of destiny," Dr. Raven declared. "Flashes showing through. A hint of a broad stream of happening behavior. One cannot know, of course. Man is always blind until he has the facts. Turning points in history have rested on a hunch. Inspired belief in one's own ability has changed the course of events more times than one can count."

He rose and walked to a book case, stood with his head tilted back.

"Somewhere," he said, "if I can find it, there is a book."

He searched and did not find it.

"No matter," he declared, "I'll run onto it later if you are still interested. It tells about an old African tribe with a strange belief. They believed that each man's spirit or consciousness or ego or whatever you may call it had a partner, a counterpart on some distant star. If I remember rightly, they even knew which star and could point it out in the evening sky."

He turned around from the book case and looked evenly at Sutton.

"That might be destiny, you know," he said. "It might, very well, at that."

He crossed the room to stand in front of the cold fireplace, hands locked behind his back, silver head tilted to one side.

"Why are you so interested in destiny?" he asked.

"Because I found destiny," said Sutton.

XIII

THE face in the visiplate was masked and Adams spoke in chilly anger: "I do not receive masked calls."

"You will this one," said the voice from behind the mask. "I am the man you talked to on the patio. Remember?"

"Calling from the future, I presume," said Adams.

"No, I am still in your time. I have been watching you."

"Watching Sutton, too?"

The masked head nodded. "You have seen him now. What do you think?"

"He's hiding something," Adams said. "And not all of him is human."

"You're going to have him killed?"

"No," said Adams. "No, I don't think I will. He knows something that we need to know. And we won't get it out of him by killing."

"What he knows," said the masked voice, "is better dead with the man who knows it."

"Perhaps," said Adams, "we could come to an understanding if you would tell me what this is all about."

"I can't tell you, Adams. I wish I could. I can't tell you the future."

"And until you do," snapped Adams, "I won't let you change the past."

And he was thinking: The man is scared and almost desperate. He could kill Sutton any time he wished, but he is afraid to do it. Sutton has to be killed by a man of his own time . . . literally has to be, for time may not tolerate the intrusion of violence from future to past.

"By the way," said the future man, "how are things on Aldebaran XII?"

ADAMS sat rigid in his chair, anger flaming in him.

"If it hadn't been for Sutton," said the masked man, "there would have been no incident on Aldebaran XII."

"But Sutton wasn't back yet," argued Adams. His voice ran down, for he remembered something. The name upon the fly leaf . . . *by Asher Sutton*. "Look, tell me. For the love of heaven, if you have anything to tell, tell it."

"You mean to say you haven't guessed what it might be?"

Adams shook his head.

"It's war," the voice said.

"But there is no war."

"Not in your time."

"But how—"

"Remember Michaelson?"

"The man who went a second into time."

The masked head nodded and the screen went blank. Adams sat and felt the chill of horror trickle through his body.

The visor buzzer purred at him and mechanically he snapped the toggle over.

It was Nelson in the screen. "Sutton just left the university. He spent an hour with Dr. Raven. In case you don't recall, Dr. Raven is a professor of comparative religions."

"Oh," said Adams. "Oh, so that is it."

He tapped his fingers on the desk, half irritated, half frightened.

It would be a shame, he thought, to kill a man like Sutton.

But it might be best.

Yes, he told himself, it might be for the best.

XIV

THE road curved ahead, a silver strip shining in the moonlight, and the sounds and smells of night lay across the land. The sharp, clean smell of growing things, the mystery smell of water. A creek ran through the marsh that lay off to the right, and Sutton, from behind the wheel, caught the flashing hint of winding, moonlit water as he took a curve. Peeping frogs made a veil of pixy sound that hugged against the hills, and fireflies were swinging lanterns that signaled through the dark.

Clark said that Sutton had died, and Clark was an engineer. He had made a graph and mathematics stated that certains strains and stresses would inevitably kill a man.

And Anderson had said Sutton wasn't human, and how was Anderson to know?

How, asked Sutton, unless he examined me? Unless he was the one who tried to probe into my mind after I had been knocked out when I walked into my room?

Adams had tipped his hand and Adams never tipped his hand unless he wanted one to see. He wanted me to know, Sutton told himself. He wanted me to know, but he couldn't tell me. He couldn't tell me he had me down on tape and film, that he was the one who had rigged up the room.

But he could let me know by making just one slip, a carefully calculated slip, like the one on Anderson. He knew that I would catch and he thinks he can jitter me.

The headlights caught, momentarily, the gray-black massive lines of a house that huddled on a hillside, and then there was another curve. A nightbird, black and ghostly, fluttered across the road and the shadow of its flight danced down the cone of light.

Adams was the one who was waiting for me. He knew, somehow, that I was coming, and he was ready. He had me tagged and ticketed before I hit the ground, and he gave me a going over before I knew what was going on.

And undoubtedly he found a whole lot more than he bargained for.

Sutton chuckled drily. And the chuckle merged into a scream that came slanting down the hill slope in a blaze of streaming fire . . . a rush of flame that ended in the marsh, that died down momentarily, then licked out in blue and red.

Brakes hissed and tires screeched on the pavement as Sutton slued the car around to bring it to a stop. Even before the machine came to a halt, he was out the door and running down the slope toward the strange, black craft that flickered in the swamp.

Water sloshed around his ankles and knife-edged grass slashed at his leg. The puddles gleamed black and oily in the light from the flaming craft. The frogs still strained their hoarse throats at the far edge of the marsh.

Something flopped and struggled in a pool of muddy, flame-stained water just a few feet from the burning ship. Sutton, plunging forward, caught the gleaming white of frightened, piteous eyeballs shining in the flame as the man lifted himself on his mud-caked arms and tried to drag his body forward. He saw the flash of teeth as pain twisted the face into grisly anguish. And his nostrils caught the smell of charred, crisped flesh.

He stooped and locked his hands beneath the armpits of the man, hauled him upright, dragged him back across the swamp. Mud sucked at his feet and he heard the splashing behind him, the horrible, dragging splash of the other's body trailing through the water and the slime.

There was dry land beneath his feet and he began the climb back up the slope toward the car. Sounds came from the bobbing head of the man he carried, thick, slobbering sounds that might have been words.

Sutton cast a quick glance over his shoulder and saw the flames mounting straight into the sky, a pillar of blue that lighted up the night. Marsh birds, roused from their nests, flew blinded and in squawking panic through the garish light.

"The atomics," said Sutton, aloud. "The atomics. . . ."

They couldn't hold for long in a flame like that. The automatics would melt down and the marsh would suddenly be a crater and the hills would be charred from horizon to horizon.

"No," said the bobbing head. "No . . . no atomics."

Sutton's foot caught in a root and he stumbled to his knees. The body of the man slid from his mud-caked grasp. The man struggled, trying to turn over. Sutton helped him and he lay on his back, his face toward the sky.

He was young, Sutton saw, a youth beneath the mask of mud and pain.

"No atomics," said the man. "I dumped them."

THERE was pride in the words, pride in a job well done. But the words had cost him heavily. Sutton saw the blood pumping through the temples beneath the burned and twisted skin. The man's jaw worked and words came out, limping, tangled words.

"There was a battle . . . back in '83 . . . I saw him coming . . . tried to time-jump. . . ." The words gurgled and got lost, then gushed out again. "Got new guns . . . set metal afire. . . ."

He turned his head and apparently saw Sutton for the first time. He started up. "Asher Sutton!" The two words were a whisper.

For a moment Sutton caught the triumphant, almost fanatic gleam that washed across the eyes of the dying man, wondered at the gesture of the half-raised arm, at the cryptic sign that the fingers made.

Then the gleam faded and the arm dropped back and the fingers separated.

Sutton knew, even before he bent with his head turned against the heart, that the man was dead.

Slowly Sutton stood up. The flame was dying down and the birds had gone. The craft lay almost buried in the mud, and its lines, he noted, were none he had ever seen.

Asher Sutton, the man had said. And his eyes had lighted up and he had made a sign just before he died. And there had been a battle back in '83.

Eighty-three what?

The man had tried to time-jump . . . who had ever heard of a time jump?

I never saw the man before, said Sutton. So help me, I don't know

him even now. And yet he cried my name and it sounded as if he knew me and was very glad to see me and he made a sign . . . a sign that went with the name.

He stared down at the dead man lying at his feet and saw the pity of it, the crumpled legs, the stiffened arms, the lolling head and the flash of moonlight on the teeth where the mouth had fallen open.

Carefully, Sutton went down on his knees, ran his hands over the body, seeking something . . . some bulging pocket that might give a clue to the man who lay there dead.

Because he knew me. And I must know how he knew me. And none of it makes sense.

There was a small book in the breast pocket of the coat and Sutton slipped it out. The title was in gold upon black leather, and even in the moonlight Sutton could read the letters that flamed from the cover:

THIS IS DESTINY
By
Asher Sutton

Sutton did not move. He crouched there on the ground, like a cowering thing, stricken by the golden letters on the leather cover.

A book!

A book he meant to write, but hadn't written yet!

A book he wouldn't write for many months to come!

And yet here it was, dog-eared and limp from reading.

He felt the chill of the fog rising from the marsh, the loneliness of a wild bird's crying.

A strange ship had plunged into the marsh, disabled and burning. A man had escaped from the ship, but on the verge of death. Before he died he had recognized Sutton and had called his name. In his pocket he had a book that was not even written.

Those were the facts. There was no explanation.

Faint sounds of human voices drifted down the night and Sutton rose swiftly to his feet, stood poised and waiting, listening. The voices came again.

Someone had heard the crash and was coming to investigate, coming down the road, calling to others who also had heard the crash.

Sutton turned and walked swiftly up the slope to the car.

There was, he told himself, no Earthly use of waiting. Those coming down the road might know the answers to his baffling questions—but they wouldn't tell him. Nobody seemed willing to tell him anything. He had to find out the answers himself.

XV

A MAN was waiting in the clump of lilac bushes across the road and there was another one crouched in the shadow of the courtyard wall.

Sutton walked slowly forward, strolling, taking his time.

"Johnny," he said, soundlessly.

"Yes, Ash."

"That is all there are? Just those two?"

"I think there is another one, but I can't place him. All of them are armed."

Sutton felt the stir of comfort in his brain, the sense of self-assurance, the sense of aid and comradeship.

"Keep me posted, Johnny."

He whistled a bar or two, from a tune that had been forgotten long ago, but still was fresh in his mind from twenty years before.

The rent-a-car garage was two blocks up the road, the Orion Arms two blocks farther down. Between him and the Arms were two men, waiting with guns. Two and maybe more.

Between the garage and hotel was nothing . . . just the landscaped beauty that was a residential, administrative Earth. An Earth dedicated to beauty and to ruling . . . planted with a garden's care, every inch of it mapped out by landscape architects with clumps of shrubs and lanes of trees and carefully tended flower beds.

An ideal place, Sutton told himself, for an ambush.

Adams? he wondered. Although it hardly could be Adams. He had something that Adams expected to find out, and killing the man who holds information that you want, no matter how irate you may be at him, is downright useless.

Or those others that Eva had told him of . . . the ones who had Benton psychologically conditioned to kill him. They tied in better than Adams did, for Adams wanted him to stay alive and these others, whoever they might be, were quite content to kill him.

He dropped his hand in his coat pocket as if searching for a cigarette and his fingers touched the steel of the gun he had used on Benton. He let his fingers wrap around it and then took his hand out of the pocket and found the cigarettes in another pocket.

Not time yet, he told himself. Time later on to use the gun, if he had to use it—if he had a chance to use it.

He stopped to light the cigarette, playing for time. The gun would be a poor weapon, he knew, but better than none at all. In the dark, he probably couldn't hit the broad side of a house, but it would make a noise and the waiting men were not counting on noise. If they hadn't minded noise, they could have stepped out minutes ago and shot him down.

"Ash," said Johnny, "there is another man. Just in that bush ahead. He expects to let you pass and then they'll have you caught in an ambush three ways."

SUTTON grunted. "Good, tell me exactly."

"The bush with the white flowers. He's on this edge of it. Quite close to the walk, so he can step around and be behind you when you pass."

Sutton puffed on the cigarette, making it glow like a red eye in the dark.

"Shall we take him, Johnny?"

"Yes, before we're taken."

Sutton resumed his stroll and now he saw the bush, four paces away, no more.

One step.

I wonder what it's all about.

Two steps.

Cut out your wondering. Act now and do your wondering later.

Three steps.

There he is. I see him.

Sutton was off the walk in a sudden leap. The gun whipped out of his pocket and it talked, two quick, ugly words.

The man behind the bush bent forward to his knees, swayed there for a moment, then flattened on his face. His gun fell from his fingers and in a single swoop, Sutton scooped it up. It was, he saw, an electronic device, a vicious thing that could kill even with a near miss, due to the field of distortion that its beam set up. A gun like that had been new and secret twenty years ago, but now, apparently, anyone could get it.

Gun in hand, Sutton wheeled and ran, twisting through the shrubbery, ducking overhanging branches, plowing through a tulip bed. Out of the corner of one eye, he caught a twinkle . . . the twinkling breath of a silent flaming gun, and the dancing path of silver that it sliced into the night.

He plunged through a ripping, tearing hedge, waded a stream, found himself in a clump of evergreen and birch. He stopped to get his breath, staring back over the way that he had come.

The countryside lay quiet and peaceful, a silvered picture painted by the moon. No one and nothing stirred. The gun long ago had ceased its flickering.

Johnny's warning came suddenly: "Ash! Behind you. Friendly . . ."

Sutton wheeled, gun half lifted.

Herkimer was running in the moonlight, like a hound hunting for a trace. "Mr. Sutton, sir . . ."

"Yes, Herkimer."

"We have to run for it."

"Yes," said Sutton, "I suppose we have. I walked into a trap. There were three of them laying for me."

"It's worse than that," said Herkimer. "It's worse even than you think. It's not only Morgan, but it's Adams, too."

"Adams?"

"He has given orders that you are to be killed on sight."

Sutton stiffened. "How do you know?"

"The girl,' said Herkimer. "Eva. The one you asked about. She told me."

Herkimer walked forward, stood face to face with Sutton.

"You have to trust me, sir. You said this morning I'd put the finger on you, but I never would. I was with you from the very first."

"But the girl," said Sutton.

"Eva is with you, too, sir. We started searching for you as soon as we found out, but we were too late to catch you. Eva is waiting with the ship."

"A ship," Sutton grimly repeated. "A ship and everything."

"It's your own ship, sir. The one you received from Benton's estate with the hunting asteroid and me."

Sutton scowled. "And you think I'm stupid enough to come with you and get into this ship and . . ."

"No, sir, I didn't think so," said Herkimer. "I'm sorry."

He moved so fast that Sutton couldn't do a thing.

He saw the fist coming and he tried to raise his gun. He felt the sudden fury grow cold within his brain. But that was before there was a sudden crushing impact. His head snapped back so that for a moment, before his eyelids closed, he saw the wheel of stars against a spinning sky. He felt his knees buckle under him.

He was out, stone cold, when his body hit the ground.

—**CLIFFORD D. SIMAK**

CONTINUED NEXT MONTH

By
RICHARD
MATHESON

THIRD FROM THE SUN

Escaping a known danger is highly advisable ...if you can know the unknown danger ahead!

HIS EYES were open five seconds before the alarm was set to go off. There was no effort in waking. It was sudden. Coldly conscious, he reached out his left hand in the dark and pushed in the stop. The alarm glowed a second, then faded.

At his side, his wife put her hand on his arm.

"Did you sleep?" he asked.

"No, did you?"

"A little," he said. "Not much."

She was silent for a few seconds. He heard her throat contract. She shivered. He knew what she was going to say.

"We're still going?" she asked.

He twisted his shoulders on the bed and took a deep breath.

"Yes," he said, and felt her fingers tighten on his arm.

"What time is it?" she asked.

"About five."

"We'd better get ready."

"Yes, we'd better."

They made no move.

"You're sure we can get on the ship without anyone noticing?" she asked.

"They think it's just another test flight. Nobody will be checking."

She didn't say anything. She moved a little closer to him. He felt how cold her skin was.

"I'm afraid," she said.

He took her hand and held it in a tight grip. "Don't be," he said. "We'll be safe."

"It's the children I'm worried about."

"We'll be safe," he repeated.

She lifted his hand to her lips and kissed it gently.

"All right," she said.

They both sat up in the darkness. He heard her stand. Her night garment rustled to the floor. She didn't pick it up. She stood still, shivering in the cold morning air.

"You're sure we don't need anything else with us?" she asked.

"No, nothing. I have all the supplies we need in the ship. Anyway. . . ."

"What?"

"We can't carry anything past the guard," he said. "He has to think you and the kids are just coming to see me off."

SHE began dressing. He threw off the covering and got up. He went across the cold floor to the closet and dressed.

"I'll get the children up," she said, "if they aren't already." He grunted, pulling clothes over his head. At the door she stopped. "Are you sure—" she began.

"Hm?"

"Won't the guard think it's funny that . . . that our neighbors are coming down to see you off, too?"

He sank down on the bed and fumbled for the clasps on his shoes. "We'll have to take that chance," he said. "We need them with us."

She sighed. "It seems so cold. So calculating."

He straightened up and saw her silhouette in the doorway.

"What else can we do?" he asked tensely. "We can't interbreed our own children."

"No," she said. "It's just. . . ."

"Just what?"

"Nothing, darling. I'm sorry."

She closed the door. Her footsteps disappeared down the hall. The door to the children's room opened. He heard their two voices. A cheerless smile raised his lips. You'd think it was a holiday, he thought.

He pulled on his shoes. At least the kids didn't know what was happening. They thought they were going to take him down to the field. They thought they'd come back and tell all their schoolmates. They didn't know they'd never come back.

He finished clasping his shoes and stood up. He shuffled over to the bureau and turned on the light. He looked at himself in the mirror. It was odd, such an undistinguished looking man planning this.

Cold. Calculating. Her words filled his mind again. Well, there was no other way. In a few years, probably less, the whole planet would go up with a blinding flash. This was the only way out. Escaping, starting all over again with a few people on a new planet.

He stared at the reflection.

"There's no other way," he said. He glanced around the bedroom.

Good-by, this part of my life. Turning off the lamp was like turning off a light in his mind. He closed the door gently behind him and slid his fingers off the worn handle.

His son and daughter were going down the ramp. They were talking in mysterious whispers. He shook his head in slight amusement.

His wife waited for him. They went down together, holding hands.

"I'm not afraid, darling," she said. "It'll be all right."

"Sure," he said. "Sure it will."

They all went in to eat. He sat down with his children. His wife poured out juice for them. Then she went to get the food.

"Help your mother, doll," he told his daughter. She got up.

"Pretty soon, haah, pop?" his son said. "Pretty soon, haah?"

"Take it easy," he cautioned. "Remember what I told you. If you say a word of it to anybody, I'll have to leave you behind."

A dish shattered on the floor. He darted a glance at his wife. She was staring at him, her lips trembling.

She averted her eyes and bent down. She fumbled at the pieces, picked up a few. Then she dropped them all, stood up and pushed them against the wall with her shoe.

"As if it mattered," she said nervously. "As if it mattered whether the place is clean or not."

The children were watching her in surprise.

"What is it?" asked the daughter.

"Nothing, darling, nothing," she said. "I'm just nervous. Go back to the table. Drink your juice. We have to eat quickly. The neighbors will be here soon."

"Pop, why are the neighbors coming with us?" asked his son.

"Because," he said vaguely. "Because they want to. Now forget it. Don't talk about it so much."

THE room was quiet. His wife brought over their food and set it down. Only her footsteps broke the silence. The children kept glancing at each other, at their father. He kept his eyes on his plate. The food tasted thick and flat in his mouth and he felt his heart thudding against the wall of his chest. Last day. This is the last day. It felt like a silly, dangerous plan.

"You'd better eat," he told his wife.

She sat down and began to eat mechanically, without enthusiasm. Suddenly the door buzzer sounded. The eating utensil skidded out of her nerveless fingers and clattered on the floor. He reached out quickly and put his hand on hers.

"All right, darling," he said. "It's all right." He turned to the children. "Go answer the door," he told them.

"Both of us?" his daughter asked.

"Both of you."

"But. . . ."

"Do as I say."

They slid off their chairs and left the room, glancing back at their parents.

When the sliding door shut off

their view, he turned back to his wife. Her face was pale and tight; she had her lips pressed together.

"Darling, please," he said. "Please. You know I wouldn't take you if I wasn't sure it was safe. You know how many times I've flown the ship before. And I know just where we're going. It's safe. Believe me, it's safe."

SHE pressed his hand against her cheek. She closed her eyes and large tears ran out under her lids and down her cheeks.

"It's not that so m-much," she said. "It's just . . . leaving, never coming back. We've been here all our lives. It isn't like . . . like moving. We can't come back. Ever."

"Listen, darling," his voice was tense and hurried, "you know as well as I do. In a matter of years, maybe less, there's going to be another war, a terrible one. There won't be a thing left. We have to leave. For our children, for ourselves. . . ."

He paused, testing the words in his mind.

"For the future of life itself," he finished weakly. He was sorry he said it. Early on a prosaic morning, over everyday food, that kind of talk didn't sound right. Even if it was true.

"Just don't be afraid," he said. "We'll be all right."

She squeezed his hand.

"I know," she said quietly. "I know."

There were footsteps coming toward them. He pulled out a tissue and gave it to her. She hastily dabbed at her face.

The door slid open. The neighbors and their son and daughter came in. The children were excited. They had trouble keeping it down.

"Good morning," the neighbor said.

The neighbor's wife went to his wife and the two of them went over by the window and talked in low voices. The children stood around, fidgeted, and looked nervously at each other.

"You've eaten?" he asked his neighbor.

"Yes," his neighbor said. "Don't you think we'd better be going?"

"I suppose so," he said.

They left all the dishes on the table. His wife went upstairs and got outer garments for the family.

He and his wife stayed on the porch a moment while the rest went out to the ground car.

"Should we lock the door?" he asked.

She smiled helplessly and ran a hand through her hair. She shrugged helplessly. "Does it matter?"

He locked the door and followed her down the walk. She turned as he came up to her.

"It's a nice house," she murmured.

"Don't think about it," he said.

They turned their backs on their home and got in the ground car.

"Did you lock it?" asked the neighbor.

"Yes."

The neighbor smiled wryly. "So did we," he said. "I tried not to, but then I had to go back."

They moved through the quiet streets. The edges of the sky were beginning to redden. The neighbor's wife and the four children were in back. His wife and the neighbor were in front with him.

"Going to be a nice day," said his neighbor.

"I suppose so," he said.

"Have you told your children?" the neighbor asked softly.

"Of course not."

"I haven't, I haven't," insisted his neighbor. "I was just asking."

"Oh."

They rode in silence a while.

"Do you ever get the feeling that we're . . . running out?" asked the neighbor.

He tightened. "No," he said. "No! We're the ones who were run out on—all of us."

"I guess it's better not to talk about it," his neighbor said hastily.

"Much better," he said.

As they drove up to the guard-house at the gate, he turned to the back.

"Remember," he said, "not a word from any of you."

THE guard, sleepy and not caring much, recognized him right away as the chief test pilot for the new ship. That was enough. The family was coming down to watch him off, he told the guard. No objection. The guard let them drive to the ship's platform.

The car stopped under the huge columns. They all got out and stared up.

Far above them, its nose pointed toward the sky, the great metal ship was just beginning to reflect the early morning glow.

"Let's go," he said. "Quickly."

As they hurried toward the ship's elevator, he stopped for a moment to look back. The guard house looked deserted. He looked around at everything and tried to fix it all in his memory.

He bent over and picked up some dirt. He put it in his pocket.

"Good-bye," he whispered.

He ran to the elevator.

The doors shut in front of them. There was no sound in the rising cubicle but the hum of the motor and a few self-conscious coughs from the children. He looked down at them. To have to leave so young, he thought, unable to help.

He closed his eyes. His wife's hand rested on his arm. He looked at her. Their eyes met and she smiled at him.

"And I thought it would be difficult," she whispered.

The elevator shuddered to a stop. The doors slid open and they went out. It was getting lighter. He hurried them along the enclosed platform.

They all climbed through the narrow doorway in the ship's side. He hesitated before following them. He wanted to say something fitting the moment. It burned in him to say something fitting the moment.

There wasn't a thing to say.

HE SWUNG in and grunted as he pulled the door shut and turned the wheel tight.

"That's it," he said. "Come on, everybody."

Their footsteps echoed on the metal decks and ladders as they went up to the control room.

The children ran to the ports and looked out. They gasped when they saw how high they were. Their mothers stood behind them, looking down at the ground. Their eyes were frightened. The children's were not.

"So high," said his daughter.

He patted her head gently. "So high," he repeated.

Then he turned abruptly and went over to the instrument panel. He stood there, hesitantly. He heard someone come up behind him.

"Shouldn't we tell the children?" asked his wife. "Shouldn't we let them know it's their last look?"

"Go ahead," he said.

He waited to hear her footsteps. There were none. He turned. She kissed him on the cheek. Then she went to tell the children.

He threw over the switch. Deep in the belly of the ship, a spark ignited the fuel. A concentrated rush of gas flooded from the vents. The bulkheads began to shake.

He heard his daughter crying. He tried not to listen, extended a trembling hand toward the lever, then glanced back suddenly. They were all staring at him. He put his hand on the lever and threw it over.

The ship quivered a brief second and then they felt it rush along the smooth incline. It flashed into the air, faster and faster. They all heard the wind rushing past.

He watched the children turn to the ports and look out again.

"Good-bye," they said.

He sank down wearily at the control panel. Out of the corner of his eye he saw his neighbor sit down next to him.

"You know just where we're going?" his neighbor asked.

"On that chart there."

His neighbor looked at the chart. His eyebrows wiggled in surprise.

"Another solar system?"

"That's right. There's a planet there with an oxygen atmosphere that can support our kind of life. We'll probably have it all to ourselves. No hatred. No war."

"We'll be safe," his neighbor said. "And the race will be safe."

He nodded and looked back at his and his neighbor's family. They were still staring out the ports.

"I said," his neighbor repeated, "which one of these planets is it?"

He leaned over the chart, pointed. "That small one there," he said.

"This one, third from the sun?"

"That's right," he said. "The green planet with the single moon."

—RICHARD MATHESON

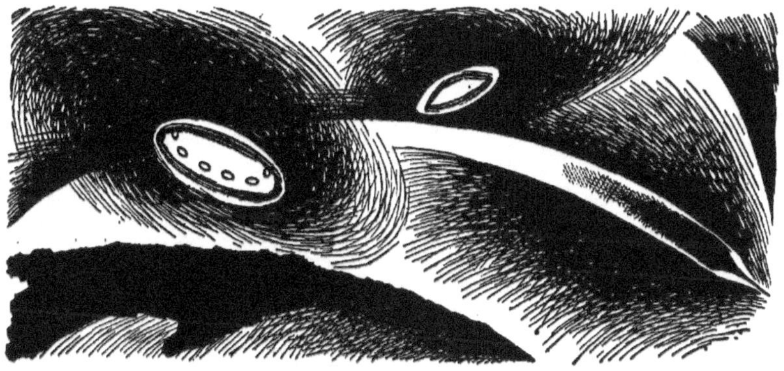

INTRODUCING A GREAT SCIENCE FICTION CONTEST

FLYING SAUCERS
Friend, Foe or Fantasy?

By WILLY LEY

THE editors of GALAXY *Science Fiction* have asked me to open the Flying Saucer Season by sniffing out the scent of the quarry, to be followed by as many bloodhound readers as may wish to join in the hunt.

Fine. I approve of the hunt. Neither a cynical nor a credulous attitude is justified in considering the Flying Saucer mystery. For one thing, about four hundred eyewitness reports have been collected. If we say that the average number of witnesses per case was three, about 1,200 persons claim to have seen these objects. One has to assume, therefore, where there is so much smoke, there must be fire somewhere.

Possibly several fires, for the persons who claim to have seen "unidentified objects" (to use a neutral term) do not agree as to size and shape. There is no question that most of the witnesses told the truth as they thought they saw it, and what they saw, or thought they saw, clearly falls into three groups:

Group One:—

Lights in the sky, generally round and without anything visible attached to them, sometimes "flying in formation," reminiscent of those strange "fiery balls" which Allied pilots saw near the wingtips of their airplanes during the last few weeks of World War II in Europe. They were called "Foo Fighters" and believed to be a secret German weapon —but they never did anything.

Group Two:—

Round or oval objects that looked metallic, flying at high speed, generally at a very high altitude, estimates of size ranging from 30 to 300 feet in diameter.

Group Three:—

Rocket-shaped craft without wings, larger in size than known military and research craft, doubly strange because they were seen in areas far away from rocket testing grounds, where experiments of such type might be conducted.

The fact that the observers do not agree makes it unlikely that one over-all explanation will fit every case. By a convenient coincidence, the explanations advanced so far also fall into three categories . . . or four, if you want to include the idea that they might be Russian missiles, which I discount from the outset. Even before China turned communist, the Soviet Union had roughly three times the land area of the United States. It has room enough to test new weapons without using our hemisphere. And if it did have such swift and powerful missiles, the cold war would have grown hot some time ago.

THE three other explanations are: (1) that the witnesses saw phenomena which are known, but not known to them; (2) that the Saucers are a secret American development; (3) that they are spaceships from another planet.

The first explanation probably accounts for a large percentage of the reports, those originating from people not professionally connected with aeronautics, meteorology and related sciences. They may have seen radar targets, Navy "skyhook" balloons which are of huge size, rare cloud formations, and even, on occasion, actual meteorites, without being able to identify them. Personally, I believe that the few reports of "luminous disks flying in formation," especially, are due to such a mistake. Meteorological instruments normally are carried by one balloon, but in special cases, clusters of five, six or more balloons are used. I consider it possible that such a balloon cluster, at maximum altitude (which means that the balloons are expanded to bursting point and therefore almost transparent) could produce an *optical effect* on a lower cloud layer which would look like luminous disks in formation.

The second explanation has two advantages. It is the easiest and also the most pleasant to believe in. The assumption that the disks are a U. S. military development which should not have been seen in the first place seems to explain why the attitude of official quarters ranges from semi-silence to outright debunking. It does, however, have a major disadvantage—it is very hard to imagine why a military missile should be given this peculiar shape.

The third explanation, championed by Donald Keyhoe in magazine and book analyses, is also quite appealing, particularly to the science fiction faithful. If the disks were spaceships from another planet, one can easily think of a number of reasons why they have avoided any contact with us. The atmospheric pressure of Earth, for example, might be too high—or too low—for them. Perhaps there is too much moisture in our air. They might need more ultra-violet light than they would get here below the ozone layer, which is at about 100,000 foot altitude.

The third explanation would also clarify a number of very old reports of "airships" dating back even before the invention of the balloon. But that explanation also suffers from a drawback. While we probably cannot yet build an atomic-powered rocket, we do have some idea of what such an atomic rocket motor could do. And then it turns out that a 30-foot disk, even with a super-excellent atomic reaction engine, could barely make the moon, and a 300-foot disk might just get to either Mars or Venus.

VENUS, of course, has an atmosphere through which no astronomer has yet looked, but we have reasons to believe that the climate below that impenetrable atmosphere is not congenial to living beings with a body chemistry like ours, not to say intelligent beings.

Mars has a thin and completely transparent atmosphere, but if it had inhabitants which could build atomic-powered space craft, we *should* see some other activity, too. And it is at least doubtful whether anybody ever did, since the phenomena observed on Mars can be explained more believably as natural occurrences than otherwise.

Therefore—the disks would probably have to be interstellar faster-than-light ships, in which case I would expect them to be about half a mile long, and, to date, none has been reported that size.

Where does this leave us? Back approximately where we started. However, several factors in my argument must be pointed out for scientific objectivity: (1) I have never seen a Flying Saucer myself, nor do I know anybody who has; (2) there may be more than one type of missile involved, which would explain the conflicting reports; (3) I have only *known* propulsive and design principles and life forms to base my reasoning on; (4) my personal belief that many reports are based on mistaken identity does not explain the rest.

The simple truth is that I don't know what to think. But, as I said at the beginning, the editors of GALAXY *Science Fiction* have declared open season on Flying Saucers. Somebody, somewhere, may be hoarding an explanation that explains all. Possibly the ingenious and extremely desirable prizes will lure out that explanation.

What is *your* theory?

—WILLY LEY

FLYING SAUCER CONTEST

This contest is meant to gain readers, certainly, but it is neither a stunt nor a hoax. Willy Ley, who introduces the contest, was a founding member and vice-president of the German Rocket Society in 1927; technical advisor to Fritz Lang's famous U F A science fiction film; "The Girl in the Moon"; and, since coming to this country in 1935 has devoted himself to research engineering for rocket development. His newest book, "Rockets, Missiles and Space Travel," is due at the end of 1950, and adds important data to the valuable literature he has already produced on this subject. When a recognized authority considers Flying Saucers a serious phenomenon, research of some kind is indicated.

As magazine editors we are limited to exploration of opinion, and this we undertake in no spirit of hoax whatever. We feel, as Mr. Ley does, that "somebody, somewhere, may be hoarding an explanation that explains all. Possibly the ingenious and extremely desirable prizes offered will lure out that explanation."

And we repeat with Mr. Ley: "What is YOUR *theory?" Tell us in 200 words or less, basing your explanation on one of Willy Ley's three hypotheses . . . or do you have one of your own?*

RULES FOR FLYING SAUCER CONTEST

1. Your theory on Flying Saucers must be contained in a letter of 200 words or less and must be accompanied by the coupon printed below. (Kindly print your name and address.)
2. All entries must be addressed to GALAXY *Flying Saucer Contest*, World Editions, Inc., Box No. 103, Brooklyn 1, New York.
3. Entries will be selected on the basis of originality, aptness to the subject, general interest, neatness and legibility.
4. There will be a total of 40 prizes awarded in the order listed below. Each winner of the first three prizes will receive an additional prize of $100 if his or her answer is accompanied by a year's subscription to GALAXY *Science Fiction*. (See coupon below.)
5. Winners will be notified by mail, and all necessary arrangements will be made for the award of prizes as stipulated.
6. In the case of merchandise awards, prizes are transferable.
7. The decision of the judges will be final. All entries become the property of World Editions, Inc. and no entries will be returned.
8. Any individual may compete with the following exceptions: Employees of World Editions, Inc., and members of their immediate families; employees of Advertising Distributors of America, Inc. (the judges of this contest) and members of their immediate families.
9. CONTEST CLOSES OCTOBER 31, 1950. All entries must be postmarked not later than midnight, October 31, 1950, and must be covered by adequate postage.

GALAXY *Flying Saucer Contest*
World Editions, Inc., Box No. 103, Brooklyn 1, N. Y.

Attached herewith is my entry to GALAXY *Flying Saucer Contest.* ☐ (check)

I am enclosing $2.50 (check or money order) for a year's subscription (12 issues) to GALAXY *Science Fiction.* ☐ (check)

NAME ______________________________

ADDRESS ______________________________

CITY ________________ ZONE ______ STATE ________

PRIZES

SPECIAL ATTENTION! If entries of the winners of first three prizes are accompanied with a year's subscription to GALAXY *Science Fiction*, a special *additional prize of $100 will be awarded to each winner.*

1. A three-day all-expense trip (transportation, lodging, meals and sightseeing) to famous Mt. Wilson Observatory, near Hollywood California.

2. A three-day all-expense trip (transportation, lodging, meals and sightseeing) to fascinating Marine Laboratory at Wood's Hole, Mass., including underwater descent with opportunity to view marine life in native habitat.

3. A three-day all-expense trip (transportation, lodging, meals and sightseeing) to a government-approved atomic energy laboratory center.

4. Three studio portraits of you, in color, (huge 8x10 photographs) using the sensational new Larjachrome process of color-print enlargement. (Worth over $100.)

5. Six professional photographs of you taken by Phil Pegler, top-flight New York photographer, at cyclotron center.

6. A ride in a sky-writing plane, piloted by one of America's best-known skywriters, arranged by the Skywriting Corporation of America.

7. An undersea trip on a late type U. S. submarine.

8. A ride in a helicopter plane arranged by the Gyrodyne Company of America.

9. A flight over New York City's skyscrapers in the famous Flamingo Orange Juice Dirigible. (For two ninth prize winners.)

10. Two No. 45 Larjachrome kits for magnificent color prints enlarged from 4x5 Kodachrome cut film transparencies—a sensational new process. (One each to two tenth prize winners.)

11. A three-day course in beauty and make-up at New York's glamorous Barbizon School of Fashion Modeling.

12. Specially arranged tour through Television studios, including stand-by visit in control room during telecast, and guest appearance in show.

13 to 18. Six No. 3 Larjachrome kits (same as those mentioned above) for 35mm. and Bantam Kodachrome transparencies. (One to each winner.)

19 to 40. A twelve-months' subscription (one for each of 22 winners) to GALAXY *Science Fiction*.

Certain prizes may be subject to change in accordance with security policy.

The Stars Are The Styx

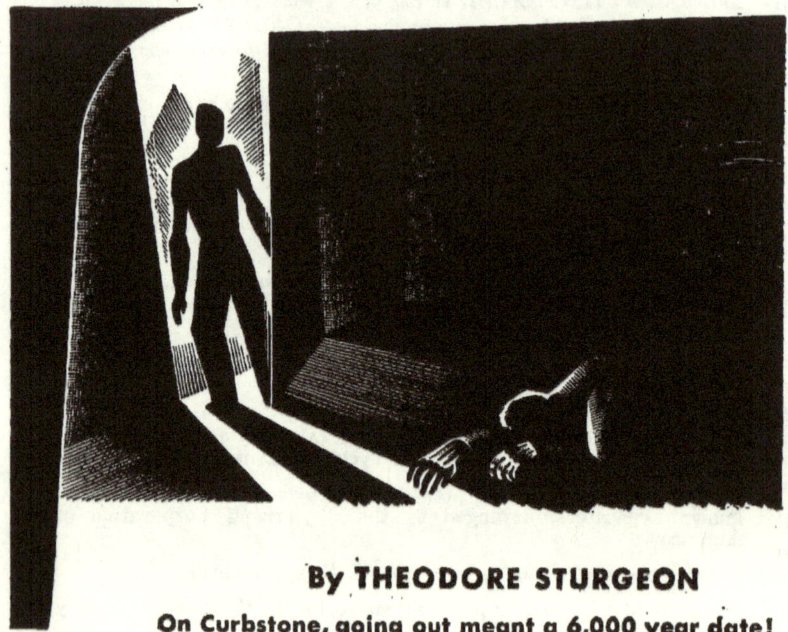

By THEODORE STURGEON

On Curbstone, going out meant a 6,000 year date!

Every few years someone thinks to call me Charon. It never lasts. I guess I don't look the part. Charon, you'll remember, was the somber ferryman who steered the boat across the River Styx, taking the departed souls over to the Other Side. He's usually pictured as a grim, taciturn character, tall and gaunt.

I get called Charon, but that's not what I look like. I'm not exactly taciturn, and I don't go around in a flapping black cloak. I'm too fat. Maybe too old, too.

It's a shrewd gag, though, calling me Charon. I do pass human souls Out, and for nearly half of them, the stars are indeed the Styx—they will never return.

I have two things I know Charon had. One is that bitter difference from the souls I deal with. They have lost only one world; the other is before them. But I'm rejected by both.

The other thing has to do with a little-known fragment of the Charon legend. And that, I think, is worth a yarn.

IT'S JUDSON'S yarn, and I wish he was here to tell it himself—which is foolish; the yarn's about why he isn't here. "Here" is Curbstone, by the way—the stepping-off place to the Other Side. It's Earth's other slow satellite, bumbling along out past the Moon. It was built 7800 years ago for heavy interplanetary transfer, though of course there's not much of that left any more. It's so easy to synthesize anything nowadays that there's just no call for imports. We make what we need from energy, and there's plenty of that around. There's plenty of everything. Even insecurity, though you have to come to Curbstone for that, and be someone like Judson to boot.

It's no secret—now—that insecurity is vital to the Curbstone project. In a cushioned existence on a stable Earth, volunteers for Curbstone are rare. But they come in—the adventurous, the dissatisfied, the yearning ones, to man the tiny ships that will, in due time, give mankind a segment of space so huge that even mankind's voracious appetite for expansion will be glutted for millenia. There is a vision that haunts all humans today—that of a network of force-beams in the form of a tremendous sphere, encompassing much of the known universe and a great deal of the unknown—through which, like thought impulses through the synaptic paths of a giant brain, matter will be transmitted instantly, and a man may step from here to the depths of space while his heart beats once. The vision frightens most and lures a few, and of those few, some are chosen to go out. Judson was chosen.

I knew he'd come to Curbstone. I'd known it for years, ever since I was on Earth and met him. He was just a youngster then, thirty or so, and boiling around under that soft-spoken, shockproof surface of his was something that had to drive him to Curbstone. It showed when he raised his eyes. They got hungry. Any kind of hunger is rare on Earth. That's what Curbstone's for. The ultimate social balance—an escape for the unbalanced.

Don't wince like that when I say 'unbalanced'. Plain talk is plain talk. You can afford to be mighty plain about social imbalance these days. It's rare and it's slight. Thing is, when a man goes through fifteen years of primary social—childhood, I'm talking about—with all the subtle tinkering that involves, and still has an imbalance, it's a thing that sticks with him no matter how slight it is. Even then, the very existence of Curbstone is enough to make most of 'em quite happy to stay where they are. The handful who do head for Curbstone do it because they have to. Once here, only about half make the final plunge. The rest go back—or live here permanently. Whatever they do, Curbstone takes care of the imbalance.

When you come right down to it, misfits are that way either because they lack something or because they have something *extra*. On Earth there's a place for everything and everything's in its place. On Curbstone you find someone who has what you lack, or who has the same extra something you have—or you leave. You go back feeling that Earth's a pretty nice safe place after all, or you go Out, and it doesn't matter to anyone else, ever, whether you're happy or not.

I WAS waiting in the entry bell when Judson arrived on Curbstone. Judson had nothing to do with that. I didn't even know he was on that particular shuttle. It's just that, aside from the fact that I happen to be Senior Release Officer on Curbstone, I like to meet the shuttles. All sorts of people come here, for all sorts of reasons. They stay here or they don't for all sorts of other reasons. I like to look at the faces that come down that ramp and guess which ones will go which way. I'm pretty good at it. As soon as I saw Judson's face I knew that this boy was bound Out. I recognized that about him even before I realized who it was.

There was a knot of us there to watch the newcomers come in. Most were there just because it's worth watching them all, the hesitant ones, the damn-it-alls, the grim ones. But two Curbstoners I noticed particularly. Hunters both. One was a lean, slick-haired boy named Wold. It was pretty obvious what he was hunting. The other was Flower. It was just as obvious what she had her long, wide-spaced eyes out for, but it was hard to tell why. Last I had heard, she had been solidly wrapped up in an Outbounder called Clinton.

I forgot about the wolf and the vixen when I recognized Judson and bellowed at him. He dropped his kit where he stood and came bounding over to me. He grabbed both my biceps and squeezed while I thumped his ribs. "I was waiting up for you, Judson," I grinned at him.

"MAN, I'm glad you're still here," he said. He was a sandy-haired fellow, all Adam's apple and guarded eyes.

"I'm here for the duration," I told him. "Didn't you know?"

"No, I—I mean. . . ."

"Don't be tactful, Jud," I said. "I belong here by virtue of the fact that there's nowhere else for me to go. Earth isn't happy about men as fat and funny-looking as I am in the era of beautiful people. And I can't go Out. I have a left axis deviation. I know that sounds political; actually it's cardiac."

"I'm sorry." He looked at my brassard. "Well, you're Mr. Big around here, anyway."

"I'm just big around *here,*" I said, swatting my belt-line. "There's Coördination Office and a half-squad of Guardians who ice this particular cake. I'm just the final check on Outbounders."

"Yeah," he said. "You don't rate. Much. The whole function of this space-station waits on whether you say yes to a departure."

"Shecks now," I said, exaggerating my embarrassment to cover up my exaggerated embarrassment. "Whatever, I wouldn't worry too much if I were you. I could be wrong—we'll have to run some more tests on you—but if ever I saw an Outbounder, it's you."

"Hi," said a silken voice. "You already know each other. How nice."

Flower.

There was something vaguely reptilian about Flower, which didn't take a thing from her brand of magnetism. Bit by bit, piece by piece, she was a so-so looking girl. Her eyes were too long, and so dark they seemed to be all pupil and the whites too white. Her nose was a bit too large and her chin a bit too small, but so help me, there never was a more perfect mouth. Her voice was like a 'cello bowed up near the bridge. She was tall, with a fragile-in-the-middle slenderness and spring-steel flanks. The overall effect was breathtaking. I didn't like her. She didn't like me either. She never spoke to me except on business, and I had practically no business with her. She'd been here a long time. I hadn't figured out why, then. But she wouldn't go Out and she wouldn't go back to Earth—which in itself was all right; we had lots of room.

LET me tell you something about modern women and therefore something about Flower—something you might not reason out unless you get as old and objective as I've somehow lived to become.

Used to be, according to what I've read, that clothes ran a lot to what I might call indicative concealment. As long as clothes had the slightest excuse of functionalism, people in general and women in particular made a large fuss over something called innate modesty—which never did exist; it had to be learned. But as long as there was weather around to blame clothes on, the myth was accepted. People exposed what the world was indifferent to in order to whip up interest in the rest. "Modesty is not so simple a virtue as honesty," one of the old books says. Clothes as weatherproofing got themselves all mixed up with clothes as ornament; fashions came and went and people followed them.

But for the past three hundred years or so there hasn't been any "weather" as such, for anyone, here or on Earth. Clothes for only aesthetic purposes became more and more the rule, until today it's up to the individual to choose what he's going to wear, if anything. An earring and a tattoo are quite as acceptable in public as forty meters of iridescent plastiweb and a two-meter coiffure.

Now, most people today are healthy, well-selected, and good to look at. Women are still as vain as ever. A woman with a bodily defect, real or imagined, has one of two choices: She can cover the defect with something artfully placed to look as if that was just the best place for it, or she can leave the defect in the open, knowing that no one today is going to judge her completely in terms of the defect. Folks nowadays generally wait until they can find out what kind of a human being you are.

But a woman who has no particular defect generally changes her clothes with her mood. It might be a sash only this morning, but a trailing drape this afternoon. Tomorrow it might be a one-sided blouse and clinging trousers. You can take it as a very significant thing when such a woman *always* covers up. She's keeping her natural warmth, as it were, under forced draft.

I didn't go into all this ancient history to impress you with my scholastics. I'm using it to illustrate a very important facet of Flower's complex character. Because Flower was one of those forced-draft jobs. Except on the sun-field and in the swimming pools, where no one ever wears clothes, Flower always affected a tunic of some kind.

The day Judson arrived, she wore a definitive example of what I mean. It was a single loose black garment with straight shoulders and no sleeves. On both sides, from a point a hand's-breath below the armpit, down to the hipbone, it was slit open. It fastened snugly under her throat with one magne-clasp, but was also slit from there to the navel. It did not quite reach to mid-thigh, and the soft material carried a light biostatic electrical charge, so that it clung to and fell away from her body as she moved. So help me, she was a walking demand for the revival of the extinct profession of peeping Tom.

This, then, was what horned in on my first few words with Judson. I should have known from the way she looked that she was planning something—something definitely for herself. I should have been doubly warned by the fact that she took the trouble to speak up just when she did—just when I told Jud he was a certifiable Outbounder if I ever saw one.

So then and there I made my big mistake. "Flower," I said, "this is Judson."

She used the second it took me to speak to suck in her lower lip, so that when she smiled slowly at Jud, the lip swelled visibly as if by blood pressure. "I *am* glad," she all but whispered.

And then she had the craft to turn the smile on me and walk away without another word.

". . . Gah!" said Judson through a tight glottis.

"That," I told him, "was beautifully phrased. Gah, indeed. Reel your eyeballs back in, Jud. We'll drop your duffel off at the Outbound quarters and—*Judson!*"

Flower had disappeared down the inner ramp. I was aware that Judson had just started to breathe again. "What?" he asked me.

I waddled over and picked up his gear. "Come on," I said, and steered him by the arm.

JUDSON had nothing to say until after we found him a room and started for my sector. "Who is she?"

"A hardy perennial," I said. "Came up to Curbstone two years ago. She's never been certified. She'll get around to it soon—or never. Are you going right ahead?"

"Just how do you handle the certification?"

"Give you some stuff to read. Pound some more knowledge into you for six, seven nights while you sleep. Look over your reflexes, physical and mental. An examination. If everything's all right, you're certified."

"Then—Out?"

I shrugged. "If you like. You come to Curbstone strictly on your own. You take your course if and when you like. And after you've been certified, you leave when you want to, with someone or not, and without telling anyone unless you care to."

"Man, when you people say 'voluntary' you're not just talking!"

"There's no other way to handle a thing like this. And you can bet that we get more people Out this way than we ever would on a compulsory basis. In the long run, I mean, and this is a long-term project . . . six thousand years long."

He walked silently for a time, and I was pretty sure I knew his thoughts. For Outbounders there is no return, and the best possible chance they have of survival is something like fifty-four per cent, a figure which was arrived at after calculations so complex that it might as well be called a guess. You don't force people Out against those odds. They go by themselves, driven by their own reasoning, or they don't go at all.

AFTER a time Judson said, "I always thought Outbounders were assigned a ship and a departure time. With certified people leaving whenever they feel like it, what's to prevent uncertified ones from doing it?"

"That I'm about to show you."

We passed the Coördination offices and headed out to the launching racks. They were shut off from Top Central Corridor by a massive gate. Over the gate floated three words in glowing letters:

SPECIES

GROUP

SELF

Seeing Jud's eyes on it, I explained, "The three levels of survival. They're in all of us. You can judge a man by the way he lines them up. The ones who have them in that order are the best. It's a good thought for Outbounders to take away with them." I watched his face. "Particularly since it's always the third item that brings 'em this far."

Jud smiled slowly. "Along with all that bumbling you carry a sting, don't you?"

"Mine is a peculiar job," I grinned back. "Come on in."

I put my palm on the key-plate. It tingled for a brief moment and then the shining doors slid back. I rolled through, stopping just inside the launching court at Judson's startled yelp.

"Well, come on," I said.

He stood just inside the doors, straining mightily against nothing at all. "Wh—wh—?" His arms were spread and his feet slipped as if he were trying to force his way through a steel wall.

Actually he was working on something a good deal stronger than that. "That's the answer to why uncertified people don't go Out," I told him. "The plate outside scanned the whorls and lines of my hand. The door opened and that Gillis-Menton field you're muscling passed me through. It'll pass anyone who's certified, too, but no one else. Now stop pushing or you'll suddenly fall on your face."

I stepped to the left bulkhead and palmed the plate there, then beckoned to Judson. He approached the invisible barrier timidly. It wasn't there. He came all the way through, and I took my hand off the scanner.

"That second plate," I explained, "works for me and certified people only. There's no way for an uncertified person to get into the launching court unless I bring him in personally. It's as simple as that. When the certified are good and ready, they go. If they want to go Out with a banquet and a parade beforehand, they can. If they want to roll out of bed some night and slip Out quietly, they can. Most of 'em do it quietly. Come on and have a look at the ships."

WE CROSSED the court to the row of low doorways along the far wall. I opened one at random and we stepped into the ship.

"It's just a room!"

"They all say that," I chuckled. "I suppose you expected a planet-type space job, only more elaborate."

"I thought they'd at least *look* like ships. This is a double room out of some luxury hotel."

"It's that, and then some." I showed him around—the capacious food lockers, the automatic air re-circulators, and, most comforting of all, the synthesizer, which meant food, fuel, tools and materials converted directly from energy to matter.

"Curbstone's more than a space station, Jud. It's a factory, for one thing. When you decide to go on your way, you'll flip that lever by the door. (You'll be catapulted out—you won't feel it, because of the stasis generator and artificial gravity.) As soon as you're gone, another ship will come up from below into this slot. By the time you're clear of Curbstone's gravitic field and slip into hyper-drive, the new ship'll be waiting for passengers."

"And that will be going on for six thousand years?"

"More or less."

"That's a powerful lot of ships."

"As long as Outbounders keep the quota, it is indeed. Nine hundred thousand—including forty-six per cent failure."

"Failure," said Jud. He looked at me and I held his gaze.

"Yes," I said. "The forty-six per cent who are not expected to get where they are going. The ones who materialize inside solid matter. The ones who go into the space-time nexus and never come out. The ones who reach their assigned synaptic junction and wait, and wait, and wait until they die of old age because no one gets to them soon enough. The ones who go mad and kill themselves or their shipmates."

I spread my hands. "The forty-six per cent."

"You can convince a man of danger," said Judson evenly, "but nobody ever believed he was really and truly going to die. Death is something that happens to other people. I won't be one of the forty-six per cent."

That was Judson. I wish he was still here.

I let the remark lie there on the thick carpet and went on with my guided tour. I showed him the casing of the intricate beam-power apparatus that contained the whole reason for the project, and gave him a preliminary look at the astrogational and manual maneuvering equipment and controls. "But don't bother your pretty little head about it just now," I added. "It'll all be crammed into you before you get certified."

We went back to the court, closing the door of the ship behind us.

"There's a lot of stuff piled into those ships," I observed, "but the one thing that can't be packed in sardine-size is the hyper-drive. I suppose you know that."

"I've heard something about it. The initial kick into second-order space comes from the station here, doesn't it? But how is the ship returned to normal space on arrival?"

"That's technology so refined it sounds like mysticism," I answered. "I don't begin to understand it. I can give you an analogy, though. It takes a power source, a compression device, and valving to fill a pneumatic tire. It takes a plain nail to let the air out again. See what I mean?"

"Vaguely. Anyway, the important thing is that Outbound is strictly one way. Those ships never come back. Right?"

"So right."

One of the doors behind us opened, and a girl stepped out of a ship. "Oh . . . I didn't know there was anyone here!" she said, and came toward us with a long, easy stride. "Am I in the way?"

"YOU—in the way, Tween?" I answered. "Not a chance."

I was very fond of Tween. To these jaded old eyes she was one of the loveliest things that ever happened. Two centuries ago, before variation limits were as rigidly set as they are now, Eugenics dreamed up her kind—olive-skinned truebreeds with the silver hair and deep ruby eyes of an albino. It was an experiment they should never have stopped. Albinoism wasn't dominant, but in Tween it had come out strongly. She wore her hair long—really long; she could tuck the ends of it under her toes and stand up straight when it was loose. Now it was braided in two ingenious halves of a coronet that looked like real silver. Around her throat and streaming behind her as she walked was a single length of flame-colored material.

"This is Judson, Tween," I said.

"We were friends back on Earth. What are you up to?"

She laughed, a captivating, self-conscious laugh. "I was sitting in a ship pretending that it was Outside. We'd looked at each other one day and suddenly said, 'Let's!' and off we'd gone." Her face was luminous. "It was lovely. And that's just what we're going to do one of these days. You'll see."

" 'We'? Oh—you mean Wold."

"Wold," she breathed, and I wished, briefly and sharply, that someone, somewhere, s o m e d a y would speak my name like that. And on the heels of that reaction came the mental picture of Wold as I had seen him an hour before, slick and smooth, watching the shuttle passengers with his dark hunting eyes. There was nothing I could say, though. My duties have their limits. If Wold didn't know a good thing when he saw it, that was his hard luck.

But looking at that shining face, I knew it would be her hard luck.

"You're certified?" Judson asked, awed.

"Oh, yes," she smiled, and I said, "Sure is, Jud. But she had her troubles, didn't you, Tween?"

We started for the gate. "I did indeed," said Tween. (I loved hearing her talk. There was a comforting, restful quality to her speech like silence when an unnoticed, irritating noise disappears.) "I just didn't have the logical aptitudes when I first came. Some things just wouldn't stick in my head, even in hypnopedia. All the facts in the universe won't help if you don't know how to put them together." She grinned. "I used to hate you."

"Don't blame you a bit." I nudged Judson. "I turned down her certification eight times. She used to come to my office to get the bad news, and she'd stand there after I'd told her and shuffle her feet and gulp a little bit. And the first thing she said then was always, 'Well, when can I start retraining?' "

SHE flushed, laughing. "You're telling secrets!"

Judson touched her. "It's all right. I don't think less of you for any of his maunderings. . . . You must have wanted that certificate very much."

"Yes," she said. "Very much."

"Could—could I ask why?"

She looked at him, in him, through him, past him. "All our lives," she said quietly, "are safe and sure and small. This—" she waved back towards the ships—"is the only thing in our experience that's none of those things. I could give you fifty reasons for going Out. But I think they all come down to that one."

We were silent for a moment, and then I said, "I'll put that in my notebook, Tween. You couldn't be more right. Modern life gives us infinite variety in everything except the magnitude of the things we do. And that stays pretty tiny." And, I thought, big, fat, superannuated station officials, rejected by one world and unqualified for the next. A small chore for a small mind.

"The only reason most of us do puny things and think puny thoughts," Judson was saying, "is that Earth has too few jobs like his in these efficient times."

"Too few men like him for jobs like his," Tween corrected.

I blinked at them both. It was me they were talking about. I don't think I changed expression much, but I felt as warm as the color of Tween's eyes.

WE PASSED through the gates, Tween first with never a thought for the barrier which did not exist for her, then Judson, waiting cautiously for my go-ahead after the inside scanning plate had examined the whorls and lines of my hand. I followed, and the great gates closed behind us.

"Want to come up to the office?" I asked Tween when we reached Central Corridor.

"Thanks, no," she said. "I'm going to find Wold." She turned to Judson. "You'll be certified quickly," she told him. "I just know. But, Judson—"

"Say it, whatever it is," said Jud, sensing her hesitation.

"I was going to say get certified first. Don't try to decide anything else before that. You'll have to take my word for it, but nothing that ever happened to you is quite like the knowledge that you're free to go through those gates any time you feel like it."

Judson's face assumed a slightly puzzled, slightly stubborn expression. It disappeared, and I knew it was a conscious effort for him to do it. Then he put out his hand and touched her heavy silver hair. "Thanks," he said.

She strode off, the carriage of her head telling us that her face was eager as she went to Wold. At the turn of the corridor she waved and was gone.

"I'm going to miss that girl," I said, and turned back to Judson. The puzzled, stubborn look was back, full force. "What's the matter?"

"What did she mean by that sisterly advice about getting certified first? What else would I have to decide about right now?"

I swatted his shoulder. "Don't let it bother you, Jud. She sees something in you that you can't see yourself, yet."

That didn't satisfy him at all. "Like what?" When I didn't answer, he asked, "You see it, too, don't you?"

We started up the ramp to my office. "I like you," I said. "I liked you the minute I laid eyes on you, years ago, when you were just a sprout."

"You've changed the subject."

"Hell I have. Now let me save my wind for the ramp." This was only slightly a stall. As the years went by, that ramp seemed to get steeper and steeper. Twice Coördination had offered to power it for me and I'd refused haughtily. I could see the time coming when I was going to be too heavy for my high-horse. All the same, I was glad for the chance to stall my answer to Judson's question. The answer lay in my liking him; I knew that instinctively. But it needed thinking through. We've conditioned ourselves too much to analyze our dislikes and to take our likes for granted.

THE outer door opened as we approached. There was a man waiting in the appointment foyer, a big fellow with a gray cape and a golden circlet around his blue-black hair. "Clinton!" I said. "How are you, son? Waiting for me?"

The inner door opened for me and I went into my office, Clinton behind me. I fell down in my specially molded chair and waved him to a relaxer. At the door Judson cleared his throat. "Shall I—uh. . . ."

Clinton looked up swiftly, an annoyed, tense motion. He raked a blazing blue gaze across Jud, and his expression changed. "Come in, for God's sake. Newcomer, hm? Sit down. Listen. You can't learn enough about this project. Or these people. Or the kind of flat spin an Outbounder can get himself into."

"Clint, this's Judson," I said. "Jud, Clint's about the itchy-footedest Outbounder of them all. What is on your mind, son?"

Clinton wet his lips. "How's about me heading Out—*alone?*"

I said, "Your privilege, if you think you'll enjoy it."

He smacked a heavy fist into his palm. "Good, then."

"Of course," I said, looking at the overhead, "the ships are built for two. I'd personally be a bit troubled about the prospect of spending—uh—however long it might be, staring at that empty bunk across the way. Specially," I added loudly, to interrupt what he was going to say, "if I had to spend some hours or weeks or maybe a decade with the knowledge that I was alone because I took off with a mad on."

"This isn't what you might call a fit of pique," snapped Clinton. "It's been years building—first because I had a need and recognized it; second because the need got greater when I started to work toward filling it; third because I found who and what would satisfy it; fourth because I was so wrong on point three."

"You *are* wrong? Or you're *afraid* you're wrong?"

He looked at me blankly. "I don't know," he said, all the snap gone out of his voice. "Not for sure."

"Well, then, you've no real problem. All you do is ask yourself whether it's worthwhile to take off alone because of a problem you haven't solved. If it is, go ahead."

He rose and went to the door. "Clinton!" My voice must have crackled; he stopped without turning, and from the corner of my eye I saw Judson sit up abruptly. I said, more quietly, "When Judson here suggested that he go away and leave us alone, why did you tell him to come in? What did you see in him that made you do it?"

Clinton's thoughtfully slitted eyes hardly masked their blazing blue as he turned them on Judson, who squirmed like a schoolboy. Clinton said, "I think it's because he looks as if he can be reached. And trusted. That answer you?"

"It does." I waved him out cheerfully. Judson said, "You have an awesome way of operating."

"On him?"

"On both of us. How do you know what you did by turning his problem back on himself? He's likely to go straight to the launching-court."

"He won't."

"You're sure?"

"Of course I'm sure," I said flatly. "If Clinton hadn't already decided *not* to take off alone—not today, anyhow—he wouldn't have come to see me and get argued out of it."

"What's really bothering him?"

"I can't say." I wouldn't say. Not to Judson. Not now, at least. Clinton was ripe to leave, and he was the kind to act when ready. He had found what he thought was the perfect human being for him to go with. She wasn't ready to go. She never in all time and eternity would be ready to go.

"All right," said Jud. "What about me? That was very embarrassing."

I LAUGHED at him. "Sometimes when you don't know exactly how to phrase something for yourself, you can shock a stranger into doing it for you. Why did I like you on sight, years ago, and now, too? Why did Clinton feel you were trustworthy? Why did Tween feel free to pass you some advice—and what prompted the advice? Why did—" No. Don't mention the most significant one of all. Leave her out of it. "—Well, there's no point in itemizing all afternoon. Clinton said it. *You can be reached.* Practically anyone meeting you knows—feels, anyhow—that you can be reached . . . touched . . . affected. We like feeling that we have an effect on someone."

Judson closed his eyes, screwed up his brow. I knew he was digging around in his memory, thinking of close and casual acquaintances . . . how many of them . . . how much they had meant to him and he to them. He looked at me. "Should I change?"

"God, no! Only—don't let it be *too* true. I think that's what Tween was driving at when she said not to jump at any decisions until you've reached the comparative serenity of certification."

"Serenity . . . I could use some of that," he murmured.

"Jud."

"Mm?"

"Did you ever try to put into one simple statement just why you came to Curbstone?"

He looked startled. Like most people, he had been living, and living ardently, without ever wondering particularly what for. And like most people, he had sooner or later had to answer the jackpot question: "What am I doing here?"

"I CAME because—because . . . no, that wouldn't be a simple statement."

"All right. Run it off, anyway. A simple statement will come out of it if there's anything really important there. Any basic is simple, Jud. Every basic is important. Complicated matters may be fascinating, frightening, funny, intriguing, worrisome, educational, or what have you; but if they're complicated, they are, by definition, not important."

He leaned forward and put his elbows on his knees. His hands wound tightly around one another, and his head went down.

"I came here . . . looking for something. Not because I thought it was here. There was just nowhere else left to look. Earth is under such strict discipline . . . discipline by comfort; discipline by constructive luxury. Every need is taken care of that you can name, and no one seems to understand that the needs you *can't* name are the important ones. And all Earth is in a state of arrested development because of Curbstone. Everything is held in check. The *status quo* rules because for six thousand years it must and will. Six thousand years of physical and social evolution will be sacrificed for the single tremendous step that Curbstone makes possible. And I couldn't find a place for myself in the static part of the plan, so the only place for me to go was to the active part."

He was quiet so long after that, I felt I had to nudge him along. "Could it be that there *is* a way to make you happy on Earth, and you just haven't been able to find it?"

"Oh, no," he said positively. Then he raised his head and stared at me. "Wait a minute. You're very close to the mark there. That—that simple statement is trying to crawl out." He frowned. This time I kept my mouth shut and watched him.

"The something I'm looking for," he said finally, in the surest tones he'd used yet, "is something I lack, or something I have that I haven't been able to name yet. If there's anything on Earth or here that can fill that hollow place, and if I find it, I won't want to go Out. I won't need to go—I *shouldn't* go. But if it doesn't exist for me here, then Out I go, as part of a big something, rather than as a something missing a part. Wait!" He chewed his lower lip. His knuckle-joints crackled as he twisted his hands together. "I'll rephrase that and you'll have your simple statement."

He took a deep breath and said, "I came to Curbstone to find out . . . whether there's something I haven't had yet that belongs to me, or whether I . . . belong to something that hasn't had me yet."

"Fine," I said. "Very damned fine. You keep looking, Jud. The answer's here, somewhere, in some form. I've never heard it put better: Do you owe, or are you owed? There are three possible courses open to you, no matter which way you decide."

"There are? Three?"

I put up fingers one at a time. "Earth. Here. Out."

"I—see."

"And you can take the course of any one of the words you saw floating over the gate to the launching court."

He stood up. "I've got a lot to think about."

"You have."

"But I've got me one hell of a blueprint."

I just grinned at him.

"You through with me?" he asked.

"For now."

"When do I start work for my certificate?"

"At the moment, you're just about four-ninths through."

"You dog! All this has been—"

"I'm a working man, Jud. I work all the time. Now beat it. You'll hear from me."

"You dog," he said again. "You old *hound*-dog!" But he left.

I sat back to think. I thought about Judson, of course. And Clinton and his worrisome solo ideas. The trip can be done solo, but it isn't a good idea. The human mind's communications equipment isn't a convenience—it's a vital necessity. Tween. How beautiful can a girl get? And the way she lights up when she thinks about going Out. She's certified now. Guess she and Wold will be taking off any time now.

Then my mind spun back to Flower. Put those pieces together . . . something should fit. Turn it this way, back—Ah! Clinton wants Out. He's been waiting and waiting for his girl to get certified. She hasn't even tried. He's not going to wait much longer. Who's his girl now . . .?

Flower.

Flower, who turned all that heat on Judson.

Why Judson? There were bigger men, smarter, better-looking ones. What was special about Judson?

I filed the whole item away in my mind—with a red priority tab on it.

THE days went by. A gong chimed and the number-board over my desk glowed. I didn't have to look up the numbers to know who it was. Fort and Mariellen. Nice kids. Slipped Out during a sleep period. I thought about them, watched the chain of checking lights flicker on, one after another. Palm-patterns removed from the Gate scanner; they'd never be used there again. Ship replaced. Quarters cleared and readied. Launching time reported to Coördination. Marriage recorded. Automatic machinery calculated, filed, punched cards, activated more automatic machinery until Fort and Mariellen were only axial alignments on the molecules of a magnetic tape . . . names . . . memories . . . dead, perhaps; gone, certainly, for the next six thousand years.

Hold tight, Earth! Wait for them, the fifty-four per cent (I hope, I ardently hope) who will come back. Their relatives, their Earthbound friends will be long dead, and all their children and theirs; so let the Outbounders come home at least to the same Earth, the same language, the same traditions. They will be the millennial traditions of a more-than-Earth, the source of the unthinkable spatial sphere made fingertip-available to humankind through the efforts of the Outbounders. Earth is prepaying six thousand years of progress in exchange for the ability to use stars for stepping-stones, to be able to make Mars in a minute, Antares and Betelgeuse afternoon stops in a delivery run. Six thousand years of sacred stasis buys all but a universe, conquers Time, eliminates the fractionation of humanity into ship-riding, minute-shackled fragments of diverging evolution among the stars. All the stars will be in the next room when the Outbounders return.

Six thousand times around Sol, with Sol moving in a moving galaxy, and the galaxy in flight through a fluxing universe. That all amounts to a resultant movement of Earth through nine Möllner degrees around the Universal Curve. For six thousand years Curbstone flings off its tiny ships, its monstrous power-plant kicking them into space-time and the automatics holding them there until all—or until enough—are positioned. Some will materialize in the known universe and some in faintly suspected nebulae; some will appear in the empty nothingnesses beyond the galactic clusters, and some will burst into normal space inside molten suns.

BUT when the time comes, and the little ships are positioned in a great spherical pattern out around space, and together they become real again, they will send to each other a blaze of tight-beam energy. Like the wiring of a great switchboard, like the synapses of a brain, each beam will find its neighbors, and through them Earth.

And then, within and all through that sphere, humanity will spread, stepping from rim to rim of the universe in seconds, instantaneously transmitting men and materials from and to the stars. Here a ship can be sent piecemeal and assembled, there a space-station. Yonder, on some unheard-of planet of an unknown star, men light years away from Earth can assemble matter transceivers and hook them up to the great sphere, and add yet another world to those already visited.

AND what of the Outbounders? Real time, six thousand years. Ship's time, from second-order spatial entry to materialization—*zero.*

Fort and Mariellen. Nice kids. Memories now; lights on a board, one after another, until they're all accounted for. At Curbstone, the quiet machinery says, "Next!"

Fort and Mariellen. Clinging together, they press down the launching lever. Effortlessly in their launching, they whirl away from Curbstone. In minutes there is a flicker of gray, or perhaps not even that. Strange stars surround them. They stare at one another. They are elsewhere . . . else*when.* Lights glow. This one says the tight-beam has gone on, pouring out toward the neighbors and, through them, to all the others. That one cries "*emergency*" and Fort whips to the manual controls and does what he can to avoid a dust-cloud, a planet . . . perhaps an alien ship.

Fort and Mariellen (or George and Viki, or Bruce, who went Out by himself, or Eleanor and Grace, or Sam and Rod—they were brothers) may materialize and die in an intolerable matter-displacement explosion so quickly that there is no time for pain. They may be holed by a meteor and watch, with glazing freezing eyes, the froth bubbling up from each other's bursting lungs. They may survive for minutes or weeks, and then fall captive to some giant planet or unsuspected sun. They may be hunted down and killed or captured by beings undreamed of.

And some of them will survive all this and wait for the blessed contact; the strident heralding of the matter transceiver with which each ship is equipped—and the abrupt appearance of a man, sixty centuries unborn when they left Curbstone, instantly transmitted from Earth to their vessel. Back with him they'll go, to an unchanged and ecstatic Earth, teeming with billions of trained, mature humans ready to fill the universe with human ways—the new humans who have left war and greed behind them, who have acquired a universe so huge that they need exploit no creature's properties, so rich and available is everything they require.

And some will survive, and wait, and die waiting because of some remotely extrapolated miscalculation. The beams never reach them; their beams contact nothing. And perhaps a few of these will not die, but will find refuge on some planet to leave a marker that will shock whatever is alive and intelligent a million years hence. Perhaps they will leave more than that. Perhaps there will be a slower, more hazardous planting of humanity in the gulfs.

But fifty-four per cent, the calculations insist, will establish the star-conquering sphere and return.

THE weeks went by. A chime: Bark and Barbara. Damn it all, no more of Barbara's banana cream pie. The filing, the sweeping, the recording, the lights. Marriage recorded.

When a man and a woman go Out together, that is marriage. There is another way to be married on Curbstone. There is a touch less speed involved in it than in joined hands pressing down a launching lever. There is not one whit less solemnity. It means what it means because it is not stamped with necessity. Children derive their names from their mothers, wed or not, and there is no distinction. Men and women, as responsible adults, do as they please within limits which are extremely wide. *Except*. . . .

By arduous trial and tragic error, humanity has evolved modern marriage. With social pressure removed from the pursuit of a mate, with the end of the ribald persecution of spinsterhood, a marriage ceases to be a rubber stamp upon what people are sure to do, with or without ceremonies. Where men and women are free to seek their own company, as and when they choose, without social penalties, they will not be trapped into hypocrisies with marriage vows. Under such conditions a marriage is entered gravely and with sincerity, and it constitutes a public statement of choice and—with the full implementation of a mature society—of inviolability. The lovely, ancient words "forsaking all others" spell out the nature of modern marriage, with the universally respected adjunct that fidelity is not a command or a restriction, but a chosen path. Divorce is swift and simple, and—almost unheard of. Married people live this way, single people live that way; the lines are drawn and deeply respected. People marry because they intend to live within the limits of marriage. The fact that a marriage exists is complete proof that it is working.

I had a word about marriage with Tween. Ran into her in the Gate corridor. I think she'd been in one of the ships again. If she was pale, her olive skin hid it. If her eyes were bloodshot, the lustrous ruby of her eyes covered it up. Maybe I saw her dragging her feet as she walked, or some such. I took her chin in my hand and tilted her head back. "Any dragons I can kill?"

She gave me a brilliant smile which lived only on her lips. "I'm wonderful," she said bravely.

"You are," I agreed. "Which doesn't necessarily have anything to do with the way you feel. I won't pry, child; but tell me—if you ever ate too many green apples, or stubbed your toe on a cactus, do you know a nice safe something you could hang on to while you cried it out?"

"I do," she said breathlessly, making the smile just as hard as she could. "Oh, I do." She patted my cheek. "You're . . . listen. Would you tell me something if I asked you?"

"About certificates? No, Tween. Not about anyone else's certificate. But—all he has to do is complete his final hypnopediae, and he just hasn't showed up."

She hated to hear it, but I'd made her laugh, too, a little. "Do you read minds, the way they all say?"

"I do not. And if I could, I wouldn't. And if I couldn't help reading 'em, I'd sure never act as if I could. In other words, no. It's just that I've been alive long enough to know what pushes people around. So's I don't care much about a person, I can judge pretty well what's bothering him.

"'Course," I added, "if I do give a damn, I can tell even better. Tween, you'll be getting married pretty soon, right?"

Perhaps I shouldn't have said that. She gasped, and for a moment she just stopped making that smile. Then, "Oh, yes," she said brightly. "Well, not exactly. What I mean is, when we go Out, you see, so we might as well not, and I imagine as soon as Wold gets his certificate, we'll . . . we kind of feel going Out is the best—I seem to have gotten something in my eye. I'm s-sor. . . ."

I let her go. But when I saw Wold next—it was down in the Euphoria Sector—I went up to him very cheerfully. There are ways I feel sometimes that make me real jovial.

I laid my hand on his shoulder. His back bowed a bit and it seemed to me I felt vertebrae grinding together. "Wold, old boy," I said heartily. "Good to see you. You haven't been around much recently. Mad?"

He pulled away from me. "A little," he said sullenly. His hair was too shiny and he had perfect teeth that always reminded me of a keyboard instrument.

"Well, drop around," I said. "I like to see young folks get ahead. You," I added with a certain amount of emphasis, "have gone pretty damn far."

"So have you," he said with even more emphasis.

"Well, then." I slapped him on the back. His eyeballs stayed in, which surprised me. "You can top me. You can go farther than I ever can. See you soon, old fellow."

I WALKED off, feeling the cold brown points of his gaze.

And as it happened, not ten minutes later I saw that *kakumba* dance. I don't see much dancing usually, but there was an animal roar from the dance-chamber that stopped me, and I ducked in to see what had the public so charmed.

The dance had gone through most of its figures, with the caller already worked up into a froth and only three couples left. As I shouldered my way to a vantage point, one of the three couples was bounced, leaving the two best. One was a tall blonde with periwigged hair and subvoltaic bracelets that passed and repassed a clatter of pastel arcs; she was dancing with one of the armor-monkeys from the Curbstone Hull Division, and they were good.

The other couple featured a slender, fluid dark girl in an open tunic of deep brown. She moved so beautifully that I caught my breath, and watched so avidly that it was seconds before I realized that it was Flower. The reaction to that made me lose more seconds in realizing that her partner was Judson. Good as the other couple were, they were better. I'd tested Jud's reflexes, and they were phenomenal, but I'd had no idea he could respond like this to anything.

The caller threw the solo light to the first couple. There was a wild burst of music and the arc-wielding blonde and her arc-wielding boy friend cut loose in an intricate frenzy of disjointed limbs and half-beat stamping. So much happened between those two people so fast that I thought they'd never get separated when the music stopped. But they untangled right with the closing bars, and a roar went up from the people watching them. And then the same blare of music was thrown at Jud and Flower.

Judson simply stood back and folded his arms, walking out a simple figure to indicate that, honest, he was dancing, too. But he gave it all to Flower.

Now I'll tell you what she did in a single sentence: she knelt before him and slowly stood up with her arms over her head. But words will never describe the process completely. It took her about twelve minutes to get all the way up. At the fourth minute the crowd began to realize that her body was trembling. It wasn't a wriggle or a shimmy, or anything as crude as that. It was a steady, apparently uncontrollable shiver. At about the eighth minute the audience began to realize it was controlled, and just how completely controlled it was. It was hypnotic, incredible. At the final crescendo she was on her tiptoes with her arms stretched high, and when the music stopped she made no flourish; she simply relaxed and stood still, smiling at Jud. Even from where I stood I could see the moisture on Jud's face.

A big man standing beside me grunted, a tight, painful sound. I turned to him; it was Clinton. Tension crawled through his jaw-muscles like a rat under a rug. I put my hand on his arm. It was rocky. "Clint."

"Wh—oh. Hi."

"Thirsty?"

"No," he said. He turned back to the dance floor, searched it with his eyes, found Flower.

"Yes, you are, son," I said. "Come on."

"Why don't you go and—" He got hold of himself. "You're right. I am thirsty."

We went to the almost deserted Card Room and dispensed ourselves some methyl-caffeine. I didn't say anything until we'd found a table. He sat stiffly looking at his drink without seeing it. Then he said, "Thanks."

"For what?"

"I was about to be real uncivilized in there."

I just waited.

He said truculently, "Well, damn it, she's free to do what she wants, isn't she? She likes to dance—good. Why shouldn't she? Damn it, what is there to get excited about?"

"Who's excited?"

"It's that Judson. What's he have to be crawling around her all the time for? She hasn't done a damn thing about getting her certificate since he got here." He drank his liquor down at a gulp. It had no apparent effect, which meant something.

"What had she done before he got here?" I asked quietly. When he didn't answer I said, "Jud's Outbound, Clint. I wouldn't worry. I can guarantee Flower won't be with him when he goes, and that will be real soon. Hold on and wait."

"Wait?" His lip curled. "I've been ready to go for weeks. I used to think of . . . of Flower and me working together, helping each other. I used to make plans for a celebration the day we got certified. I used to look at the stars and think about the net we'd help throw around them, pull 'em down, pack 'em in a basket. Flower and me, back on Earth after six thousand years, watching humanity come into its own, knowing we'd done something to help. I've been waiting, and you say wait some more."

"This," I said, "is what you call an unstable situation. It can't stay the way it is and it won't. Wait, I tell you: wait. There's got to be a blow-off."

There was.

IN MY office the chime sounded. Moira and Bill. Certificates denied to Hester, Elizabeth, Jenks,

Mella. Hester back to earth. Hallowell and Letitia, marriage recorded. Certificates granted to Aaron, Musette, n'Guchi, Mancinelli, Judson.

Judson took the news quietly, glowing. I hadn't seen much of him recently. Flower took up a lot of his time, and training the rest. After he was certified and I'd gone with him to test the hand-scanner by the gate and give him his final briefing, he cut out on the double, I guess to give Flower the great news. I remember wondering how he'd like her reaction.

WHEN I got back to my office Tween was there. She rose from the foyer couch as I wheezed in off the ramp. I took one look at her and said, "Come inside." She followed me through the inner door. I waved my hand over the infra-red plate and it closed. Then I put out my arms.

She bleated like a new-born lamb and flew to me. Her tears were scalding, and I don't think human muscles are built for the wrenching those agonized sobs gave her. People should cry more. They ought to learn how to do it easily, like laughing or sweating. Crying piles up. In people like Tween, who do nothing if they can't smile and make a habit-pattern of it, it really piles up. With a reservoir like that, and no developed outlet, things get torn when the pressure builds too high.

I just held her tight so she wouldn't explode. The only thing I said to her was "sh-h-h" once when she tried to talk while she wept. One thing at a time.

It took a while, but when she was finished she was finished. She didn't taper off. She was weak from all that punishment, but calm. She talked.

"He isn't a real thing at all," she said bleakly. "He's something I made up out of starshine, out of wanting so much to be a part of something as big as this project. I never felt I had anything big about me except that. I wanted to join it with something bigger than I was, and, together, we'd build something so big that it would be worthy of Curbstone.

"I thought it was Wold. I *made* it be Wold. Oh, none of this is his fault. I could have seen what he was, and I just wouldn't. What I did with him, what I felt for him, was just as crazy as if I'd convinced myself he had wings and then hated him because he wouldn't fly. He isn't anything but a h-hero. He struts to the newcomers and the rejected ones pretending he's a man who will one day give himself to humanity and the stars. He . . . probably believes that about himself. But he won't complete his training, and he . . . now I know, now I can see it—he tried everything he could think of to stop me from being certified. I was no use to him with a certificate. He couldn't treat me as his pretty, slightly stupid little girl, once I was certified. And he couldn't get his own certificate because if he did he'd have to go Out, one of these days, and that's something he can't face.

"He—*wants* me to leave him. If I will, if it's my decision, he can wear my memory like a black band on his arm, and delude himself for the rest of his life that his succession of women is just a search for something to replace me. Then he'll always have an excuse; he'll never, never have to risk his neck. He'll be the shattered hero, and women as stupid as I was will try to heal the wounds he's arranged for me to give him."

"You don't hate him?" I asked her quietly.

"No. Oh, no, *no!* I told you, it wasn't his fault. I—loved *something.* A man lived in my heart, lived there for years. He had no name and no face. I gave him Wold's name and Wold's face and just wouldn't believe it wasn't Wold. I did it. Wold didn't. I don't hate him. I don't like him. I just don't . . . *anything.*"

I PATTED her shoulder. "Good. You're cured. If you hated him, he'd still be important. What are you going to do?"

"What shall I do?"

"I'd never tell you what to do about a thing like this, Tween. You know that. You've got to figure out your own answers. I can advise you to use those new-opened eyes of yours carefully, though. And don't think that that man who lives in your heart doesn't exist anywhere else. He does. Right here on this station, maybe. You just haven't been able to see him before."

"Who?"

"God, girl, don't ask me that! Ask Tween next time you see her; no one will ever know for sure but Tween."

"You're so wise. . . ."

"Nah. I'm old enough to have made more mistakes than most people, that's all, and I have a good memory."

She rose shakily. I put out a hand and helped her. "You're played out, Tween. Look—don't go back yet. Hide out for a few days and get some rest and do some thinking. There's a suite on this level. No one will bother you, and you'll find everything there you need, including silence and privacy."

"That would be good," she said softly. "Thank you."

"All right . . . listen. Mind if I send someone in to talk to you?"

"Talk? Who?"

"Let me play it as it comes."

The ruby eyes sent a warm wave to me, and she smiled. I thought, I wish I was as confident of myself as she is of me. "It's 412," I said, "the third door to your left. Stay there as long as you want to. Come back when you feel like it."

She came close to me and tried to say something. I thought for a second she was going to kiss me on the mouth. She didn't; she kissed my hand. "I'll swat your bottom!"

I roared, flustered. "Git, now, dammit!" She laughed . . . she always had a bit of laughter tucked away in her, no matter what, bless her cotton head. . . .

As soon as she was gone, I turned to the annunciator and sent out a call for Judson. *Hell,* I thought, *you can try, can't you?* Waiting, I thought about Judson's hungry, upward look, and that hole in his head . . . that quality of reachableness, and what happened when he was reached by the wrong thing. Lord, responsive people certainly make the worst damn fools of all!

He was there in minutes, looking flushed, excited, happy, and worried all at once. "Was on my way here when your call went out," he said.

"SIT down, Jud. I have a small project in mind. Maybe you could help."

He sat. I looked for just the right words to use. I couldn't say anything about Flower. She had her hooks into him; if I said anything about her, he'd defend her. And one of the oldest phenomena in human relations is that we come to be very fond of the thing we find ourselves defending, even if we didn't like it before. I thought again of the hunger that lived in Jud, and what Tween might see of it with her newly opened eyes.

"Jud—"

"I'm married," he blurted.

I sat very still. I don't think my face did anything at all.

"It was the right thing for me to do," he said, almost angrily. "Don't you see? You know what my problem is—it was you who found it for me. I was looking for something that should belong to me . . . or something to belong to."

"Flower," I said.

"Of course. Who else? Listen, that girl's got trouble, too. What do you suppose blocks her from taking her certificate? She doesn't think she's *worthy* of it."

My, I said. Fortunately, I said it to myself.

Jud said, "No matter what happens, I've done the right thing. If I can help her get her certificate, we'll go Out together, and that's what we're here for. If I can't help her do that, but find that she fills that place in me that's been so empty for so long, well and good—that's what *I'm* here for. We can go back to Earth and be happy."

"You're quite sure of all this."

"Sure I'm sure! Do you think I'd have gone ahead with the marriage if I weren't sure?"

Sure you would, I thought. I said, "Congratulations, then. You know I wish you the best."

He stood up uncertainly, started to say something, and apparently couldn't find it. He went to the door, turned back. "Will you come for dinner tonight?" I hesitated. He said, "Please. I'd appreciate it."

I cocked an eyebrow. "Answer me straight, Jud. Is dinner your idea or Flower's?"

He laughed embarrassedly. "Damn it, you always see too much. Mine . . . sort of . . . I mean, it isn't that she dislikes you, but . . . well, hell, I want the two of you to be friends, and I think you'd understand her and me, too, a lot better if you made the effort."

I could think of things I'd much rather do than have dinner with Flower. A short swim in boiling oil, for example. I looked up at his anxious face. Oh, hell. "I'd love to," I said. "Around eight?"

"Fine! Gee," he said, like a school kid. "Gee, thanks." He shuffled, not knowing whether to go right away or not. "Hey," he said suddenly. "You sent out a call for me. What's this project you wanted me for?"

"Nothing, Jud," I said tiredly. "I've . . . changed my mind. See you later, son."

THE dinner was something special. Steaks. Jud had broiled them himself. I got the idea that he'd selected them, too, and set the table. It was Flower, though, who got me something to sit on. She looked me over, slowly and without concealing it, went to the table, pulled the light formed-aluminum chair away, and dragged over a massive relaxer. She then smiled straight at me. A little unnecessary, I thought; I'm bulky, but those aluminum chairs have always held up under me so far.

I won't give it to you round by round. The meal passed with Flower either in a sullen silence or manufacturing small brittle whips of conversation. When she was quiet, Jud tried to goad her into talking. When she talked, he tried to turn the conversation away from me. The occasion, I think, was a complete success—for Flower. For Jud it must have been hell. For me—well, it was interesting.

Item: Flower poked and prodded at her steak, and when she got a lull in the labored talk Jud and I were squeezing out, she began to cut meticulously around the edges of the steak. "If there is anything I can't stand the sight or the smell of," she said clearly, "it's fat."

Item: She said, "Oh, Lord" this and "Lord sakes" that in a drawl that made it come out "Lard" every time.

Item: I sneezed once. She whipped a tissue over to me swiftly and politely enough, and then said "Render unto sneezers . . . ." which stood as a cute quip until she nudged her husband and said, *"Render!"* at which point things got real hushed.

Item: When she had finished, she leaned back and sighed. "If I ate like that all the time, I'd be as big as—" She looked straight at me and stopped. Jud, flushing miserably, tried to kick her under the table; I know, because it was me he kicked. Flower finished, "—as big as a lifeboat." But she kept looking at me, easily and insultingly.

Item—You get the idea. All I

can say for myself is that I got through it all. I wouldn't give her the satisfaction of driving me out until I'd had all she could give me. I wouldn't be overtly angry, because if I did, she'd present me to Jud ever after as the man who hated her. If Jud ever had wit enough, this evening could be remembered as the time she was insufferably insulting, and that was all I wanted.

It was over at last, and I made my excuses as late as I possibly could without staying overnight. As I left, she took Jud's arm and held it tight until I was out of sight, thereby removing the one chance he had to come along a little way and apologize to me.

He didn't get close enough to speak to me for four days, and when he did, I had the impression that he had lied to be there, that Flower thought he was somewhere else. He said rapidly, "About the other night, you mustn't think that—"

And I cut him off as gently and firmly as I could: "I understand it perfectly, Jud. Think a minute and you'll know that."

"Look, Flower was just out of sorts. I'll work on her. Next time you come there'll be a real difference. You'll see."

"I'm sure I will, Jud. But drop it, will you? There's no harm done." And I thought, next time I come will be six months after the Outbounders get back. That gives me sixty centuries or so to get case-hardened.

ABOUT a week after Jud's wedding, I was in the Upper Central corridor where it ramps into the Gate passageway. Now whether it was some sixth sense, or whether I actually did smell something, I don't know. I got a powerful, sourceless impression of methyl-caffeine in the air, and at the same time I looked down the passage and saw the Gate just closing.

I got down there altogether too fast to do my leaky valves any good. I palmed the doors open and sprinted across the court. When anything my size and shape gets to sprinting, it's harder to stop it than let it keep going. One of the ship ports was open and I was heading for it. It started to swing closed. I lost all thought of trying to slow down and put what little energy I could find into pumping my old legs faster.

With a horrible slow-motion feeling of disaster, I felt one toe tip my other heel, and my center of gravity began to move forward faster than I was traveling. I was in mid-air for an age—long enough to chew and swallow a tongue—and then I hit on my stomach, rocked forward on my receding chest and two of my chins, and slid. I had my hands out in front of me. My left hit the bulkhead and buckled. My right shot through what was left of the opening of the door, which crunched shut on my forearm. Then my forehead hit the sill and I blacked out.

When the lights dimmed on

again, I was spread out on a ship's bunk, apparently alone. My left arm hurt more than I could bear, and my right arm hurt worse, and both of them together couldn't match what was going on in my head.

A man appeared from the service cubicle when I let out a groan. He had a bowl of warm water and the ship's B first-aid kit in his hands. He crossed quickly to me, and began to stanch the blood from between some of my chins. It wasn't until then that my blurring sight made out who he was.

"Clinton, you hub-forted son of a bastich!" I roared at him. "Leave the chin alone and get some plexicaine into those arms!"

HE HAD the gall to laugh at me. "One thing at a time, old man. You are bleeding. Let's try to be a patient, not an impatient."

"Impatient, out-patient," I yelped, "get that plex into me! I am just not the strong, silent type!"

"Okay, okay." He got the needle out of the kit, squirted it upward, and plunged it deftly into my arms. A good boy. He hit the bicep on one, the forearm on the other, and got just the right ganglia. The pain vanished. That left my head, but he fed me an analgesic and that cataclysmic ache began to recede.

"I'm afraid the left is broken," he said. "As for the right—well, if I hadn't seen that hand come crawling in over the sill like a pet puppy, and reversed the door control, I'd have cut your fingernails off clear up to the elbow. What in time did you think you were doing?"

"I can't remember; maybe I've got a concussion. For some reason or other it seemed I had to look inside the ship. Can you splint this arm?"

"Let's call the medic."

"You can do just as well."

He went for the C kit and got a traction splint out. He whipped the prepared cushioning around the swelling arm, clamped the ends of the splint at wrist and elbow, and played an infra-red lamp on it. In a few seconds the splint began to lengthen. When the broken forearm was a few millimeters longer than the other, he shut off the heat and the thermoplastic splint automatically set and snugged into the cushioning. Clinton threw off the clamps. "That's good enough for now. All right, are you ready to tell me what made you get in my way?"

"No."

"Stop trying to look like an innocent babe! Your stubble gives you away. You knew I was going to solo, didn't you?"

"No one said anything to me."

"No one ever has to," he said in irritation, and then chuckled. "Man, I wish I could stay mad at you. All right—what next?"

"You're not going to take off?"

"With you in here? Don't be foolish. The station'd lose too much and I wouldn't be gaining a thing. Damn you! I'd worked up the most glamorous drunk on methyl-caffeine, and you had to get me all anxious and drive away the fumes. . . . Well, go ahead. I'll play it your way. What do we do?"

"Stop trying to make a Machiavelli out of me," I growled. "Give me a hand back to my quarters and I'll let you go do whatever you want."

"It's never that simple with you," he half-grinned. "Okay. Let's go."

When I got to my feet—with more of his help than I like to admit—my heart began to pound. He must have felt it, because he said nothing while we stood there and waited for it to behave itself. Clinton was a good lad.

We negotiated the court and the Gate all right, but slowly. When we got to the foot of my ramp, I shook my head. "Not that," I wheezed. "Couldn't make it. Down this way."

WE WENT down the lateral corridor to 412. The door slid back for me.

"Hi!" I called. "Company."

"What? Who is it?" came the crystal voice. Tween appeared. "Oh—oh! I didn't want to see anyone just—why, what's happened?"

My eyelids flickered. I moaned. Clinton said, "I think we better get him spread out. He's not doing so well."

Tween ran to us and took my arm gently above the splint. They got me to a couch and I collapsed on it.

"Damn him," said Clinton good-humoredly. "He seems to be working full time to keep me from going Out."

There was such a long silence that I opened one eye to look at them. Tween was staring at him as if she had never seen him before—as, actually, she hadn't, with her eyes so full of Wold.

"Do you really want to go Out?" she asked softly.

"More than. . . ." He looked at her hair, her lovely face. "I don't think I've seen you around much. You're—Tween, aren't you?"

She nodded and they stopped talking. I snapped my eyes shut because they were sure to look at me just for something to do.

"Is he all right?" she asked.

"I think he's—yes, he's asleep. Don't wonder. He's been through a lot."

"Let's go in the other room where we can talk together without disturbing him."

They closed the door. I could barely hear them. It went on for a long time, with occasional silences. Finally I heard what I'd been listening for: "If it hadn't been for him, I'd be gone now. I was just about to solo."

"No! Oh, I'm glad. . . . I'm glad you didn't."

One of those silences. Then, "So am I, Tween. Tween. . . ." in a whisper of astonishment.

I got up off the couch and silently let myself out. I went back to my quarters, even managing to climb the ramp. I felt real fine.

I HEARD an ugly rumor.

I'd seen a lot and I'd done a lot, and I regarded myself as pretty shockproof, but this one jolted me to the core. I took refuge in the old ointment, "It can't be, it just can't be," but in my heart I knew it could.

I got hold of Judson. He was hollow-eyed and much quieter than usual. I asked him what he was doing these days, though I knew.

"Boning up on the fine points of astrogation," he told me. "I've never hit anything so fascinating. It's one thing to have the stuff shoveled into your head when you're asleep, and something else again to experience it all, note by note, like music."

"But you're spending an awful lot of time in the archives, son."

"It takes a lot of time."

"Can't you study at home?"

I think he only just then realized what I was driving at. "Look," he said quietly, "I have my troubles. I have things wrong with me. But I'm not blind. I'm not stupid. You wouldn't tell me to my face that I couldn't handle problems that are strictly my own, would you?"

"I would if I were sure," I said. "Damn it, I'm not. And I'm not going to pry for details."

"I'm glad of that," he said soberly. "Now we don't have to talk about it at all, do we?"

In spite of myself, I laughed aloud.

"What's funny?"

"I am, Jud, boy. I been—handled."

He saw the point, and smiled a little with me. "Hell, I know what you've been hinting at. But you're not close enough to the situation to know all the angles. I am. When the time comes, I'll take care of it. Until then, it's no one's problem but my own."

He picked up his star-chart reels and I knew that one single word more would be one too many. I squeezed his arm and let him go.

Five people, I thought: Wold, Judson, Tween, Clinton, Flower. Take away two and that leaves three. Three's a crowd—in this case, a very explosive kind of crowd.

Nothing, *nothing* justifies infidelity in a modern marriage. But the ugly rumors kept trickling in.

"I want my certificate," Wold said.

I looked up at him and a bushel of conjecture flipped through my mind. So you want your certificate? Why? And why just now, of all times? What can a man do with a certificate that he can't do without one—aside from going Out? Because, damn you, you'll never go Out. Not of your own accord, you won't.

All this, but none of it slipped out. I said, "All right. That's what I'm here for, Wold." And we got to work.

He worked hard, and smoothly and easily, the way he talked, the way he moved. I am constantly astonished at how small accomplished people can make themselves at times.

He was certified easy as breathing. And can you believe it, I worked with him, saw how hard he was working, helped him through, and never realized what it was he was after?

After going through the routines of certification for him, I wasn't happy. There was something wrong somewhere . . . something missing. This was a puzzle that ought to fall together easily, and it wouldn't. I wish—Lord, how I wish I could have thought a little faster.

I let a day go by after Wold was certified. I couldn't sleep, and I couldn't eat, and I couldn't analyze what it was that was bothering me. So I began to cruise, to see if I could find out.

I went to the archives. "Where's Judson?"

The girl told me he hadn't been there for forty-eight hours.

I looked in the Recreation Sector, in the libraries, in the stereo and observation rooms. Some kind of rock-bottom good sense kept me from sending out a general call for him. But it began to be obvious that he just wasn't around. Of course, there were hundreds of rooms and corridors in Curbstone that were unused—they wouldn't be used until the interplanetary project was completed and the matter transmitters started working. But Jud wasn't the kind to hide from anything.

I squared my shoulders and realized that I was doing a lot of speculation to delay looking in the obvious place. I think, more than anything else, I was afraid that he would *not* be there. . . .

I passed my hand over the door announcer. In a moment she answered; she had apparently come in from the sun-field and hadn't bothered to see who it was. She was warm brown from head to toe, all spring-steel and velvet. Her long eyes were sleepy and her mouth was pouty. But when she recognized me, she stood squarely in the doorway.

I think that in the back of every human mind is a machine that works out all the answers and never makes mistakes. I think mine had had enough data to figure out what was happening, what was going to happen, for a long while now. Only I hadn't been able to read the answer until now. Seeing Flower, in that split second, opened more than one door for me. . . .

"*You* want something?" she asked. The emphasis was hard and very insulting.

I went in. It was completely up to her whether she moved aside or was walked down. She moved aside. The door swung shut.

"Where's Jud?"

"I don't know."

I LOOKED into those long secret eyes and raised my hand. I think I was going to hit her. Instead I put my hand on her chest and shoved. She fell, unhurt but terrified, across a relaxer. "What do you th—"

"You won't see him again," I

said, and my voice bounced harshly off the acoust-absorbing walls. "He's gone. *They're* gone."

"They?" Her face went pasty under the deep tan.

"You ought to be killed," I said. "But I think it's better if you live with it. You couldn't hold either of them, or anyone else."

I went out.

MY HEAD was buzzing and my knitting arm throbbed. I moved with utter certainty; never once did it occur to me to ask myself: "Why did I say that?" All the ugly pieces made sense.

I found Wold in the Recreation Sector. He was tanked. I decided against speaking to him, went straight to the launching court and tried the row of ship ports. There was no one there, no one in any of them. My eye must have photographed something in the third ship, because I felt compelled to go back there and look again.

I stared hard at the deep-flocked floor. The soft pile of it looked right and yet not-right. I went to the control panel and unracked an emergency torch, turned it to needle-focus and put it, lit, on the floor. A horizontal beam will tell you things no other light knows about.

I turned the light on the door and slowly swung the sharp streak across the carpet. The monotone, amorphous surface took on streaks and ridges, shadows and shadings. A curved scuff inside. Two parallel ones, long, where something had been dragged. A blurred sector where something heavy had lain long enough to press the springy fibers down for a while, over by the left-hand bunk.

I looked at the bunk. It was unruffled, which meant nothing; the resilient surface was meant to leave no impressions. But at the edge was a single rubbed spot, as if something had spilled there and been wiped hard.

I went to the service cubicle. Everything seemed in order, except one of the cabinet doors, which wouldn't quite close. I looked inside.

It was a food locker. The food was there all right, each container socketed in place in the prepared shelves. But on, between, and among them were micro-reels for the book projector.

I frowned and looked further. Reels were packed into the disposal lock, the towel dispenser, the spare-parts chest for the air exchanger.

Something was where the book-reels belonged, and the reels had been hidden by someone who could not leave them in sight or carry them off.

And where did the reels belong?

I went back to the central chamber and the left-hand bunk. I touched the stud that should have rolled the bunk outward, opening the top, so that the storage space under it could be reached. The bunk didn't move.

I examined the stud. It was coated

over with quick-setting leak-sealer. The stuff was tough but resilient. I got a steel rod and a hammer from the tool-rack and, placing the rod against the stud, hit it once. The leak-sealer cracked off. The bed rolled forward and opened.

It was useless to move him or touch him, or, for that matter, to say anything. Judson was dead, his head twisted almost all the way around. His face was bluish and his eyes stared. He was pushed, jammed, wedged into the small space.

I hit the stud again and the bunk rolled back. Moving without any volition that I could analyze, feeling nothing but a great angry numbness, I cleaned up. I put the rod and the hammer away and fluffed up the piling of the carpeting by the bunk. Then I went and stood in the service cubicle and began to wait.

Wait. Not just stay—wait. I knew he'd be back, just as I suddenly and belatedly understood what it was that every factor in five people had made inevitable. I was coldly hating myself for not having known it sooner.

The great, the admirable, the adventurous in modern civilization were Outbounders. To one who wanted and needed personal power, there would be an ultimate goal, greater even than being an Outbounder. And that would be to stand between an Outbounder and his destiny.

For months Flower had blocked Clinton. When she saw she must ultimately lose him to the stars, she went hunting. She saw Judson—reachable, restless Jud—and she heard my assurance that he would soon go Out. Then and there Judson was doomed.

Wold needed admiration the way Flower needed power. To be an Outbounder and wait for poor struggling Tween suited him perfectly. Tween's certification gave him no alternative but to get rid of her; he couldn't bring himself to go Out.

Once I had taken care of Tween for him, there remained one person on the entire project who could keep him from going Out—and she was married to Jud. Having married, Jud would stay married. Wold did what he could to smash that marriage. When Jud still hung on, wanting to help Flower; wanting to show me that he had made the right choice, there remained one alternative for Wold. Evidence of that lay cramped and staring under the bunk.

But Wold wasn't finished. He wouldn't be finished while Jud's body remained on Curbstone. In Wold's emotional state, he would have to go somewhere and drink to figure out the next step. There was no way of sending a ship Out without riding it. So—I waited.

HE CAME back all right. I was cramped, then, and one foot was asleep. I curled and uncurled the toes frantically when I saw the door begin to move, and tried to flatten my big bulk back down out of sight.

He was breathing hard. He put his lips together and blew like a winded horse, wiped his lips on his forearm. He seemed to have difficulty in focusing his eyes. I wondered how much liquor he had poured into that empty place where most men keep their courage.

He took a fine coil of single-strand plastic cord out of his belt-pouch. Fumbling for the end, he found it and dropped the coil., With the exaggerated care of a drunk, he threw a bowline and drew the loop tight, pulled the bight through the loop so he had a running noose. He made this fast to a triangular bracket over the control panel, led it along the edge of the chart-rack and down to the launching control lever. He bent two half-hitches in the cord, slipped it over the end of the lever and drew it tight. The cord now bound the lever in the up—"off"—position.

From the bulkhead he unfastened the clamps which held the heavy-duty fire extinguisher and lifted it down. It weighed half as much as he did. He set it on the floor in front of the control panel, brought the dangling end of the cord through the U-shaped clamp gudgeons on the extinguisher, took a loose half-hitch around the bight, and, lifting the extinguisher between his free arm and his body, pulled the knot tight. Another half-hitch secured it.

Now the heavy extinguisher dangled in mid-air under the control panel. The cord which supported it ran up to the handle of the launching lever and from there, bending over the edge of the chart-rack, to the bracket.

Panting, Wold took out a cigarette and shook it alight. He drew on it hungrily, and then put it on the chart-rack, resting it against the plastic cord.

When the cigarette burned down to the cord, the thermoplastic would melt through with great enthusiasm. The cord would break, the extinguisher would fall, dragging the lever down. And Out would go all the evidence, to be hidden forever, as far as Wold was concerned, and 6,000 years from anyone else.

Wold stepped back to survey his work just as I stepped forward out of the service cubicle. I brought up my broken arm and swung it with all my weight—and that is really weight—against the side of his head. The cast, though not heavy, was hard, and it must have hit him like a crowbar.

He went down like an elevator, hitched to his knees, and for a second seemed about to topple. His head sagged. He shook it, slowly looked up and saw me.

"I could use one of those needle-guns," I said. "Or I could kick you cold and let Coördination handle you. There are regulations for things like you. But I'd rather do it this way. Get up."

"I never. . . ."

"Get up!" I bellowed, and kicked at him.

He threw his arms around my leg and rolled. As I started down, I pulled the leg in close and whipped it out again. We both hit with a crash on opposite sides of the room. The bunk broke my fall; he was not so lucky. He rose groggily, sliding his back up the door. I lumbered across, deliberately crashed into him, and heard ribs crack as the wind gushed out of his lungs.

I STOOD back a little as he began to sag. I hit him savagely in the face, and his face came back and hit my hand again as his head bounced off the door. I let him fall, then knelt beside him.

There are things you can do to a human body if you know enough physiology—pressures on this and that nerve center which paralyze and cramp and immobilize whole motor-trunk systems. I did these things, and got up, finally, leaving him twisted, sweating in agony. I wheezed over to the control bank and looked critically at the smoldering cigarette. Less than a minute.

"I know you can hear me," I whispered with what breath I could find. "I'd . . . like you to know . . . that you'll be a hero. Your name will . . . be on the Great Roll of the . . . Outbounders. You always . . . wanted that without any . . . effort on your part . . . now you've got it."

I went out. I stopped and leaned back against the wall beside the door. In a few seconds it swung silently shut. I forced back the waves of gray that wanted to engulf me, turned and peered into the port. It showed only blackness.

Jud . . . Jud, boy . . . you always wanted it, too. You almost got cheated out of it. You'll be all right now, son. . . .

I TOTTERED across the court and out the gate. There was someone standing there. She flew to me, pounded my chest with small hard hands. "Did he go? Did he really go?"

I brushed her off as if she had been a midge, and closed one eye so I could get a single image. It was Flower, without her come-on tunic. Her hair was disarrayed and her eyes were bloodshot.

"*They* left," I croaked. "I told you they would. Jud and Wold . . . you couldn't stop them."

"Together? They left *together?*"

"That's what Wold got certified for." I looked bluntly up and down her supple body. "Like everybody else who goes Out together, they had *some*thing in common."

I pushed past her and went back to my office. Lights were blazing over the desk. Judson and Wold. Ship replaced. Quarters cleaned. Palm-key removed and filed. I sat and looked blindly until they were all lit and the board blanked out.

I thought, this pump of mine won't last much longer under this kind of treatment.

I thought, I keep convincing myself that I handle things impartially and fairly, without getting involved.

I felt bad. Bad.

I thought, this is a job without authority, without any real power. I certify 'em, send 'em along, check 'em out. A clerk's job. And because of that I have to be God. I have to make up my own justice, and execute it myself. Wold was no threat to me or to Curbstone, yet it was in me to give oblivion to him and purgatory to Flower.

I felt frightened and disgusted and puny.

Someone came in, and I looked up blindly. For a moment I could make out nothing but a silver-haloed figure and a muted, wordless murmuring. I forced my eyes to focus, and I had to close them again, as if I had looked into the sun.

Her hair was unbound beneath a diamond ring that circled her brows. The silver silk cascaded about her, brushing the floor behind her, mantling her warm-toned shoulders, capturing small threads of light and weaving them in and about the gleaming light that was her hair. Her deep pigeon's-blood eyes shone and her lips trembled.

"Tween. . . ."

The soft murmuring became words, laughter that wept with happiness, small shaking syllables of rapture. "He's waiting. He wanted to say good-by to you, too . . . but he asked me to do it for him. He said you'd like that better."

I could only nod.

She came close to the desk. "I love him. I love him more than I thought anyone could. Somehow, loving him that much, I can . . . love you, too."

She bent over the desk and kissed my mouth. Her lips were cool. She —blurred then. Or maybe it was my eyes. When I could see again, she was gone.

The chime, and the lights, one after another.

Marriage recorded. . . .

Suddenly I relaxed and I knew I could live with the viciousness of what I had done to Wold and to Flower. It had been my will that Judson go Out, and that Tween be happy, and I had been crossed, and I had taken vengeance. And that was small, and decidedly human— not godlike at all.

So, I thought, every day I find something out about people. And, today, I'm people. I felt the pudgy lips that Tween had kissed. I'm old and I'm fat, I thought, and by the Lord, I'm people.

When they call me Charon, they forget what it must be like to be denied both worlds instead of only one.

And they forget the other thing— the little-known fragment of the Charon legend. To the Etruscans, he was more than a ferryman.

He was an executioner.

—THEODORE STURGEON

FORECAST

Next month's installment of Clifford D. Simak's novel, "Time Quarry," develops adrenal-agitating momentum. The plot against Asher Sutton, returned to Earth after 20 years to find himself sentenced to assassination, becomes a savagely civilized—and worriedly meticulous—war against a simple idea with stupendous implications. "Time Quarry," incidentally, will be published early next year by Simon & Schuster, in exactly the form in which it appears in GALAXY *Science Fiction*, with minor editing differences. Our policy will continue to be to publish all book-length novels *complete.*

Anthony Boucher, after editing and reviewing science fiction, finally resumes writing it. His novelet, "Transfer Point," about the Last Man on Earth, who wasn't actually, and the Last Woman, who should have been, makes us wonder what superb stories we've missed these past few years. We'll keep him writing. . . .

Fredric Brown, between novels, found time to do two yarns, and we bought both. The second, "Honeymoon in Hell," resolves a problem currently coloring the front pages, and does so by a crisis in the maternity rooms and the willing, even eager, cooperation of two bitter and attractive enemies.

Short stories include "Coming Attraction" by Fritz Leiber, a piece of shock writing that may turn out to be more than fiction; Isaac Asimov's chillingly charming "Misbegotten Missionary," an altruistic little creature with an unwittingly alarming message to preach . . . and enforce; "Jaywalker" by Ross Rocklynne, which proves that a challenge to death is the paradoxical answer to widowhood; plus whatever other shorts we can squeeze in with our regular features. We can see a good many of our short stories, the stuff of which s-f anthologies are made, appearing in hard covers before too long. We approve; they are important enough to be in permanent form, along with our novels. But read them here *first.*

Later Than You Think

By FRITZ LEIBER

It's much later. The question is . . . how late?

OBVIOUSLY the Archeologist's study belonged to an era vastly distant from today. Familiar similarities here and there only sharpened the feeling of alienage. The sunlight that filtered through the windows in the ceiling had a wan and greenish cast and was augmented by radiation from some luminous material impregnating the walls and floor. Even the wide desk and the commodious hassocks glowed with a restful light. Across the former were scattered metal-backed wax tablets, styluses, and a pair of large and oddly formed spectacles. The crammed bookcases were not particularly unusual, but the books were bound in metal and the script on their spines would have been utterly unfamiliar to the most erudite of modern linguists. One of the books, lying open on a hassock, showed leaves of a thin, flexible, rustless metal covered with luminous characters. Between the bookcases were phosphorescent oil paintings, mainly of sea bottoms, in somber greens and browns. Their style, neither wholly realistic nor abstract, would have baffled the historian of art.

A blackboard with large colored crayons hinted equally at the schoolroom and the studio.

In the center of the room, midway to the ceiling, hung a fish with irridescent scales of breathtaking beauty. So invisible was its means of support that—also taking into account the strange paintings and the greenish light—one would have sworn that the object was to create an underwater scene.

The Explorer made his entrance in a theatrical swirl of movement. He embraced the Archeologist with a warmth calculated to startle that crusty old fellow. Then he settled himself on a hassock, looked up and asked a question in a speech and idiom so different from any we know that it must be called another means of communication rather than another language. The import was, "Well, what about it?"

If the Archeologist were taken aback, he concealed it. His expression showed only pleasure at being reunited with a long-absent friend.

"What about what?" he queried.

"About your discovery!"

"What discovery?" The Archeologist's incomprehension was playful.

The Explorer threw up his arms. "Why, what else but your discovery, here on Earth, of the remains of an intelligent species? It's the find of the age! Am I going to have to coax you? Out with it!"

"I didn't make the discovery," the other said tranquilly. "I only supervised the excavations and directed the correlation of material. *You* ought to be doing the talking. *You're* the one who's just returned from the stars."

"Forget that." The Explorer brushed the question aside. "As soon as our spaceship got within radio range of Earth, they started to send us a continuous newscast covering the period of our absence. One of the items, exasperatingly brief, mentioned your discovery. It captured my imagination. I couldn't wait to hear the details." He paused, then confessed, "You get so eager out there in space—a metal-filmed droplet of life lost in immensity. You rediscover your emotions. . . ." He changed color, then finished rapidly, "As soon as I could decently get away, I came straight to you. I wanted to hear about it from the best authority—yourself."

THE Archeologist regarded him quizzically. "I'm pleased that you should think of me and my work, and I'm very happy to see you again. But admit it now, isn't there something a bit odd about your getting so worked up over this thing? I can understand that after your long absence from Earth, any news of Earth would seem especially important. But isn't there an additional reason?"

The Explorer twisted impatiently. "Oh, I suppose there is. Disappointment, for one thing. We were hoping to get in touch with intelligent life out there. We were specially trained in techniques for establishing mental contact with alien intelligent life forms. Well, we found some planets with life upon them, all right. But it was primitive life, not worth bothering about."

Again he hesitated embarrassedly. "Out there you get to thinking of the preciousness of intelligence. There's so little of it, and it's so lonely. And we so greatly need intercourse with another intelligent species to give depth and balance to our thoughts. I suppose I set too much store by my hopes of establishing a contact." He paused. "At any rate, when I heard that what we were looking for, you had found here at home—even though dead and done for—I felt that at least it was something. I was suddenly very eager. It is odd, I know, to get so worked up about an extinct species—as if my interest could mean anything to them now—but that's the way it hit me."

SEVERAL small shadows crossed the windows overhead. They might have been birds, except they moved too slowly.

"I think I understand," the Archeologist said softly.

"So get on with it and tell me about your discovery!" the Explorer exploded.

"I've already told you that it wasn't my discovery," the Archeologist reminded him. "A few years after your expedition left, there was begun a detailed resurvey of Earth's mineral resources. In the course of some deep continental borings, one party discovered a cache—either a very large box or a rather small room—with metallic walls of great strength and toughness. Evidently its makers had intended it for the very purpose of carrying a message down through the ages. It proved to contain artifacts; models of buildings, vehicles, and machines, objects of art, pictures, and books—hundreds of books, along with elaborate pictorial dictionaries for interpreting them. So now we even understand their languages."

"Languages?" interrupted the Explorer. "That's queer. Somehow one thinks of an alien species as having just one language."

"Like our own, this species had several, though there were some words and symbols that were alike in all their languages. These words and symbols seem to have come down unchanged from their most distant prehistory."

The Explorer burst out, "I am not interested in all that dry stuff! Give me the wet! What were they like? How did they live? What did they create? What did they want?"

The Archeologist gently waved aside the questions. "All in good time. If I am to tell you everything you want to know, I must tell it my own way. Now that you are back on Earth, you will have to reacquire those orderly and composed habits of thought which you have partly lost in the course of your wild interstellar adventurings."

"Curse you, I think you're just trying to tantalize me."

The Archeologist's expression showed that this was not altogether untrue. He casually fondled an animal that had wriggled up onto his desk, and which looked rather more like an eel than a snake. "Cute little brute, isn't it?" he remarked. When it became apparent that the Explorer wasn't to be provoked into another outburst, he continued, "It became my task to interpret the contents of the cache, to reconstruct its makers' climb from animalism and savagery to civilization, their rather rapid spread across the world's surface, their first fumbling attempts to escape from the Earth."

"THEY had spaceships?"

"It's barely possible. I rather hope they did, since it would mean the chance of a survival elsewhere, though the negative results of your expedition rather lessen that." He went on, "The cache was laid down when they were first attempting space flight, just after their discovery of atomic power, in the first flush of their youth. It was probably created in a kind of exuberant fancifulness, with no serious belief that it would ever serve the purpose for which it was intended." He looked at the Explorer strangely. "If I am not mistaken, we have laid down similar caches."

After a moment the Archeologist continued, "My reconstruction of their history, subsequent to the laying down of the cache, has been largely hypothetical. I can only guess at the reasons for their decline and fall. Supplementary material has been very slow in coming in, though we are still making extensive excavations at widely separated points. Here are the last reports." He tossed the Explorer a small metal-leaf pamphlet. It flew with a curiously slow motion.

"That's what struck me so queer right from the start," the Explorer observed, putting the pamphlet aside after a glance. "If these creatures were relatively advanced, why haven't we learned about them before? They must have left so many things—buildings, machines, engineering projects, some of them on a large scale. You'd think we'd be turning up traces everywhere."

"I have four answers to that," the Archeologist replied. "The first is the most obvious. Time. Geologic ages of it. The second is more subtle. What if we should have been looking in the wrong place? I mean, what if the creatures occupied a very different portion of the Earth than our own? Third, it's possible that atomic energy, out of control, finished the race and destroyed its traces. The present distribution of radioactive compounds throughout the Earth's surface lends some support to this theory.

"Fourth," he went on, "it's my belief that when an intelligent species begins to retrogress, it tends to destroy, or, rather, debase all the things it has laboriously created. Large buildings are torn down to make smaller ones. Machines are broken up and worked into primitive tools and weapons. There is a kind of unraveling or erasing. A cultural Second Law of Thermodynamics begins to operate, whereby the intellect and all its works are gradually degraded to the lowest level of meaning and creativity."

"BUT why?" The Explorer sounded anguished. "Why should any intelligent species end like that? I grant the possibility of atomic power getting out of hand, though one would have thought they'd have taken the greatest precautions. Still, it could happen. But that fourth answer—it's morbid."

"Cultures and civilizations die," said the Archeologist evenly. "That has happened repeatedly in our own history. Why not species? An individual dies—and is there anything intrinsically more terrible in the death of a species than in the death of an individual?"

He paused. "With respect to the members of this one species, I think that a certain temperamental instability hastened their end. Their appetites and emotions were not sufficiently subordinated to their understanding and to their sense of drama—their enjoyment of the comedy and tragedy of existence. They were impatient and easily incapacitated by frustration. They seem to have been singularly guilty in their pleasures, behaving either like gloomy moralists or gluttons.

"Because of taboos and an overgrown possessiveness," he continued, "each individual tended to limit his affection to a tiny family; in many cases he focused his love on himself alone. They set great store by personal prestige, by the amassing of wealth and the exercise of power. Their notable capacity for thought and manipulative activity was expended on things rather than persons or feelings. Their technology outstripped their psychology. They skimped fatally when it came to hard thinking about the purpose of life and intellectual activity, and the means for preserving them."

Again the slow shadows drifted overhead.

"And finally," the Archeologist said, "they were a strangely haunted species. They seem to have been obsessed by the notion that others, greater than themselves, had prospered before them and then died, leaving them to rebuild a civilization from ruins. It was from those others that they thought they derived the few words and symbols common to all their languages."

"Gods?" mused the Explorer.

The Archeologist shrugged. "Who knows?"

THE Explorer turned away. His excitement had visibly evaporated, leaving behind a cold and miserable residue of feeling. "I am not sure I want to hear much more about them," he said. "They sound too much like us. Perhaps it was a mistake, my coming here. Pardon me, old friend, but out there in space even *our* emotions become undisciplined. Everything becomes indescribably poignant. Moods are tempestuous. You shift in an instant from zenith to nadir—and remember, out there you can see both.

"I was very eager to hear about this lost species," he added in a sad voice. "I thought I would feel a kind of fellowship with them across the eons. Instead, I touch only corpses. It reminds me of when, out in space, there looms up before your prow, faint in the starlight, a dead sun. They were a young race. They thought they were getting somewhere. They promised themselves an eternity of effort. And all the while there was wriggling toward them out of that future for which they yearned . . . oh, it's so completely futile and unfair."

"I disagree," the Archeologist said spiritedly. "Really, your absence from Earth has unsettled you even more than I first surmised. Look at the matter squarely. Death comes to everything in the end. Our past is strewn with our dead. That species died, it's true. But what they achieved, they achieved. What happiness they had, they had. What they did in their short span is as significant as what they might have done had they lived a billion years. The present is always more important than the future. And no creature can have all the future—it must be shared, left to others."

"Maybe so," the Explorer said slowly. "Yes, I guess you're right. But I still feel a horrible wistfulness about them, and I hug to myself the hope that a few of them escaped and set up a colony on some planet we haven't yet visited." There was a long silence. Then the Explorer turned back. "You old devil," he said in a manner that showed his gayer and more boisterous mood had returned, though diminished, "you still haven't told me anything definite about them."

"So I haven't," replied the Archeologist with guileful innocence. "Well, they were vertebrates."

"Oh?"

"Yes. What's more, they were mammals."

"MAMMALS? I was expecting something different."

"I thought you were."

The Explorer shifted. "All this matter of evolutionary categories is pretty cut-and-dried. Even a knowledge of how they looked doesn't mean much. I'd like to approach them in a more intimate way. How did they think of themselves? What did they call themselves? I know the word won't mean anything to me, but it will give me a feeling—of recognition."

"I can't say the word," the Archeologist told him, "because I haven't the proper vocal equipment. But I know enough of their script to be able to write it for you as they would have written it. Incidentally, it is one of those words common to all their languages, that they attributed to an earlier race of beings."

The Archeologist extended one of his eight tentacles toward the blackboard. The suckers at its tip firmly grasped a bit of orange crayon. Another of his tentacles took up the spectacles and adjusted them over his three-inch protruding pupils.

The eel-like glittering pet drifted back into the room and nosed curiously about the crayon as it traced:

RAT

—FRITZ LEIBER

paul pierce

CONTAGION

By KATHERINE MacLEAN

Minos was such a lovely planet. Not a thing seemed wrong with it. Excepting the food, perhaps. And a disease that wasn't really.

IT WAS like an Earth forest in the fall, but it was not fall. The forest leaves were green and copper and purple and fiery red, and a wind sent patches of bright greenish sunlight dancing among the leaf shadows.

The hunt party of the *Explorer* filed along the narrow trail, guns ready, walking carefully, listening to the distant, half familiar cries of strange birds.

A faint crackle of static in their earphones indicated that a gun had been fired.

"Got anything?" asked June Walton. The helmet intercom carried her voice to the ears of the others without breaking the stillness of the forest.

"Took a shot at something," explained George Barton's cheerful voice in her earphones. She rounded a bend of the trail and came upon Barton standing peering up into the trees, his gun still raised. "It looked like a duck."

"This isn't Central Park," said Hal Barton, his brother, coming into sight. His green spacesuit struck an incongruous note against the bronze and red forest. "They won't all look like ducks," he said soberly.

"Maybe some will look like drag-

ons. Don't get eaten by a dragon, June," came Max's voice quietly into her earphones. "Not while I still love you." He came out of the trees carrying the blood sample kit, and touched her glove with his, the grin on his ugly beloved face barely visible in the mingled light and shade. A patch of sunlight struck a greenish glint from his fishbowl helmet.

THEY walked on. A quarter of a mile back, the space ship *Explorer* towered over the forest like a tapering skyscraper, and the people of the ship looked out of the viewplates at fresh winds and sunlight and clouds, and they longed to be outside.

But the likeness to Earth was danger, and the cool wind might be death, for if the animals were like Earth animals, their diseases might be like Earth diseases, alike enough to be contagious, different enough to be impossible to treat. There was warning enough in the past. Colonies had vanished, and traveled spaceways drifted with the corpses of ships which had touched on some plague planet.

The people of the ship waited while their doctors, in airtight spacesuits, hunted animals to test them for contagion.

The four medicos, for June Walton was also a doctor, filed through the alien homelike forest, walking softly, watching for motion among the copper and purple shadows.

They saw it suddenly, a lighter moving copper patch among the darker browns. Reflex action swung June's gun into line, and behind her someone's gun went off with a faint crackle of static, and made a hole in the leaves beside the specimen. Then for a while no one moved.

This one looked like a man, a magnificently muscled, leanly graceful, humanlike animal. Even in its callused bare feet, it was a head taller than any of them. Red-haired, hawk-faced and darkly tanned, it stood breathing heavily, looking at them without expression. At its side hung a sheath knife, and a crossbow was slung across one wide shoulder.

They lowered their guns.

"It needs a shave," Max said reasonably in their earphones, and he reached up to his helmet and flipped the switch that let his voice be heard. "Something we could do for you, Mac?"

The friendly drawl was the first voice that had broken the forest sounds. June smiled suddenly. He was right. The strict logic of evolution did not demand beards; therefore a non-human would not be wearing a three day growth of red stubble.

Still panting, the tall figure licked dry lips and spoke. "Welcome to Minos. The Mayor sends greetings from Alexandria."

"English?" gasped June.

"We were afraid you would take off again before I could bring word to you. . . . It's three hundred miles. . . . We saw your scout plane pass twice, but we couldn't attract its attention."

JUNE looked in stunned silence at the stranger leaning against the tree. Thirty-six light years—thirty-six times six trillion miles of monotonous space travel—to be told that the planet was already settled! "We didn't know there was a colony here," she said. "It is not on the map."

"We were afraid of that," the tall bronze man answered soberly. "We have been here three generations and yet no traders have come."

Max shifted the kit strap on his shoulder and offered a hand. "My name is Max Stark, M.D. This is June Walton, M.D., Hal Barton, M.D., and George Barton, Hal's brother, also M.D."

"Patrick Mead is the name," smiled the man, shaking hands casually. "Just a hunter and bridge carpenter myself. Never met any medicos before."

The grip was effortless but even through her airproofed glove June could feel that the fingers that touched hers were as hard as padded steel.

"What—what is the population of Minos?" she asked.

He looked down at her curiously for a moment before answering. "Only one hundred and fifty." He smiled. "Don't worry, this isn't a city planet yet. There's room for a few more people." He shook hands with the Bartons quickly. "That is—you are people, aren't you?" he asked startlingly.

"Why not?" said Max with a poise that June admired.

"Well, you are all so—so—" Patrick Mead's eyes roamed across the faces of the group. "So varied."

They could find no meaning in that, and stood puzzled.

"I mean," Patrick Mead said into the silence, "all these—interesting different hair colors and face shapes and so forth—" He made a vague wave with one hand as if he had run out of words or was anxious not to insult them.

"Joke?" Max asked, bewildered.

June laid a hand on his arm. "No harm meant," she said to him over the intercom. "We're just as much of a shock to him as he is to us."

She addressed a question to the tall colonist on outside sound. "What should a person look like, Mr. Mead?"

He indicated her with a smile. "Like you."

June stepped closer and stood looking up at him, considering her own description. She was tall and tanned, like him; had a few freckles, like him; and wavy red hair, like his. She ignored the brightly humorous blue eyes.

"In other words," she said, "everyone on the planet looks like you and me?"

Patrick Mead took another look at their four faces and began to grin. "Like me, I guess. But I hadn't thought of it before. I did not think that people could have different colored hair or that noses could fit so many ways onto faces. I was judging by my own appearance, but I suppose any fool can walk on his hands and say the world is upside down!" He laughed and sobered. "But then why wear spacesuits? The air is breathable."

"For safety," June told him. "We can't take any chances on plague."

Pat Mead was wearing nothing but a loin cloth and his weapons, and the wind ruffled his hair. He looked comfortable, and they longed to take off the stuffy spacesuits and feel the wind against their own skins. Minos was like home, like Earth. . . . But they were strangers.

"Plague," Pat Mead said thoughtfully. "We had one here. It came two years after the colony arrived and killed everyone except the Mead families. They were immune. I guess we look alike because we're all related, and that's why I grew up thinking that it is the only way people can look."

Plague. "What was the disease?" Hal Barton asked.

"Pretty gruesome, according to my father. They called it the melting sickness. The doctors died too soon to find out what it was or what to do about it."

"You should have trained for more doctors, or sent to civilization for some." A trace of impatience was in George Barton's voice.

Pat Mead explained patiently, "Our ship, with the power plant and all the books we needed, went off into the sky to avoid the contagion, and never came back. The crew must have died." Long years of hardship were indicated by that statement, a colony with electric power gone and machinery stilled, with key technicians dead and no way to replace them? June realized then the full meaning of the primitive sheath knife and bow.

"Any recurrence of melting sickness?" asked Hal Barton.

"No."

"Any other diseases?"

"Not a one."

Max was eying the bronze redheaded figure with something approaching awe. "Do you think all the Meads look like that?" he said to June on the intercom. "I wouldn't mind being a Mead myself!"

THEIR job had been made easy by the coming of Pat. They went back to the ship laughing, exchanging anecdotes with him. There was nothing now to keep Minos from being the home they wanted, except the melting sickness, and, forewarned against it, they could take precautions.

The polished silver and black column of the *Explorer* seemed to rise higher and higher over the trees as they neared it. Then its symmetry blurred all sense of specific size as they stepped out from among the trees and stood on the edge of the meadow, looking up.

"Nice!" said Pat. "Beautiful!" The admiration in his voice was warming.

"It was a yacht," Max said, still looking up, "second hand, an old-time beauty without a sign of wear. Synthetic diamond-studded control board and murals on the walls. It doesn't have the new speed drives, but it brought us thirty-six light years in one and a half subjective years. Plenty good enough."

The tall tanned man looked faintly wistful, and June realized that he had never had access to a full library, never seen a movie, never experienced luxury. He had been born and raised on Minos.

"MAY I go aboard?" Pat asked hopefully.

Max unslung the specimen kit from his shoulder, laid it on the carpet of plants that covered the ground and began to open it.

"Tests first," Hal Barton said. "We have to find out if you people still carry this so-called melting sickness. We'll have to de-microbe you and take specimens before we let you on board. Once on, you'll be no good as a check for what the other Meads might have."

Max was taking out a rack and a stand of preservative bottles and hypodermics.

"Are you going to jab me with those?" Pat asked with interest.

"You're just a specimen animal to me, bud!" Max grinned at Pat Mead, and Pat grinned back. June saw that they were friends already, the tall pantherish colonist, and the wry, black-haired doctor. She felt a stab of guilt because she loved Max and yet could pity him for being smaller and frailer than Pat Mead.

"Lie down," Max told him, "and hold still. We need two spinal fluid samples from the back, a body cavity one in front, and another from the arm."

Pat lay down obediently. Max knelt, and, as he spoke, expertly swabbed and inserted needles with the smooth speed that had made him a fine nerve surgeon on Earth.

High above them the scout helioplane came out of an opening in the ship and angled off toward the west, its buzz diminishing. Then, suddenly, it veered and headed back, and Reno Unrich's voice came tinnily from their earphones:

"What's that you've got? Hey, what are you docs doing down there?" He banked again and came to a stop, hovering fifty feet away. June could see his startled face looking through the glass at Pat.

Hal Barton switched to a narrow radio beam, explained rapidly and pointed in the direction of Alexandria. Reno's plane lifted and flew away over the odd-colored forest.

"The plane will drop a note on your town, telling them you got through to us," Hal Barton told Pat, who was sitting up watching Max dexterously put the blood and spinal fluids into the right bottles without exposing them to air.

"We won't be free to contact your people until we know if they still carry melting sickness," Max added. "You might be immune so it doesn't show on you, but still carry enough germs—if that's what caused it—to wipe out a planet."

"If you do carry melting sickness," said Hal Barton, "we won't be able to mingle with your people until we've cleared them of the disease."

"Starting with me?" Pat asked.

"Starting with you," Max told him ruefully, "as soon as you step on board."

"More needles?"

"Yes, and a few little extras thrown in."

"Rough?"

"It isn't easy."

A few minutes later, standing in the stalls for spacesuit decontamination, being buffeted by jets of hot disinfectant, bathed in glares of sterilizing ultraviolet radiation, June remembered that and compared Pat Mead's treatment to theirs.

In the *Explorer*, stored carefully in sealed tanks and containers, was the ultimate, multi-purpose cureall. It was a solution of enzymes so like the key catalysts of the human cell nucleus that it caused chemical derangement and disintegration in any non-human cell. Nothing could live in contact with it but human cells; any alien intruder to the body would die. Nucleocat Cureall was its trade name.

But the cureall alone was not enough for complete safety. Plagues had been known to slay too rapidly and universally to be checked by human treatment. Doctors are not reliable; they die. Therefore spaceways and interplanetary health law demanded that ship equipment for guarding against disease be totally mechanical in operation, rapid and efficient.

Somewhere near them, in a series of stalls which led around and around like a rabbit maze, Pat was being herded from stall to stall by peremptory mechanical voices, directed to soap and shower, ordered to insert his arm into a slot which took a sample of his blood, given solutions to drink, bathed in germicidal ultraviolet, shaken by sonic blasts, breathing air thick with sprays of germicidal mists, being directed to put his arms into other slots where they were anesthesized and injected with various immunizing solutions.

Finally, he would be put in a room of high temperature and extreme dryness, and instructed to sit for half an hour while more fluids were dripped into his veins through long thin tubes.

All legal spaceships were built for safety. No chance was taken of allowing a suspected carrier to bring an infection on board with him.

JUNE stepped from the last shower stall into the locker room, zipped off her spacesuit with a sigh of relief, and contemplated herself in a wall mirror. Red hair, dark blue eyes, tall. . . .

"I've got a good figure," she said thoughtfully.

Max turned at the door. "Why this sudden interest in your looks?" he asked suspiciously. "Do we stand here and admire you, or do we finally get something to eat?"

"Wait a minute." She went to a wall phone and dialed it carefully, using a combination from the ship's directory. "How're you doing, Pat?"

The phone picked up a hissing of water or spray. There was a startled chuckle. "Voices, too! Hello, June. How do you tell a machine to go jump in the lake?"

"Are you hungry?"

"No food since yesterday."

"We'll have a banquet ready for you when you get out," she told Pat and hung up, smiling. Pat Mead's voice had a vitality and enjoyment which made shipboard talk sound like sad artificial gaiety in contrast.

They looked into the nearby small laboratory where twelve squealing hamsters were protestingly submitting to a small injection each of Pat's blood. In most of them the injection was followed by one of antihistaminics and adaptives. Otherwise the hamster defense system would treat all non-hamster cells as enemies, even the harmless human blood cells, and fight back against them violently.

One hamster, the twelfth, was given an extra large dose of adaptive, so that if there were a disease, he would not fight it or the human cells, and thus succumb more rapidly.

"How ya doing, George?" Max asked.

"Routine," George Barton grunted absently.

On the way up the long spiral ramps to the dining hall, they passed a viewplate. It showed a long scene of mountains in the distance on the horizon, and between them, rising step by step as they grew farther away, the low rolling hills, bronze and red with patches of clear green where there were fields.

Someone was looking out, standing very still, as if she had been there a long time—Bess St. Clair, a Canadian woman. "It looks like Winnipeg," she told them as they paused. "When are you doctors going to let us out of this blithering barberpole? Look," she pointed. "See that patch of field on the south hillside, with the brook winding through it? I've staked that hillside for our house. When do we get out?"

RENO ULRICH'S tiny scout plane buzzed slowly in from the distance and began circling lazily.

"Sooner than you think," Max told her. "We've discovered a castaway colony on the planet. They've done our tests for us by just living here. If there's anything here to catch, they've caught it."

"People on Minos?" Bess's handsome ruddy face grew alive with excitement.

"One of them is down in the medical department," June said. "He'll be out in twenty minutes."

"May I go see him?"

"Sure," said Max. "Show him the way to the dining hall when he gets out. Tell him we sent you."

"Right!" She turned and ran down the ramp like a small girl going to a fire. Max grinned at June and she grinned back. After a year and a half of isolation in space, everyone was hungry for the sight of new faces, the sound of unfamiliar voices.

They climbed the last two turns to the cafeteria, and entered to a rich subdued blend of soft music and quiet conversations. The cafeteria was a section of the old dining room, left when the rest of the ship had been converted to living and working quarters, and it still had the original finely grained wood of the ceiling and walls, the sound absorbency, the soft music spools and the intimate small light at each table where people leisurely ate and talked.

THEY stood in line at the hot foods counter, and behind her June could hear a girl's voice talking excitedly through the murmur of conversation.

"—new man, honest! I saw him through the viewplate when they came in. He's down in the medical department. A real frontiersman."

The line drew abreast of the counters, and she and Max chose three heaping trays, starting with hydroponic mushroom steak, raised in the growing trays of water and chemicals; sharp salad bowl with rose tomatoes and aromatic peppers; tank-grown fish with special sauce; four different desserts, and assorted beverages.

Presently they had three tottering trays successfully maneuvered to a table. Brant St. Clair came over. "I beg your pardon, Max, but they are saying something about Reno carrying messages to a colony of savages, for the medical department. Will he be back soon, do you know?"

Max smiled up at him, his square face affectionate. Everyone liked the shy Canadian. "He's back already. We just saw him come in."

"Oh, fine." St. Clair beamed. "I had an appointment with him to go out and confirm what looks like a nice vein of iron to the northeast. Have you seen Bess? Oh—there she is." He turned swiftly and hurried away.

A very tall man with fiery red hair came in surrounded by an eagerly talking crowd of ship people. It was Pat Mead. He stood in the doorway, alertly scanning the dining room. Sheer vitality made him seem even larger than he was. Sighting June, he smiled and began to thread toward their table.

"Look!" said someone. "There's the colonist!" Shelia, a pretty, jeweled woman, followed and caught his arm. "Did you *really* swim across a river to come here?"

Overflowing with good-will and curiosity, people approached from all directions. "Did you actually walk three hundred miles? Come, eat with us. Let me help choose your tray."

Everyone wanted him to eat at their table, everyone was a specialist and wanted data about Minos. They all wanted anecdotes about hunting wild animals with a bow and arrow.

"He needs to be rescued," Max said. "He won't have a chance to eat."

June and Max got up firmly, edged through the crowd, captured Pat and escorted him back to their table. June found herself pleased to be claiming the hero of the hour.

PAT sat in the simple, subtly designed chair and leaned back almost voluptuously, testing the way it gave and fitted itself to him. He ran his eyes over the bright tableware and heaped plates. He looked around at the rich grained walls and soft lights at each table. He said nothing, just looking and feeling and experiencing.

'When we build our town and leave the ship," June explained, "we will turn all the staterooms back into the lounges and ballrooms and cocktail bars that used to be inside."

"Oh, I'm not complaining," Pat said negligently. He cocked his head to the music, and tried to locate its source.

"That's big of you," said Max with gentle irony.

They fell to, Pat beginning the first meal he had had in more than a day.

Most of the other diners finished when they were halfway through, and began walking over, diffidently at first, then in another wave of smiling faces, handshakes, and introductions. Pat was asked about crops, about farming methods, about rainfall and floods, about farm animals and plant breeding, about the compatibility of imported Earth seeds with local ground, about mines and strata.

There was no need to protect him. He leaned back in his chair and drawled answers with the lazy ease of a panther; where he could think of no statistic, he would fill the gap with an anecdote. It developed that he enjoyed spinning campfire yarns and especially being the center of interest.

Between bouts of questions, he ate with undiminished and glowing relish.

June noticed that the female specialists were prolonging the questions more than they needed, clustering around the table laughing at his jokes, until presently Pat was almost surrounded by pretty faces, eager questions, and chiming laughs. Shelia the beautiful laughed most chimingly of all.

June nudged Max, and Max shrugged indifferently. It wasn't anything a man would pay attention to, perhaps. But June watched Pat for a moment more, then glanced uneasily back to Max. He was eating and listening to Pat's answers and did not feel her gaze. For some reason Max looked almost shrunken to her. He was shorter than she had realized; she had forgotten that he was only the same height as herself. She was dimly aware of the clear lilting chatter of female voices increasing at Pat's end of the table.

"That guy's a menace," Max said, and laughed to himself, cutting another slice of hydroponic mushroom steak. "What's eating you?" he added, glancing aside at her when he noticed her sudden stillness.

"Nothing," she said hastily, but she did not turn back to watching Pat Mead. She felt disloyal. Pat was only a superb animal. Max was the man she loved. Or—was he? Of course he was, she told herself angrily. They had gone colonizing together because they wanted to spend their lives together; she had never thought of marrying any other man. Yet the sense of dissatisfaction persisted, and along with it a feeling of guilt.

Len Marlow, the protein tank-culture technician responsible for the mushroom steaks, had wormed his way into the group and asked Pat a question. Now he was saying, "I don't dig you, Pat. It sounds like you're putting the people into the tanks instead of the vegetables!" He glanced at them, looking puzzled. "See if you two can make anything of this. It sounds medical to me."

Pat leaned back and smiled, sipping a glass of hydroponic burgundy. "Wonderful stuff. You'll have to show us how to make it."

Len turned back to him. "You people live off the country, right? You hunt and bring in steaks and eat them, right? Well, say I have one of those steaks right here and I want to eat it, what happens?"

"GO AHEAD and eat it. It just wouldn't digest. You'd stay hungry."

"Why?" Len was aggrieved.

"Chemical differences in the basic protoplasm of Minos. Different amino linkages, left-handed instead of right-handed molecules in the carbohydrates, things like that. Nothing will be digestible here until you are adapted chemically by a little test-tube evolution. Till then you'd starve to death on a full stomach."

Pat's side of the table had been loaded with the dishes from two trays, but it was almost clear now and the dishes were stacked neatly to one side. He started on three desserts, thoughtfully tasting each in turn.

"Test-tube evolution?" Max repeated. "What's that? I thought you people had no doctors."

"It's a story." Pat leaned back again. "Alexander P. Mead, the head of the Mead clan, was a plant geneticist, a very determined personality and no man to argue with. He didn't want us to go through the struggle of killing off all Minos plants and putting in our own, spoiling the face of the planet and upsetting the balance of its ecology. He decided that he would adapt our genes to this planet or kill us trying. He did it all right."

"Did which?" asked June, suddenly feeling a sourceless prickle of fear.

"Adapted us to Minos. He took human cells—"

SHE listened intently, trying to find a reason for fear in the explanation. It would have taken many human generations to adapt to Minos by ordinary evolution, and that only at a heavy toll of death and hunger which evolution exacts. There was a shorter way: Human cells have the ability to return to their primeval condition of independence, hunting, eating and reproducing alone.

Alexander P. Mead took human cells and made them into phagocytes. He put them through the hard savage school of evolution—a thousand generations of multiplication, hardship and hunger, with the alien indigestible food always present, offering its reward of plenty to the cell that reluctantly learned to absorb it.

"Leucocytes can run through several thousand generations of evolution in six months," Pat Mead finished. "When they reached to a point where they would absorb Minos food, he planted them back in the people he had taken them from."

"What was supposed to happen then?" Max asked, leaning forward.

"I don't know exactly how it worked. He never told anybody much about it, and when I was a little boy he had gone loco and was wandering ha-ha-ing around waving a test tube. Fell down a ravine and broke his neck at the age of eighty."

"A character," Max said.

Why was she afraid? "It worked then?"

"Yes. He tried it on all the Meads the first year. The other settlers didn't want to be experimented on until they saw how it worked out. It worked. The Meads could hunt and plant while the other settlers were still eating out of hydroponics tanks."

"It worked," said Max to Len. "You're a plant geneticist and a tank culture expert. There's a job for you."

"Uh-*uh!*" Len backed away. "It sounds like a medical problem to me. Human cell control—right up your alley."

"It is a one-way street," Pat warned. "Once it is done, you won't be able to digest ship food. I'll get no good from this protein. I ate it just for the taste."

Hal Barton appeared quietly beside the table. "Three of the twelve test hamsters have died," he reported, and turned to Pat. "Your people carry the germs of melting sickness, as you call it. The dead hamsters were injected with blood taken from you before you were de-infected. We can't settle here unless we de-infect everybody on Minos. Would they object?"

"We wouldn't want to give you folks germs," Pat smiled. "Anything for safety. But there'll have to be a vote on it first."

The doctors went to Reno Ulrich's table and walked with him to the hangar, explaining. He was to carry the proposal to Alexandria, mingle with the people, be persuasive and wait for them to vote before returning. He was to give himself shots of cureall every two hours on the hour or run the risk of disease.

RENO was pleased. He had dabbled in sociology before retraining as a mechanic for the expedition. "This gives me a chance to study their mores." He winked wickedly. "I may not be back for several nights." They watched through the viewplate as he took off, and then went over to the laboratory for a look at the hamsters.

Three were alive and healthy, munching lettuce. One was the control; the other two had been given shots of Pat's blood from before he entered the ship, but with no additional treatment. Apparently a hamster could fight off melting sickness easily if left alone. Three were still feverish and ruffled, with a low red blood count, but recovering. The three dead ones had been given strong shots of adaptive and counter histamine, so their bodies had not fought back against the attack.

June glanced at the dead animals hastily and looked away again. They lay twisted with a strange semi-fluid limpness, as if ready to dissolve. The last hamster, which had been given the heaviest dose of adaptive, had apparently lost all its hair before death. It was hairless and pink, like a still-born baby.

"We can find no micro-organisms," George Barton said. "None at all. Nothing in the body that should not be there. Leucosis and anemia. Fever only for the ones that fought it off." He handed Max some temperature charts and graphs of blood counts.

June wandered out into the hall. Pediatrics and obstetrics were her field; she left the cellular research to Max, and just helped him with laboratory routine. The strange mood followed her out into the hall, then abruptly lightened.

Coming toward her, busily telling a tale of adventure to the gorgeous Shelia Davenport, was a tall, red-headed, magnificently handsome man. It was his handsomeness which made Pat such a pleasure to look upon and talk with, she guiltily told herself, and it was his tremendous vitality. . . . It was like meeting a movie hero in the flesh, or a hero out of the pages of a book—Deerslayer, John Clayton, Lord Greystoke.

She waited in the doorway to the laboratory and made no move to join them, merely acknowledged the two with a nod and a smile and a casual lift of the hand. They nodded and smiled back.

"Hello, June," said Pat and continued telling his tale, but as they passed he lightly touched her arm.

"Oh, pioneer!" she said mockingly and softly to his passing profile, and knew that he had heard.

THAT night she had a nightmare. She was running down a long corridor looking for Max, but every man she came to was a big bronze man with red hair and bright blue eyes who grinned at her.

The pink hamster! She woke suddenly, feeling as if alarm bells had been ringing, and listened carefully, but there was no sound. She had had a nightmare, she told herself, but alarm bells were still ringing in her unconscious. Something was wrong.

Lying still and trying to preserve the images, she groped for a meaning, but the mood faded under the cold touch of reason. Damn intuitive thinking! A pink hamster! Why did the unconscious have to be so vague? She fell asleep again and forgot.

They had lunch with Pat Mead that day, and after it was over Pat delayed June with a hand on her shoulder and looked down at her for a moment. "I want you, June," he said and then turned away, answering the hails of a party at another table as if he had not spoken. She stood shaken, and then walked to the door where Max waited.

She was particularly affectionate with Max the rest of the day, and it pleased him. He would not have been if he had known why. She tried to forget Pat's blunt statement.

June was in the laboratory with Max, watching the growth of a small tank culture of the alien protoplasm from a Minos weed, and listening to Len Marlow pour out his troubles.

"And Elsie tags around after that big goof all day, listening to his stories. And then she tells me I'm just jealous, I'm imagining things!" He passed his hand across his eyes. "I came away from Earth to be with Elsie. . . . I'm getting a headache. Look, can't you persuade Pat to cut it out, June? You and Max are his friends."

"Here, have an aspirin," June said. "We'll see what we can do."

"Thanks." Len picked up his tank culture and went out, not at all cheered.

MAX sat brooding over the dials and meters at his end of the laboratory, apparently sunk in thought. When Len had gone, he spoke almost harshly.

"Why encourage the guy? Why let him hope?"

"Found out anything about the differences in protoplasm?" she evaded.

"Why let him kid himself? What chance has he got against that hunk of muscle and smooth talk?"

"But Pat isn't after Elsie," she protested.

"Every scatter-brained woman on this ship is trailing after Pat with her tongue hanging out. Brant St. Clair is in the bar right now. He doesn't say what he is drinking about, but do you think Pat is resisting all these women crowding down on him?"

"There are other things besides looks and charm," she said, grimly trying to concentrate on a slide under her binocular microscope.

"Yeah, and whatever they are, Pat has them, too. Who's more competent to support a woman and a family on a frontier planet than a handsome bruiser who was born here?"

"I meant," June spun around on her stool with unexpected passion, "there is old friendship, and there's fondness, and memories, and loyalty!" She was half shouting.

"They're not worth much on the second-hand market," Max said. He was sitting slumped on his lab stool, looking dully at his dials. "Now *I'm* getting a headache!" He smiled ruefully. "No kidding, a real headache. And over other people's troubles yet!"

Other people's troubles. . . . She got up and wandered out into the long curving halls. "I want you June," Pat's voice repeated in her mind. Why did the man have to be so overpoweringly attractive, so glaring a contrast to Max? Why couldn't the universe manage to run on without generating troublesome love triangles?

SHE walked up the curving ramps to the dining hall where they had eaten and drunk and talked yesterday. It was empty except for one couple talking forehead to forehead over cold coffee.

She turned and wandered down the long easy spiral of corridor to the pharmacy and dispensary. It was empty. George was probably in the test lab next door, where he could hear if he was wanted. The automatic vendor of harmless euphorics, stimulants and opiates stood in the corner, brightly decorated in pastel abstract designs, with its automatic tabulator graph glowing above it.

Max had a headache, she remembered. She recorded her thumbprint in the machine and pushed the plunger for a box of aspirins, trying to focus her attention on the problem of adapting the people of the ship to the planet Minos. An aquarium tank with a faint solution of histamine would be enough to convert a piece of human skin into a community of voracious active phagocytes individually seeking something to devour, but could they eat enough to live away from the rich sustaining plasma of human blood?

After the aspirins, she pushed another plunger for something for herself. Then she stood looking at it, a small box with three pills in her hand—Theobromine, a heart strengthener and a confidence-giving euphoric all in one, something to steady shaky nerves. She had used it before only in emergency. She extended a hand and looked at it. It was trembling. Damn triangles!

While she was looking at her hand there was a click from the automatic drug vendor. It summed the morning use of each drug in the vendors throughout the ship, and recorded it in a neat addition to the end of each graph line. For a moment she could not find the green line for anodynes and the red line for stimulants, and then she saw that they went almost straight up.

There were too many being used —far too many to be explained by jealousy or psychosomatic peevishness. This was an epidemic, and only one disease was possible!

The disinfecting of Pat had not succeeded. Nucleocat Cureall, killer of all infections, had not cured! Pat had brought melting sickness into the ship with him!

Who had it?

The drugs vendor glowed cheerfully, uncommunicative. She opened a panel in its side and looked in on restless interlacing cogs, and on the inside of the door saw printed some directions. . . . "To remove or examine records before reaching end of the reel—"

After a few fumbling minutes she had the answer. In the cafeteria at breakfast and lunch, thirty-eight men out of the forty-eight aboard ship had taken more than his norm of stimulant. Twenty-one had taken aspirin as well. The only woman who had made an unusual purchase was herself!

She remembered the hamsters that had thrown off the infection with a short sharp fever, and checked back in the records to the day before. There was a short rise in aspirin sales to women at late afternoon. The women were safe.

It was the men who had melting sickness!

Melting sickness killed in hours, according to Pat Mead. How long had the men been sick?

AS SHE was leaving, Jerry came into the pharmacy, recorded his thumbprint and took a box of aspirin from the machine.

She felt all right. Self-control was working well and it was pleasant still to walk down the corridor smiling at the people who passed. She took the emergency elevator to the control room and showed her credentials to the technician on watch.

"Medical Emergency." At a small control panel in the corner was a large red button, precisely labeled. She considered it and picked up the control room phone. This was the hard part, telling someone, especially someone who had it—Max.

She dialed, and when the click on the end of the line showed he had picked the phone up, she told Max what she had seen.

"No women, just the men," he repeated. "That right?"

"Yes."

"Probably it's chemically alien, inhibited by one of the female sex hormones. We'll try sex hormone shots, if we have to. Where are you calling from?"

She told him.

"That's right. Give Nucleocat Cureall another chance. It might work this time. Push that button."

She went to the panel and pushed the large red button. Through the long height of the *Explorer,* bells woke to life and began to ring in frightened clangor, emergency doors thumped shut, mechanical apparatus hummed into life and canned voices began to give rapid urgent directions.

A plague had come.

SHE obeyed the mechanical orders, went out into the hall and walked in line with the others. The captain walked ahead of her and the gorgeous Shelia Davenport fell into step beside her. "I look like a positive hag this morning. Does that mean I'm sick? Are we all sick?"

June shrugged, unwilling to say what she knew.

Others came out of all rooms into the corridor, thickening the line. They could hear each room lock as the last person left it, and then, faintly, the hiss of disinfectant spray. Behind them, on the heels of the last person in line, segments of the ship slammed off and began to hiss.

They wound down the spiral corridor until they reached the medical treatment section again, and there they waited in line.

"It won't scar my arms, will it?" asked Shelia apprehensively, glancing at her smooth, lovely arms.

The mechanical voice said, "Next. Step inside, please, and stand clear of the door."

"Not a bit," June reassured Shelia, and stepped into the cubicle.

Inside, she was directed from cubicle to cubicle and given the usual buffeting by sprays and radiation, had blood samples taken and was injected with Nucleocat and a series of other protectives. At last she was directed through another door into a tiny cubicle with a chair.

"You are to wait here," commanded the recorded voice metallically. "In twenty minutes the door will unlock and you may then leave. All people now treated may visit all parts of the ship which have been protected. It is forbidden to visit any quarantined or unsterile part of the ship without permission from the medical officers."

Presently the door unlocked and she emerged into bright lights again, feeling slightly battered.

She was in the clinic. A few men sat on the edge of beds and looked sick. One was lying down. Brant and Bess St. Clair sat near each other, not speaking.

Approaching her was George Barton, reading a thermometer with a puzzled expression.

"What is it, George?" she asked anxiously.

"Some of the women have slight fever, but it's going down. None of the fellows have any—but their white count is way up, their red count is way down, and they look sick to me."

She approached St. Clair. His usually ruddy cheeks were pale, his pulse was light and too fast, and his skin felt clammy. "How's the headache? Did the Nucleocat treatment help?"

"I feel worse, if anything."

"Better set up beds," she told George. "Get everyone back into the clinic."

"We're doing that," George assured her. "That's what Hal is doing."

She went back to the laboratory. Max was pacing up and down, absently running his hands through his black hair until it stood straight up. He stopped when he saw her face, and scowled thoughtfully. "They are still sick?" It was more a statement than a question.

She nodded.

"The Cureall didn't cure this time," he muttered. "That leaves it up to us. We have melting sickness and according to Pat and the hamsters, that leaves us less than a day to find out what it is and learn how to stop it."

Suddenly an idea for another test struck him and he moved to the work table to set it up. He worked rapidly, with an occasional uncoordinated movement betraying his usual efficiency.

It was strange to see Max troubled and afraid.

She put on a laboratory smock and began to work. She worked in silence. The mechanicals had failed. Hal and George Barton were busy staving off death from the weaker cases and trying to gain time for Max and her to work. The problem of the plague had to be solved by the two of them alone. It was in their hands.

Another test, no results. Another test, no results. Max's hands were shaking and he stopped a moment to take stimulants.

She went into the ward for a moment, found Bess and warned her quietly to tell the other women to be ready to take over if the men became too sick to go on. "But tell them calmly. We don't want to frighten the men." She lingered in the ward long enough to see the word spread among the women in a widening wave of paler faces and compressed lips; then she went back to the laboratory.

Another test. There was no sign of a micro-organism in anyone's blood, merely a growing horde of leucocytes and phagocytes, prowling as if mobilized to repel invasion.

LEN MARLOW was wheeled in unconscious, with Hal Barton's written comments and conclusions pinned to the blanket.

"I don't feel so well myself," the assistant complained. "The air feels thick. I can't breathe."

June saw that his lips were blue. "Oxygen short," she told Max.

"Low red corpuscle count," Max

answered. "Look into a drop and see what's going on. Use mine; I feel the same way he does." She took two drops of Max's blood. The count was low, falling too fast.

Breathing is useless without the proper minimum of red corpuscles in the blood. People below that minimum die of asphyxiation although their lungs are full of pure air. The red corpuscle count was falling too fast. The time she and Max had to work in was too short.

"PUMP some more CO_2 into the air system," Max said urgently over the phone. "Get some into the men's end of the ward."

She looked through the microscope at the live sample of blood. It was a dark clear field and bright moving things spun and swirled through it, but she could see nothing that did not belong there.

"Hal," Max called over the general speaker system, "cut the other treatments, check for accelerating anemia. Treat it like monoxide poisoning—CO_2 and oxygen."

She reached into a cupboard under the work table, located two cylinders of oxygen, cracked the valves and handed one to Max and one to the assistant. Some of the bluish tint left the assistant's face as he breathed and he went over to the patient with reawakened concern.

"Not breathing, Doc!"

Max was working at the desk, muttering equations of hemoglobin catalysis.

"Len's gone, Doc," the assistant said more loudly.

"Artificial respiration and get him into a regeneration tank," said June, not moving from the microscope. "Hurry! Hal will show you how. The oxidation and mechanical heart action in the tank will keep him going. Put anyone in a tank who seems to be dying. Get some women to help you. Give them Hal's instructions."

The tanks were ordinarily used to suspend animation in a nutrient bath during the regrowth of any diseased organ. It could preserve life in an almost totally destroyed body during the usual disintegration and regrowth treatments for cancer and old age, and it could encourage healing as destruction continued . . . but they could not prevent ultimate death as long as the disease was not conquered.

The drop of blood in June's microscope was a great dark field, and in the foreground, brought to gargantuan solidity by the stereo effect, drifted neat saucer shapes of red blood cells. They turned end for end, floating by the humped misty mass of a leucocyte which was crawling on the cover glass. There were not enough red corpuscles, and she felt that they grew fewer as she watched.

She fixed her eye on one, not blinking in fear that she would miss what might happen. It was a tidy red button, and it spun as it drifted, the current moving it aside in a curve as it passed by the leucocyte.

Then, abruptly, the cell vanished.

June stared numbly at the place where it had been.

Behind her, Max was calling over the speaker system again: "Dr. Stark speaking. Any technician who knows anything about the life tanks, start bringing more out of storage and set them up. Emergency."

"We may need forty-seven," June said quietly.

"We may need forty-seven," Max repeated to the ship in general. His voice did not falter. "Set them up along the corridor. Hook them in on extension lines."

His voice filtered back from the empty floors above in a series of dim echoes. What he had said meant that every man on board might be on the point of heart stoppage.

JUNE looked blindly through the binocular microscope, trying to think. Out of the corner of her eyes she could see that Max was wavering and breathing more and more frequently of the pure, cold, burning oxygen of the cylinders. In the microscope she could see that there were fewer red cells left alive in the drop of his blood. The rate of fall was accelerating.

She didn't have to glance at Max to know how he would look—skin pale, black eyebrows and keen brown eyes slightly squinted in thought, a faint ironical grin twisting the bluing lips. Intelligent, thin, sensitive, his face was part of her mnd. It was inconceivable that Max could die. He couldn't die. He couldn't leave her alone.

She forced her mind back to the problem. All the men of the *Explorer* were at the same point, whereever they were.

Moving to Max's desk, she spoke into the intercom system: "Bess, send a couple of women to look through the ship, room by room, with a stretcher. Make sure all the men are down here." She remembered Reno. "Sparks, heard anything from Reno? Is he back?"

Sparks replied weakly after a lag. "The last I heard from Reno was a call this morning. He was raving about mirrors, and Pat Mead's folks not being real people, just carbon copies, and claiming he was crazy; and I should send him the psychiatrist. I thought he was kidding. He didn't call back."

"Thanks, Sparks." Reno was lost.

Max dialed and spoke to the bridge over the phone. "Are you okay up there? Forget about engineering controls. Drop everything and head for the tanks while you can still walk."

June went back to the work table and whispered into her own phone. "Bess, send up a stretcher for Max. He looks pretty bad."

There had to be a solution. The life tanks could sustain life in a damaged body, encouraging it to regrow more rapidly, but they merely slowed death as long as the disease was not checked. The postponement could not last long, for destruction could go on steadily in the tanks until the nutritive solution would hold no life except the triumphant microscopic killers that caused melting sickness.

There were very few red blood corpuscles in the microscope field now, incredibly few. She tipped the microscope and they began to drift, spinning slowly. A lone corpuscle floated through the center. She watched it as the current swept it in an arc past the dim off-focus bulk of the leucocyte. There was a sweep of motion and it vanished.

For a moment it meant nothing to her; then she lifted her head from the microscope and looked around. Max sat at his desk, head in hand, his rumpled short black hair sticking out between his fingers at odd angles. A pencil and a pad scrawled with formulas lay on the desk before him. She could see his concentration in the rigid set of his shoulders. He was still thinking; he had not given up.

"MAX, - just saw a leucocyte grab a red blood corpuscle. It was unbelievably fast."

"Leukemia," muttered Max without moving. "Galloping leukemia yet! That comes under the heading of cancer. Well, that's part of the answer. It might be all we need." He grinned feebly and reached for the speaker set. "Anybody still on his feet in there?" he muttered into it, and the question was amplified to a booming voice throughout the ship. "Hal, are you still going? Look, Hal, change all the dials, change the dials, set them to deep melt and regeneration. One week. This is like leukemia. Got it? This is like leukemia."

June rose. It was time for her to take over the job. She leaned across his desk and spoke into the speaker system. "Doctor Walton talking," she said. "This is to the women. Don't let any of the men work any more; they'll kill themselves. See that they all go into the tanks right away. Set the tank dials for deep regeneration. You can see how from the ones that are set."

Two exhausted and frightened women clattered in the doorway with a stretcher. Their hands were scratched and oily from helping to set up tanks.

"That order includes you," she told Max sternly and caught him as he swayed.

Max saw the stretcher bearers and struggled upright. "Ten more minutes," he said clearly. "Might think of an idea. Something not right in this setup. I have to figure how to prevent a relapse, how the thing started."

He knew more bacteriology than she did; she had to help him think. She motioned the bearers to wait, fixed a breathing mask for Max from a cylinder of CO_2 and the opened one of oxygen. Max went back to his desk.

She walked up and down, trying

to think, remembering the hamsters. The melting sickness, it was called. Melting. She struggled with an impulse to open a tank which held one of the men. She wanted to look in, see if that would explain the name.

Melting Sickness. . . .

Footsteps came and Pat Mead stood uncertainly in the doorway. Tall, handsome, rugged, a pioneer. "Anything I can do?" he asked.

She barely looked at him. "You can stay out of our way. We're busy."

"I'd like to help," he said.

"Very funny." She was vicious, enjoying the whip of her words. "Every man is dying because you're a carrier, and you want to help."

HE STOOD nervously clenching and unclenching his hands. "A guinea pig, maybe. I'm immune. All the Meads are."

"Go away." God, why couldn't she think? What makes a Mead immune?

"Aw, let 'im alone," Max muttered. "Pat hasn't done anything." He went waveringly to the microscope, took a tiny sliver from his finger, suspended it in a slide and slipped it under the lens with detached habitual dexterity. "Something funny going on," he said to June. "Symptoms don't feel right."

After a moment he straightened and motioned for her to look. "Leucocytes, phagocytes—" He was bewildered. "My own—".

She looked in, and then looked back at Pat in a growing wave of horror. "They're not your own, Max!" she whispered.

Max rested a hand on the table to brace himself, put his eye to the microscope, and looked again. June knew what he saw. Phagocytes, leucocytes, attacking and devouring his tissues in a growing incredible horde, multiplying insanely.

Not his phagocytes! Pat Mead's! The Meads' evolved cells had learned too much. They were contagious. And not Pat Mead's. . . . How much alike *were* the Meads? . . . Mead cells contagious from one to another, not a disease attacking or being fought, but acting as normal leucocytes in whatever body they were in! The leucocytes of tall, red-headed people, finding no strangeness in the bloodstream of any of the tall, red-headed people. No strangeness. . . . A toti-potent leucocyte finding its way into cellular wombs..

The womblike life tanks. For the men of the *Explorer,* a week's cure with deep melting to de-differentiate the leucocytes and turn them back to normal tissue, then regrowth and reforming from the cells that were there. From the cells that *were* there. *From the cells that were there. . . .*

"Pat—"

"I know." Pat began to laugh, his face twisted with sudden understanding. "I understand. I get it. I'm a contagious personality. That's funny, isn't it?"

Max rose suddenly from the microscope and lurched toward him, fists clenched. Pat caught him as he fell, and the bewildered stretcher bearers carried him out to the tanks.

FOR a week June tended the tanks. The other women volunteered to help, but she refused. She said nothing, hoping her guess would not be true.

"Is everything all right?" Elsie asked her anxiously. "How is Jerry coming along?" Elsie looked haggard and worn, like all the women, from doing the work that the men had always done.

"He's fine," June said tonelessly, shutting tight the door of the tank room. "They're all fine."

"That's good," Elsie said, but she looked more frightened than before.

June firmly locked the tank room door and the girl went away.

The other women had been listening, and now they wandered back to their jobs, unsatisfied by June's answer, but not daring to ask for the actual truth. They were there whenever June went into the tank room, and they were still there—or relieved by others; June was not sure—when she came out. And always some one of them asked the unvarying question for all the others, and June gave the unvarying answer. But she kept the key. No woman but herself knew what was going on in the life tanks.

Then the day of completion came. June told no one of the hour. She went into the room as on the other days, locked the door behind her, and there was the nightmare again. This time it was reality and she wandered down a path between long rows of coffinlike tanks, calling, "Max! Max!" silently and looking into each one as it opened.

But each face she looked at was the same. Watching them dissolve and regrow in the nutrient solution, she had only been able to guess at the horror of what was happening. Now she knew.

They were all the same lean-boned, blond-skinned face, with a pin-feather growth of reddish down on cheeks and scalp. All horribly—and handsomely—the same.

A medical kit lay carelessly on the floor beside Max's tank. She stood near the bag. "Max," she said, and found her throat closing. The canned voice of the mechanical mocked her, speaking glibly about waking and sitting up. "I'm sorry, Max. . . ."

The tall man with rugged features and bright blue eyes sat up sleepily and lifted an eyebrow at her, and ran his hand over his red-fuzzed head in a gesture of bewilderment.

"What's the matter, June?" he asked drowsily.

She gripped his arm. "Max—"

He compared the relative size of his arm with her hand and said wonderingly, "You shrank."

"I know, Max. I know."

He turned his head and looked at his arms and legs, pale blond arms and legs with a down of red hair. He touched the thick left arm, squeezed a pinch of hard flesh. "It isn't mine," he said, surprised. "But I can feel it."

Watching his face was like watching a stranger mimicking and distorting Max's expressions. Max in fear. Max trying to understand what had happened to him, looking around at the other men sitting up in their tanks. Max feeling the terror that was in herself and all the men as they stared at themselves and their friends and saw what they had become.

"We're all Pat Mead," he said harshly. "All the Meads are Pat Mead. That's why he was surprised to see people who didn't look like himself."

"Yes, Max."

"Max," he repeated. "It's me, all right. The nervous system didn't change." His new blue eyes held hers. "My love didn't, either. Did yours? Did it, June?"

"No, Max." But she couldn't know yet. She had loved Max with the thin, ironic face, the rumpled black hair and the twisted smile that never really hid his quick sympathy. Now he was Pat Mead. Could he also be Max? "Of course I still love you, darling."

He grinned. It was still the wry smile of Max, though fitting strangely on the handsome new blond face. "Then it isn't so bad. It might even be pretty good. I envied him this big, muscular body. If Pat or any of these Meads so much as looks at you, I'm going to knock his block off. Understand?"

SHE laughed and couldn't stop. It wasn't that funny. But it was still Max, trying to be unafraid, drawing on humor. Maybe the rest of the men would also be their old selves, enough so the women would not feel that their men were strangers.

Behind her, male voices spoke characteristically. She did not have to turn to know which was which: "This is one way to keep a guy from stealing your girl," that was Len Marlow; "I've got to write down all my reactions," Hal Barton; "Now I can really work that hillside vein of metal," St. Clair. Then others complaining, swearing, laughing bitterly at the trick that had been played on them and their flirting, tempted women. She knew who they were. Their women would know them apart, too.

"We'll go outside," Max said. "You and I. Maybe the shock won't be so bad to the women after they see me." He paused. "You didn't tell them, did you?"

"I couldn't. I wasn't sure. I—was hoping I was wrong."

She opened the door and closed it quickly. There was a small crowd on the other side.

"Hello, Pat," Elsie said uncertainly, trying to look past them into the tank room before the door shut.

"I'm not Pat, I'm Max," said the

tall man with the blue eyes and the fuzz-reddened skull. "Listen—"

"Good heavens, Pat, what happened to your hair?" Shelia asked.

"I'm Max," insisted the man with the handsome face and the sharp blue eyes. "Don't you get it? I'm Max Stark. The melting sickness is Mead cells. We caught them from Pat. They adapted us to Minos. They also changed us all into Pat Mead."

The women stared at him, at each other. They shook their heads.

"They don't understand," June said. "I couldn't have if I hadn't seen it happening, Max."

"It's Pat," said Shelia, dazedly stubborn. "He shaved off his hair. It's some kind of joke."

Max shook her shoulders, glaring down at her face. "I'm Max. Max Stark. They all look like me. Do you hear? It's funny, but it's not a joke. Laugh for us, for God's sake!"

"It's too much," said June. "They'll have to see."

She opened the door and let them in. They hurried past her to the tanks, looking at forty-six identical blond faces, beginning to call in frightened voices:

"Jerry!"

"Harry!"

"Lee, where are you, sweetheart—"

June shut the door on the voices that were growing hysterical, the women terrified and helpless, the men shouting to let the women know who they were.

"It isn't easy," said Max, looking down at his own thick muscles. "But you aren't changed and the other girls aren't. That helps."

Through the muffled noise and hysteria, a bell was ringing.

"It's the airlock," June said.

Peering in the viewplate were nine Meads from Alexandria. To all appearances, eight of them were Pat Mead at various ages, from fifteen to fifty, and the other was a handsome, leggy, red-headed girl who could have been his sister.

Regretfully, they explained through the voice tube that they had walked over from Alexandria to bring news that the plane pilot had contracted melting sickness there and had died.

They wanted to come in.

JUNE and Max told them to wait and returned to the tank room. The men were enjoying their new height and strength, and the women were bewilderedly learning that they could tell one Pat Mead from another, by voice, by gesture of face or hand. The panic was gone. In its place was a dull acceptance of the fantastic situation.

Max called for attention. "There are nine Meads outside who want to come in. They have different names, but they're all Pat Mead."

They frowned or looked blank, and George Barton asked, "Why didn't you let them in? I don't see any problem."

"One of them," said Max soberly,

"is a girl. *Patricia* Mead. The girl wants to come in."

There was a long silence while the implication settled to the fear center of the women's minds. Shelia the beautiful felt it first. She cried, "No! Please don't let her in!" There was real fright in her tone and the women caught it quickly.

Elsie clung to Jerry, begging, "You don't want me to change, do you, Jerry? You like me the way I am! Tell me you do!"

THE other girls backed away. It was illogical, but it was human. June felt terror rising in herself. She held up her hand for quiet, and presented the necessity to the group.

"Only half of us can leave Minos," she said. "The men cannot eat ship food; they've been conditioned to this planet. We women can go, but we would have to go without our men. We can't go outside without contagion, and we can't spend the rest of our lives in quarantine inside the ship. George Barton is right—there is no problem."

"But we'd be changed!" Shelia shrilled. "I don't want to become a Mead! I don't want to be somebody else!"

She ran to the inner wall of the corridor. There was a brief hesitation, and then, one by one, the women fled to that side, until there were only Bess, June and four others left.

"See!" cried Shelia. "A vote! We can't let the girl in!"

No one spoke. To change, to be someone else—the idea was strange and horrifying. The men stood uneasily glancing at each other, as if looking into mirrors, and against the wall of the corridor the women watched in fear and huddled together, staring at the men. One man in forty-seven poses. One of them made a beseeching move toward Elsie and she shrank away.

"No, Jerry! I won't let you change me!"

Max stirred restlessly, the ironic smile that made his new face his own unconsciously twisting into a grimace of pity. "We men can't leave, and you women can't stay," he said bluntly. "Why not let Patricia Mead in. Get it over with!"

June took a small mirror from her belt pouch and studied her own face, aware of Max talking forcefully, the men standing silent, the women pleading. Her face . . . her own face with its dark blue eyes, small nose, long mobile lips . . . the mind and the body are inseparable; the shape of a face is part of the mind. She put the mirror back.

"I'd kill myself!" Shelia was sobbing. "I'd rather die!"

"You won't die," Max was saying. "Can't you see there's only one solution—"

They were looking at Max. June stepped silently out of the tank room, and then turned and went to the airlock. She opened the valves that would let in Pat Mead's sister.

—KATHERINE MacLEAN

GALAXY'S

FIVE STAR SHELF

SHADOW ON THE HEARTH, by Judith Merril. Doubleday, Inc., $3.00. 277 *pages.*

THIS is a book which never should have had to be written. But now that it has been, one can only honor the woman who wrote it for painting one of the most terrifyingly real pictures of an atomic war that science fiction has ever produced.

There are those who will say that this is not really science fiction, since there is no "new" science in it, and no high-flying adventure—only the horrible desperation of ordinary people faced with catastrophe. But as science fiction matures, it becomes more and more obvious that one of its important functions is to portray just such reactions to events growing out of actual or probable scientific developments. This Judith Merril has done.

Briefly, the story tells what happens to a suburban housewife and her family when New York City is atom bombed. Little that is "big-scale" occurs in the safe, smug community twenty miles from where the bombs fall. Most of the utilities eventually fail; schools close; food is rationed. There is some radiation poisoning, due largely to radioactive rain. Evacuees from New York complicate conditions, bringing in occasional bands of looters.

Most of the action takes place within the comfortable middle-class home of the heroine. The unimaginable terror of an atomic war is brought intimately close through impersonal radio announcements, official voices on the telephone (until it breaks down) a handful of actual contacts with the outer world at the front door and in the house, and—most vividly of all—the children's own reactions to the unprecedented new conditions. Through their eyes and those of their mother, one sees civilization waver and dissolve in a general, brutal chaos.

Both as an overwhelming argument for peace and a masterly example of sensitive and perceptive story-telling, unadorned by high-pressure writing or hysterics, *Shadow on the Hearth* is unreservedly recommended to everyone who is able to enjoy science fiction above the level of space operas.

THE RAT RACE, by Jay Franklin. Fantasy Publishing Company, $3.00. 371 *pages.*

THERE have been incredible pieces of pseudo-science fantasy in the past, and there will be more. But this book really should take a prize.

The "science" in it is Conan Doyle stuff: mere personality transfer from one body to another under the impact of an atomic explosion. But consider the story built around this simple little idea! Jay Franklin is well known as political commentator, biographer of Fiorello LaGuardia, and general insider-about-Washington. He wrote this story in 1947, and sold it to *Collier's* as a serial. All the events in it are supposed to have taken place before the end of the war—and consequently *The Rat Race* is, in essence, a try at rewriting the history of the war's last year from the "insider's" point of view. Here are some of the "rewritings" that crop up in the story:

A thorium bomb was developed by the Navy for only $50,000,000 while the Manhattan project was spending billions on uranium. The Navy's one thorium bomb was sabotaged aboard the U. S. S. *Alaska,* mythical battleship carrying the bomb to reduce Japan. In this explosion the hero's personality is transferred from the battleship to the body of a fat, lecherous stockbroker in Manhattan—but let that part of the story go. It isn't important.

President Roosevelt was murdered. Not by the enemy, Germany; not by the Russians, either; but by a "friendly nation" who wanted to keep him from spoiling the rich takings at the peace table with his idealism. Turns out Woodrow Wilson was crippled by the same kind of drugs for the same reason, too.

All the important security agencies in Washington agreed to permit Hitler's chief spy in the United States to remain at large, pursuing his usual activities with their assistance because it was important to Big Business and Government to have an open line through to Hitler for preservation of top-level contacts.

The Secret Service has an uncomfortable habit of incarcerating anyone it wants out of the way in Saint Elizabeth's, Washington, D. C.'s huge psychiatric hospital, if it cannot get any evidence against such people.

The hero passes himself off as a member of a mythical intelligence unit called "Z-2". This non-existent unit had an agent "in the Jap squadron that attacked Pearl Harbor and one of our men was military secretary to Rommel in North Africa." In the end, however, although the hero had just thought up "Z-2", it turns out to have been real!

It is finally found that the soul of the man whose body the hero is occupying passed into the body of Ponto, a dog—an idea used previously in a famous story, "A Matter of Form," by the editor of this magazine, which interested readers will find in *The Big Book of Science Fiction,* Groff Conklin, editor, Crown Publishers Inc., $3.00 (advt.) And the end of the book is the most incredible thing of all—for the hero who tells the story in the first person casually kills himself off without ever giving himself a chance to write it down!

If this is science fiction, then I am definitely a three-eyed man from Mars. (Photograph sent on receipt of $1.00.) However, it is fascinating reading, and for those who like to believe the worst, it can be considered *the* exposé to end all exposés. Certainly Franklin wanted to have his readers haunted by the idea that some of what he was writing was actually true. Maybe it was and just doesn't sound it.

BEYOND TIME AND SPACE, edited by August Derleth. Pellegrini & Cudahy, $4.50. 643 *pages.*
FLIGHT INTO SPACE, edited by Donald A. Wollheim. Frederick Fell, $2.75. 251 *pages.*
THE BIG BOOK OF SCIENCE FICTION, edited by Groff Conklin. Crown Publishers, Inc., $3.00. 350,000 *words.*

THREE new anthologies which embarrass your reviewer no end to discuss. On the first two the great question is whether to be as critical as one thinks one should be, or to lay off because, as a competing anthologist, one might be thought to be tearing down the opposition. And on the last one—what to say at all? Well. . . .

Mr. Derleth performs a big favor for science fiction lovers by bringing together, in the first half of the book, some of the great classics of the past, from Plato on Atlantis to Frank Stockton's "A Tale of Negative Gravity," and Johannes Kepler's "Somnium" to Grant Allen's fine "Pausodyne."

When we come to the second half, the stories by current writers, my own personal tastes begin to interfere violently, and I drop criticism only to remark that it does contain good stories by Heard, Leiber and Sturgeon. Of the others, they seem to me much less science fiction than tales of the weird, the supernatural or the fantastic. Many of these stories will, I am sure, please many people, but I do not think they represent modern science fiction.

As regards *Flight Into Space,* my task is even more difficult. Here the stories certainly are science fiction—but science fiction on a level which is so different from what one hopes to find modern writers doing that there is no basis for critical evaluation. Robert Abernathy's spritely "Peril of the Blue World," which shows how scientific machinery can delude the most advanced scientists when faced with superstition, is one excellent tale. It is also a pleasure to have Clare Winger Harris' and Miles J. Breuer's "A Baby on Neptune," a classic from the early days of *Amazing Stories*.

The book contains twelve stories, one for each planet, the sun, the moon and the asteroids. It is probably a must for collectors, but for the "lay reader," so-called, turning from the slick and beautifully machined realism of the modern detective story to science fiction for a new kind of relaxation, I fear that most of the tales in this book are too implausible, too portentous, and, frankly, too badly written for easy acceptance. They are on the juvenile level; the really adult audience which science fiction needs deserves a better selection of stories about the solar system than this one.

As for the third and most recently published anthology on the list, all your reviewer will say at this point is that it contains 32 stories, runs to roughly 350,000 words, and sells for a bargain-basement price. It attempts to cover the field of modern science fiction from Karel Capek's *R. U. R.* down to some of the newest writers such as Katherine MacLean and Peter Phillips, Damon Knight and Noel Loomis. Not every story is a masterpiece; not every one is a gem of fine writing. But all were selected to be read by a mature person without insulting his taste or intelligence.

SEVEN SCIENCE FICTION NOVELS OF H. G. WELLS. Dover Publications, $3.95. 1015 *pages.*

HERE is wonderful news for science fiction fans of all schools. The huge omnibus volume of H. G. Wells' scientific romances has been reissued at a price anyone can afford. People who have long wanted to reread these out-of-print classics, and the younger generation which has never had a chance to read them at all, may now do so. The book contains The Time Machine, The Island of Dr. Moreau, The Invisible Man, The War of the Worlds, The First Men in the Moon, The Food of the Gods, and In the Days of the Comet. Men Like Gods is not included, but Dover hopes to bring it out separately in the not too distant future, and also hopes (cheers!) to reissue Wells' one-volume collected short stories. We will keep you posted on the future reprint plans of this publisher, one of the most recent in the field of regular trade houses to take up science fiction.

—GROFF CONKLIN

The Last Martian

The worries of a drunk are strange indeed. This one feared his people were all dead on another world. Silly, of course. Only...

By FREDRIC BROWN

IT WAS an evening like any evening, but duller than most. I was back in the city room after covering a boring banquet, at which the food had been so poor that, even though it had cost me nothing, I'd felt cheated. For the hell of it, I was writing a long and glowing account of it, ten or twelve column inches. The copyreader, of course, would cut it to a passionless paragraph or two.

Slepper was sitting with his feet up on the desk, ostentatiously doing nothing, and Johnny Hale was putting a new ribbon on his typewriter. The rest of the boys were out on routine assignments.

Cargan, the city ed, came out of his private office and walked over to us.

"Any of you guys know Barney Welch?" he asked us.

A silly question. Barney runs Barney's Bar right across the street from the Trib. There isn't a Trib reporter who doesn't know Barney well enough to borrow money from him. So we all nodded.

"He just phoned," Cargan said. "He's got a guy down there who claims to be from Mars."

"Drunk or crazy, which?" Slepper wanted to know.

"Barney doesn't know, but he said there might be a gag story in it if we want to come over and talk to the guy. Since it's right across the street and since you three mugs are just sitting on your prats, anyway, one of you dash over. But no drinks on the expense account."

Slepper said, "I'll go," but Cargan's eyes had lighted on me. "You free, Bill?" he asked. "This has got to be a funny story, if any, and you got a light touch on the human interest stuff."

"Sure," I grumbled. "I'll go."

"Maybe it's just some drunk being funny, but if the guy's really insane, phone for a cop, unless you think you can get a gag story. If there's an arrest, you got something to hang a straight story on."

Slepper said, "Cargan, you'd get your grandmother arrested to get a story. Can I go along with Bill, just for the ride?"

"No, you and Johnny stay here.

We're not moving the city room across the street to Barney's." Cargan went back into his office.

I slapped a "thirty" on to end the banquet story and sent it down the tube. I got my hat and coat. Slepper said, "Have a drink for me, Bill. But don't drink so much you lose that light touch."

I said, "Sure," and went on over to the stairway and down.

I walked into Barney's and looked around. Nobody from the Trib was there except a couple of pressmen playing gin rummy at one of the tables. Aside from Barney himself, back of the bar, there was only one other man in the place. He was a tall man, thin and sallow, who was sitting by himself in one of the booths, staring morosely into an almost empty beer glass.

I THOUGHT I'd get Barney's angle first, so I went up to the bar and put down a bill. "A quick one," I told him. "Straight, water on the side. And is tall-and-dismal over there the Martian you phoned Cargan about?"

He nodded once and poured my drink.

"What's my angle?" I asked him. "Does he know a reporter's going to interview him? Or do I just buy him a drink and rope him, or what? How crazy is he?"

"You tell me. Says he just got in from Mars two hours ago and he's trying to figure it out. He says he's the last living Martian. He doesn't know you're a reporter, but he's all set to talk to you. I set it up."

"How?"

"Told him I had a friend who was smarter than any usual guy and could give him good advice on what to do. I didn't tell him any name because I didn't know who Cargan would send. But he's all ready to cry on your shoulder."

"Know *his* name?"

Barney grimaced. "Yangan Dal, he says. Listen, don't get him violent or anything in here. I don't want no trouble."

I downed my shot and took a sip of chaser. I said, "Okay, Barney. Look, dish up two beers for us and I'll go over and take 'em with me."

Barney drew two beers and cut off their heads. He rang up sixty cents and gave me my change, and I went over to the booth with the beers.

"Mr. Dal?" I said. "My name is Bill Everett. Barney tells me you have a problem I might help you on."

He looked up at me. "You're the one he phoned? Sit down, Mr. Everett. And thanks very much for the beer."

I slid into the booth across from him. He took the last sip of his previous beer and wrapped nervous hands around the glass I'd just bought him.

"I suppose you'll think I'm crazy," he said. "And maybe you'll be right, but—I don't understand it myself. The bartender thinks I'm crazy, I guess. Listen, are you a doctor?"

"Not exactly," I told him. "Call me a consulting psychologist."

"Do you think I'm insane?'

I said, "Most people who are don't admit they might be. But I haven't heard your story yet."

He took a draught of the beer and put the glass down again, but kept his hands tightly around the glass, possibly to keep them from shaking.

He said, "I'm a Martian. *The last one.* All the others are dead. I saw their bodies only two hours ago."

"You were on Mars only two hours ago? How did you get here?"

"I don't know. That's the horrible thing. I don't know. All I know is that the others were dead, their bodies starting to rot. It was awful. There were a hundred million of us, and now I'm the last one."

"A hundred million. That's the population of Mars?"

"About that. A little over, maybe. But that *was* the population. They're all dead now, except me. I looked in three cities, the three biggest ones. I was in Skar, and when I found all the people dead there, I took a targan—there was no one to stop me—and flew it to Undanel. I'd never flown one before, but the controls were simple. Everyone in Undanel was dead, too. I refueled and flew on. I flew low and watched and there was no one alive. I flew to Zandar, the biggest city—over three million people. And all of them were dead and starting to rot. It was horrible, I tell you. Horrible. I can't get over the shock of it."

"I can imagine," I said.

"YOU *can't.* Of course it was a dying world, anyway; we didn't have more than another dozen generations left to us, you understand. Two centuries ago, we numbered three billion—most of them starving. It was the kryl, the disease that came from the desert wind and that our scientists couldn't cure. In two centuries it reduced us to one-thirtieth of our number and it still kept on.'

"Your people died, then, of this—kryl?"

"No. When a Martian dies of kryl, he withers. The corpses I saw were not withered." He shuddered and drank the rest of his beer. I saw that I'd neglected mine and downed it. I raised two fingers at Barney, who was watching our way and looking worried.

My Martian went on talking. "We tried to develop space travel, but we couldn't. We thought some of us might escape the kryl, if we came to Earth or to other worlds. We tried, but we failed. We couldn't even get to Deimos or Phobos, our moons."

"You didn't develop space travel? Then how—"

"I don't know. *I don't know,* and I tell you it's driving me wild. I don't know how I got here. I'm Yangan Dal, *a Martian. And I'm here, in this body.* It's driving me wild, I tell you."

Barney came with the beers. He

looked worried enough, so I waited until he was out of hearing before I asked, "In this body? Do you mean—"

"Of course. This isn't *I*, this body I'm in. You don't think Martians would look exactly like humans, do you? I'm three feet tall, weigh what would be about twenty pounds here on Earth. I have four arms with six-fingered hands. This body I'm in—it frightens me. I don't understand it, any more than I know how I got here."

"Or how you happen to talk English? Or can you account for that?"

"Well—in a way I can. This body; its name is Howard Wilcox. It's a bookkeeper. It's married to a female of this species. It works at a place called the Humbert Lamp Company. I've got all its memories and I can do everything it could do; I know everything it knew, or knows. In a sense, I *am* Howard Wilcox. I've got stuff in my pockets to prove it. But it doesn't make sense, because I'm Yangan Dal, and I'm a Martian. I've even got this body's tastes. I like beer. And if I think about this body's wife, I—well, I love her."

I stared at him and pulled out my cigarettes, held out the package to him. "Smoke?"

"This body—Howard Wilcox—doesn't smoke. Thanks, though. And let me buy us another round of beers. There's money in these pockets."

I signaled Barney.

"When did this happen? You say only two hours ago? Did you ever suspect before then that you were a Martian?"

"Suspect? I *was* a Martian What time is it?"

I looked at Barney's clock. "A little after nine."

"Then it's a little longer than I thought. Three and a half hours. It would have been half past five when I found myself in this body, because it was going home from work then, and from its memories I know it had left work half an hour before then, at five."

"And did you—it—go home?"

"No, I was too confused. It wasn't *my* home. I'm a *Martian.* Don't you understand that? Well, I don't blame you if you don't, because I don't, either. But I walked. And I—I mean Howard Wilcox—got thirsty and he—I—" He stopped and started over again. "This body got thirsty and I stopped in here for a drink. After two or three beers, I thought maybe the bartender there could give me some advice and I started talking to him."

I LEANED forward across the table. "Listen, Howard," I said, "you were due home for dinner. You're making your wife worry like anything about you unless you phoned her. Did you?"

"Did I— Of course not. I'm not Howard Wilcox." But a new type of worry came into his face.

"You'd better phone her," I said.

"What's there to lose? Whether you are Yangan Dal or Howard Wilcox, there's a woman sitting home worrying about you or him. Be kind enough to phone her. Do you know the number?"

"Of course. It's my own—I mean it's Howard Wilcox's—"

"Quit tying yourself into grammatical knots and go make that phone call. Don't worry about thinking up a story yet; you're too confused. Just tell her you'll explain when you get home, but that you're all right."

He got up like a man in a daze and headed for the phone booth.

I went over to the bar and had another quickie, straight.

Barney said, "Is he—uh—"

"I don't know yet," I said. "There's something about it I still don't get."

I GOT back to the booth.

He was grinning weakly. He said, "She sounded madder than hoptoads. If I—if Howard Wilcox does go home, his story had better be good." He took a gulp of beer. "Better than Yangan Dal's story, anyway." He was getting more human by the moment.

But then he was back into it again. He stared at me. "I maybe should have told you how it happened from the beginning. I was shut up in a room on Mars. In the city of Skar. I don't know why they put me there, but they did. I was locked in. And then for a long time they didn't bring me food, and I got so hungry that I worked a stone loose from the floor and started to scrape my way through the door. I was starving. It took me three days—Martian days, about six Earth days—to get through, and I staggered around until I found the food quarters of the building I was in. There was no one there and I ate. And then—"

"Go on," I said. "I'm listening."

"I went out of the building and everyone was lying in the open, in the streets, dead. Rotting." He put his hands over his eyes. "I looked in some houses, other buildings. I don't know why or what I was looking for, but nobody had died indoors. Everybody was lying dead in the open, and none of the bodies were withered, so it wasn't kryl that killed them.

"Then, as I told you, I stole the targan—or I guess I really didn't steal it, because there was no one to steal it from—and flew around looking for someone alive. Out in the country it was the same way—everybody lying in the open, near the houses, dead. And Undanel and Zandar, the same.

"Did I tell you Zandar's the biggest city, the capital? In the middle of Zandar there's a big open space, the Games Field, that's more than an Earth-mile square. And all the people in Zandar were there, or it looked like all. Three million bodies, all lying together, like they'd gathered there to die, out in the open.

Like they'd known. Like everyone, everywhere else, was out in the open, but here they were all together, the whole three million of them.

"I saw it from the air, as I flew over the city. And there was something in the middle of the field, on a platform. I went down and hovered the targan—it's a little like your helicopters, I forgot to mention—I hovered over the platform to see what was there. It was some kind of a column made of solid copper. Copper on Mars is like gold is on Earth. There was a push-button set with precious stones set in the column. And a Martian in a blue robe lay dead at the foot of the column, right under the button. As though he'd pushed it—and then died. And everybody else had died, too, with him. Everybody on Mars, except me.

"And I lowered the targan onto the platform and got out and I pushed the button. I wanted to die, too; everybody else was dead and I wanted to die, too. *But I didn't. I was riding on a streetcar on Earth, on my way home from work, and my name was—"*

I signaled Barney.

"Listen, Howard," I said. "We'll have one more beer and then you'd better get home to your wife. You'll catch hell from her, even now, and the longer you wait, the worse it'll be. And if you're smart, you'll take some candy or flowers along and think up a really good story on the way home. And *not* the one you just told me."

He said, "Well—"

I said, "Well me no wells. Your name is Howard Wilcox and you'd better get home to your wife. I'll tell you what *may* have happened. We know little about the human mind, and many strange things happen to it. Maybe the medieval people *had* something when they believed in possession. Do you want to know what I think happened to you?"

"What? For Heaven's sake, if you can give me *any* explanation—except tell me that I'm crazy—"

"I think you *can* drive yourself batty if you let yourself think about it, Howard. Assume there's some natural explanation and then forget it. I can make a random guess what may have happened."

BARNEY came with the beers and I waited until he'd gone back to the bar.

I said, "Howard, just possibly a man—I mean a Martian—named Yangan Dal did die this afternoon on Mars. Maybe he really was the last Martian. And maybe, somehow, his mind got mixed up with yours at the moment of his death. I'm not saying that's what happened, but it isn't impossible to believe. Assume it was that, Howard, and fight it off. Just act as though you are Howard Wilcox—and look in a mirror if you doubt it. Go home and square things with your wife, and then go to work tomorrow morning and forget it. Don't you think that's the best idea?"

"Well, maybe you're right. The evidence of my senses—"

"Accept it. Until and unless you get better evidence."

We finished off our beers and I put him into a taxi. I reminded him to stop for candy or flowers and to work up a good and reasonable alibi, instead of thinking about what he'd been telling me.

I WENT back upstairs in the Trib building and into Cargan's office and closed the door behind me.

I said, "It's all right, Cargan. I straightened him out."

"What had happened?"

"He's a Martian, all right. And he was the last Martian left on Mars. Only he didn't know we'd come here; he thought we were all dead."

"But how— How could he have been overlooked? How could he not have known?"

I said, "He's an imbecile. He was in a mental institution in Skar and somebody slipped up and left him in his room when the button was pushed that sent us here. He wasn't out in the open, so he didn't get the mentaport rays that carried our psyches across space. He escaped from his room and found the platform in Zandar, where the ceremony was, and pushed the button himself. There must have been enough juice left to send him after us."

Cargan whistled softly. "Did you tell him the truth? And is he smart enough to keep his trap shut?"

I shook my head. "No, to both questions. His I. Q. is about fifteen, at a guess. But that's as smart as the average Earthman, so he'll get by here all right. I convinced him he really was the Earthman his psyche happened to get into."

"Lucky thing he went into Barney's. I'll phone Barney in a minute and let him know it's taken care of. I'm surprised he didn't give the guy a mickey before he phoned us."

I said, "Barney's one of us. He wouldn't have let the guy get out of there. He'd have held him till we got there."

"But you let him go. Are you sure it's safe? Shouldn't you have—"

"He'll be all right," I said. "I'll assume responsibility to keep an eye on him until we take over. I suppose we'll have to institutionalize him again after that. But I'm glad I didn't have to kill him. After all, he *is* one of us, imbecile or not. And he'll probably be so glad to learn he isn't the *last* Martian that he won't mind having to return to an asylum."

I went back into the city room and to my desk. Slepper was gone, sent out somewhere on something. Johnny Hale looked up from the magazine he was reading. "Get a story?" he asked.

"Nah," I said. "Just a drunk being the life of the party. I'm surprised at Barney for calling."

—FREDRIC BROWN

By

ISAAC ASIMOV

Darwinian Pool Room

Creation's meaning is an awesome secret. Or maybe not.

"OF COURSE the ordinary conception of Genesis I is all wrong," I said. "Take a pool room, for instance."

The other three mentally took a pool room. We were sitting in broken down swivel-chairs in Dr. Trotter's laboratory, but it was no trick at all for them to convert the lab benches into pool tables, the tall ring-stands into cues, the reagent bottles into billiard balls and then wait for me to do something with the imaginary layout.

Thetier even raised one finger, closed his eyes and muttered softly. "Pool room!" Trotter, as usual, said nothing at all, but nursed his second cup of coffee. The coffee, also as usual, was horrible, but then I was the newcomer to the group and had not yet calloused my gastric lining.

"Now consider the end of a game of pocket pool," I said. "You've got each ball, except the cue-ball, of course, in a given pocket—"

"Wait a while," said Thetier, always the purist. "It doesn't matter which pocket."

"Beside the point. When the

game is over, the balls are in various pockets. Right? Now suppose you walk into the pool room when the game is all over, and observe only that final position and try to reconstruct the course of previous events. You have several alternatives.

"Not if you know the rules of the game," said Madend.

"Assume complete ignorance," I said. "You *can* decide that the balls were pocketed by being struck with the cue-ball, which in turn was struck by the cue. This would be the truth, but not an explanation that is very likely to occur to you spontaneously. It is much more likely that you would decide that the balls were individually placed in their corresponding pockets by hand, or always existed in the pockets as you found them."

"All right," said Thetier, "if you're going to skip back to Genesis, you will claim that by analogy we can account for the universe as either having always existed, having been created arbitrarily as it is now, or having developed through evolution. So what?"

"That's not the alternative I'm proposing at all," I said. "Let us accept the idea of creation for a purpose, and consider only the methods by which such a creation could have been accomplished. It's easy to suppose that God said, 'Let there be light,' and there was light, but it's not esthetic."

"It's simple," said Madend, "and 'Occam's Razor' demands that of alternate possibilities, the simpler be chosen."

"Then why don't you play pool by putting the balls in the pockets by hand? That's simpler, too, but it isn't the game. Now if you started with the primordial atom—"

"What is that?" asked Trotter craftily.

"Well, call it all the mass-energy of the universe compressed into a single sphere, in a state of minimum entropy—completely at rest, motionless. Now explode that in such a way that all the constituent particles of matter and quanta of energy act, react and interact in a pre-calculated way, so that just our present universe is created. Wouldn't that be much more satisfactory than simply waving your hand and saying, 'Let there be light'?"

"YOU mean," said Madend, "like stroking the cue-ball against one of the billiard-balls and sending all fifteen into their predestined pockets?"

"In an esthetic pattern," I said.

"There's more poetry in the thought of a huge act of direct will," said Madend.

"That depends on whether you look at the matter as a mathematician or a theologian," I said. "As a matter of fact, Genesis I could be made to fit the billiard-ball scheme. The Creator could have spent His time calculating all the necessary variables and relationships into six gigantic equations. Count one 'day' for each equation. After having applied the initial explosive impetus, He would then 'rest' on the seventh 'day', said seventh 'day' being the entire interval of time from that beginning to 4,004 B.C. That interval, in which the infinitely complex pattern of billiard balls is sorting itself out, is obviously of no interest to the writers of the Bible. All two billion years of it could be considered merely the developing single act of creation."

"You're postulating a teleological universe," said Trotter, "one in which purpose is implied."

"Sure," I said. "Why not? A conscious act of creation without a purpose is ridiculous. Besides which, if you try to consider the course of evolution as the blind outcome of non-purposive forces, you end up with some very puzzling problems."

"AS FOR instance?" asked Madend.

"As for instance," I said, "the passing away of the dinosaurs."

"What's so hard to understand about that?"

"There's no logical reason for it. Try to name some."

"Law of diminishing returns," said Madend. "The brontosaurus got so massive, it took legs like tree-trunks to support him, and at that he had to stand in water and let buoyancy do most of the work. And he had to eat all the time to keep himself supplied with calories. I mean *all the time.* As for the carnivores, they afflicted such armor upon themselves in their race against one another, offensive and defensive, that they were just crawling tanks, puffing under tons of bone and scale. It got to the point where it just didn't pay off."

"Okay," I said, "so the big babies die off. But most of the dinosaurs were *little* running creatures whose mass and armor had not become excessive. What happened to them?"

"As far as the small ones are concerned," put in Thetier, "there's the question of competition. If some of the reptiles developed hair and warm blood, they could adapt themselves to variations in climate more efficiently. They wouldn't have to stay out of direct sunlight. They would not get sluggish as soon as the temperature dropped below eighty Fahrenheit. They would develop intelligence of a sort. Therefore, they would win the race for food."

"That doesn't satisfy me," I said. "In the first place, I don't think the various saurians were quite such pushovers. They held out for some three hundred million years, you know, which is 299 million more than genus Homo. Secondly, cold-blooded animals still survive, notably insects and amphibia—"

"High rate of reproduction," said Thetier.

"*And* plenty of reptiles. The snakes, lizards, and turtles are still very much in business. For that matter, what about the ocean? The saurians adapted to that in the shape of ichthyosaurs and plesiosaurs. They vanished, too, and there were no newly developed forms of life based on radical evolutionary advances to compete with them. As near as I can make out, the highest form of ocean life are the fish—mammals aside—and they came before the ichthyosaurs. How do you account for that? The fish are just as cold-blooded and even more primitive. And in the ocean, there's no question of mass and diminishing returns since the water does all the work of support. The sulfur-bottom whale is larger than any dinosaur that ever lived. Another thing. What's the use of talking about the inefficiency of cold blood and saying that, at temperatures below 80, cold-blooded animals become sluggish? Fish are very happy at continuous temperatures of about 35, and there is nothing sluggish about a shark."

"THEN why did the dinosaurs quietly steal off the Earth, leaving their bones behind?" asked Madend.

"They were part of the plan. Once they had served their purpose, they were gotten rid of."

"How? In a properly arranged Velikovskian catastrophe? A striking comet? The finger of God?"

"No, of course not. They died out naturally and of necessity according to the original pre-calculation."

"Then we ought to be able to find out what that natural, necessary cause of extinction was."

"Not necessarily. It might have been some obscure failure of the saurian biochemistry, deliberately provided for, some developing vitamin deficiency—"

"It's too complicated," said Thetier.

"It just seems complicated," I maintained. "Supposing it were necessary to pocket a given billiard-ball by making a four-cushion shot. Would you quibble at the complicated course of the cue-ball? A direct hit would be less complicated, but would accomplish nothing. And despite the apparent complication, the stroke would be no more difficult to the master. It would still be a single motion of the cue, merely in a different direction. The ordinary properties of elastic materials and the laws of conservation of momentum would then take over."

"I take it then," said Trotter, "that you suggest that the course of evolution represents the simplest way in which one could have progressed from original chaos to man."

"That's right. Not a sparrow falls without a purpose, and not a pterodactyl, either."

"And where do we go from here?"

"Nowhere. Evolution is finished with the development of man. The old rules don't apply any more."

"Oh, don't they?" said Madend. "You rule out the continuing occurrence of environmental variation and of mutations?"

"In a sense, I do," I insisted. "More and more, man is controlling his environment, and more and more he is understanding the mechanism of mutations. Before man appeared on the scene, creatures could neither foresee and guard themselves against shifts in climatic conditions, nor could they understand the increasing danger from newly developing species before the danger had become overwhelming. But now ask yourself this question: What species of organism can possibly replace us and how is it going to accomplish the task?"

"We can start off," said Madend, "by considering the insects. I think they're doing the job already."

"THEY haven't prevented us from increasing in population about ten-fold in the last two hundred and fifty years. If man were ever to concentrate on the struggle with the insects, instead of spending most of his spare effort on other types of fighting, said insects would not last long. We could clean them off the planet."

"What about bacteria, or, better still, viruses?" asked Madend. "The influenza virus of 1918 did a respectable job of getting rid of a sizable percentage of us."

"Sure," I said, "just about one per cent. Even the Black Death of the 14th Century only managed to kill one-third of the population of Europe, and that at a time when medical science was non-existent. It was allowed to run its course at will, under the most appalling conditions of medieval poverty, filth and squalor, and still two-thirds of our very tough species managed to survive. Disease can't do it."

"What about man himself developing into a sort of superman and displacing the old-timers?" suggested Thetier.

"Not likely," I said. "The only part of the human being which is worth anything, as far as being boss of the world is concerned, is his nervous system; the cerebral hemispheres of the brain, in particular. They are the most specialized part of his organism and therefore a dead end. If there is anything the course of evolution demonstrates, it is that, once a certain degree of specialization sets in, flexibility is lost. Further development can proceed only in greater specialization."

"Isn't that exactly what's wanted?" said Thetier.

"Maybe it is, but as Madend pointed out, specializations have a way of reaching a point of diminishing returns. It's the size of the human head at birth that makes the process difficult and painful. It's the complexity of the human mentality that makes mental and emotional maturity lag so far behind sexual maturity in man, with *its* consequent harvest of troubles. It's the delicacy of mental equipment that makes most or all of the race neurotic. How much further can we go without complete disaster?"

"THE development," said Madend, "might be in greater stability, or quicker maturity, rather than higher brain-power."

"Maybe, but there are no signs of it. Cro-Magnon man existed ten thousand years ago, and there are indications that modern man is his inferior, if anything, in brain-power. And in physique, too."

"Ten thousand years," said Trotter, "isn't much, evolutionarily speaking. Besides, there is always the possibility of other species of animals developing intelligence, or something better—and don't say there couldn't be anything better."

"We'd never let them. That's the point. It would take hundreds of thousands of years for, let us say, apes or insects to become intelligent, and we'd wipe them out—or else use them as slaves."

"All right," said Thetier. "What about obscure biochemical deficiencies, such as you insisted on in the case of the dinosaurs? Take Vitamin C, for instance. The only organisms that can't make their own are guinea-pigs and primates, *including man.* Suppose this trend continues and we become impossibly dependent on too many essential food factors. Or what if the apparent increase in the susceptibility of man to cancer continues?" Then what will happen?"

"That's no problem," I said. "It's the essence of the new situation, that we are producing all known food-factors artificially, and may eventually have a completely synthetic diet.

And there's no reason to think we won't learn how to prevent or cure cancer some day."

Trotter got up. He had finished his coffee, but was still nursing his cup. "All right, then, you say we've hit a dead end. But what if all this has been taken into the original account? The Creator was prepared to spend three hundred million years letting the dinosaurs develop something or other that would eventually result in mankind—or so you say. Why can't He have figured out a way in which man could use his intelligence and his control of the environment to prepare the next stage of the game? That might be a very tricky part of the pool game."

That stopped me. "How do you mean?"

Trotter smiled at me. "Oh, I was just thinking that it might not be entirely coincidence, and that a new race may be coming and an old one going, entirely through the efforts of this cerebral mechanism." He tapped his temple.

"In what way?"

"Stop me if I'm wrong, but aren't the sciences of nucleonics and cybernetics reaching simultaneous peaks? Aren't we inventing hydrogen bombs and thinking machines *at the same time?* Is that coincidence —or part of the divine purpose?"

That was about all for that lunch hour. It had begun as logic-chopping just to kill time, but since then —I've been wondering.

—ISAAC ASIMOV

CAPTAIN FUTURE
WIZARD OF SCIENCE
COMET
FICTION AND FACT OF THE PRIZE-RING
FIGHT
THE BLACK UHLAN
HEADQUARTERS DETECTIVE
MURDER TREADMILL
G-MAN JUGGERNAUT
MASKED RIDER WESTERN
BORROWED HOSSES
FIGHTING ACES OF WAR SKIES
WINGS
10 STORY WESTERN
ADVENTURE NOVELS
Thrilling Stories of the Sky Trails
Air STORIES
THE NIGHT HAWK
GEORGE BRUCE
AIR WAR
THE ALL-STORY
ARMY Romances
BASKETBALL STORIES
Battle Stories
O'LEARY IN ACTION IN ETHIOPIA
All Star Issue of Favorite War Authors
BLACK BOOK DETECTIVE
GOLDEN FLEECE
ROMAN HOLIDAY
HIGH-SEAS ADVENTURES
THE SEA ROGUE
INDIAN Stories
BRIDE of the TOMAHAWK PACK
MY LIFE WITH SITTING BULL
LONE RANGER
MAGIC CARPET MAGAZINE
PEARLS FROM MACAO
MARVEL SCIENCE STORIES
NEW DETECTIVE
NO BODY BUT YOU
North-West ROMANCES
GIRLS of WHITE WATER TRAIL
Oriental Stories
The PHANTOM DETECTIVE
PLANET stories
QUEEN OF THE MARTIAN CATACOMBS
POPULAR DETECTIVE
DEATH IN A COTTAGE
MURDER INSURANCE
PRIVATE DETECTIVE
LOVE STORIES OF THE REAL WEST
RANCH ROMANCES
Maid of the Valley
RANGE RIDERS
SIX-GUN VALLEY
Vice Squad DETECTIVE
SECRET of the HOUSE of HORROR
TOP-NOTCH STORIES ... TOP-NOTCH WRITERS
UNDERWORLD DETECTIVE
FIVE FATAL MINUTES
KILLER'S BAIT
THRILLING WONDER STORIES
THE FEDERALS IN ACTION
G-MEN
GIVE 'EM HELL
THE BLUE LOTUS
SCIENCE FICTION
PLANET OF THE KNOB HEADS
SPICY-ADVENTURE STORIES
HELL'S RIVER

www.ingramcontent.com/pod-product-compliance
Lightning Source LLC
LaVergne TN
LVHW090952080826
845145LV00003B/987

* 9 7 8 1 6 4 7 2 0 3 8 2 5 *